KNOT SO DAMAGED

A DARK MAFIA AGE GAP OMEGAVERSE

ALEXCIS MORRIS

Book Cover by Artista Grafico Covers

Editing by C J Editing

CONTENTS

To all my Alpha obsessed readers,

You have been so patient with me.

Now get on your knees, spread those pages and STFUATMKLAGO

CONTENT WARNING

Knot So Damaged is a dark mafia Omegaverse. There is a variety of triggering content throughout. if you find a trigger that hasn't been listed, please contact me at alexcismorrisauthor@outlook.com

These triggers include but are not limited to:

-Abuse

-Kidnapping including that of a child

-Use of weapons

-Use of poisons

-Death of family unit

-Sexual Assault and threatening of sexual assault

-BDSM (mild)

-Degradation and Praise

-Characters with complex mental health issues

-Pregnancy and birth in the epilogue

-Brutal murder scenes

-Mentions of Rape

-Torture

INTRODUCTION TO OMEGAVERSE

If this is your first time reading Omegaverse, welcome! If you already know the ins and outs of OV, you are more than welcome to skip this bit.

Omegaverse is an alternate world where humans are split up into designations: Alpha, Beta, Omega. Omegaverse can vary from author to author and how they choose to write their worlds. In this world, there is no shifting. The designations, specifically Alpha and Omega divert to very primal instincts.

Alphas are considered to be the top of the heirarchy. They are natural leaders, bigger, dominant and tend to have aggressive tendencies. They have a knot at the base of their penis that swells during intercourse that will lock inside of the omega. This is called knotting. They can go into a rut. This is most easily explained as a strong sexual urge to mate. It's an equivalent to an Omega's heat. This is very similar to that of a wolf shifter, just without the actual shifting.

Betas are regular humans. They do not have any of the primal urges that Alphas or Omegas have. They are the neutral ground.

Omegas are the more submissive designation. They are naturally more calm and gentle who are able to tone down an Alphas aggression. In return, an Alpha helps to provide protection, comfort and relief for an Omega during the heats. A heat is a period of 3-5 days where the Omega goes into a haze like state and is desperate to mate over and over.

Each designation releases pheromones, a specific scent that is unique to each person. These scents can attract and help to identify that persons scent match mate. They will then be able to form packs of three plus people.

If you have any further questions, please don't hesitate to send me a message or email!

CHAPTER ONE

VALENTINA

The guy sitting on the couch beneath me is practically drooling as I swing my hips to the music thumping through the club. I have already slapped his hands away from me more times than I want to count.

The only thing that doesn't stop me from moving on to the next paying customer is the big bills he keeps sliding under the thin string of my thong.

All the girls are on tonight. Fridays are always a full house.

I need to get my bag while I can.

I refuse to walk away tonight without a decent stack in my pocket.

It's not that I am greedy. It's the fact that I *need* the money.

Two mouths, even if one is still pint-sized, is expensive. Not to mention rent, electricity and water, necessities that have a tendency to break the bank.

I allow myself to drift into the back of my mind like I normally do on nights like tonight. I find it easier that way. To disappear into myself. To allow whatever song is playing to consume me.

My body sways, rolls and grinds. My thong is the only thing covering my body from the multitude of eyes I can feel locked in on my flesh.

I have no doubt in my mind that these men will be getting antsy.

They always want more. Down to our thongs is never enough.

This particular club doesn't have any restrictions in place when it comes to full nudity. In fact, they prefer if we take everything off.

As long as we get paid for it.

They have no problems taking our house fee from us at the end of the night. And a little bit off the top if you are a newbie. I caught onto their slight of hand quickly. Some of the other girls aren't so lucky.

Hands landing on my hips have me coming back to the present. I frown down at the suit, slapping his hands away from me, again.

"Come on, Cherry. I will give it to you good if you allow me to take you home."

I snort. I don't think this dickhead would be able to tell my thigh from my pussy lips right now. During the entirety of our dance, he has been downing drink after drink. Every word that spills from his lips is slurred.

While I know I could get him to pay, I refuse to do full service work, no matter how much the other girls convince me it will be worth my while.

I refuse to allow another person to touch me that way ever again.

Bearing my body to them is bad enough.

Having a man—an Alpha at that—get me to that point of vulnerability ever again isn't an option. Even thinking about it already has my heart racing.

Never. Fucking. Again.

I refuse to cower. To bare my neck and show submission to a person that would just take advantage of me the moment he can.

I will never be that damaged girl again.

The one that allowed herself to be taken by a pack. Used and abused time and time again.

The greasy-haired guy beneath me continues to try his luck. The questioning slowly becomes more forceful each time I deny him.

The next time I need to slap his hand away, I decide enough is enough.

Stepping off the chair, I give myself a second to get used to the height of the pleasers I am wearing, not wanting to roll my ankle like they threaten every time I put them on.

I put on the fakest smile I can possibly manage, knowing that if I showed how I really felt, it would put me at risk of not having any more customers tonight.

"Thank you so much, Sir. I hope you have a good night."

As quick as I can manage, I swipe up the scraps of fabric that was my outfit of the night and turn, making a quick exit to the dressing rooms.

I hear commotion behind me but I don't look back. My heart races with each step I take until I finally make it into the backrooms, my dressing area welcomes me back with the right amount of comfort I so desperately need right now.

I practically fall into the creaky office chair. My form slumps as I rest my head on the bench that is overflowing with a ridiculous amount of makeup, glitter and hair products.

I don't know how long I stay there for as I try to regain control of my emotions.

Each breath feels as though it is pulled into my lungs by knives. I know that if I don't get a grip now, I will continue to spiral until I need extra assistance in order to come back out.

I don't need to give anyone that kind of ammunition against me. That kind of control. Even if some of these girls I am starting to consider as friends.

I refuse to trust anyone ever again. I have well and truly learned my lesson.

It's only when I hear noises coming down the hallway do I lift my head up and pretend I wasn't on the verge of a mental breakdown.

I paint a fake smile on my face, hoping that it's enough of a disguise. It has done me well over the past couple of years at least.

"Hey babe, how has your night been?"

I smile over at my best friend, Luna, her presence setting a part of me at ease. I sigh as I begin pulling the crumpled bills out of my money bag.

"Pretty good. Mr. CEO tried his luck a little harder tonight but the man pays well." I shrug, faking nonchalance.

Luna rolls her eyes, sorting her own money into piles. It's clear she has had a good night based on the amount of big bills she is pulling out.

"You really need to let Ben know that he is getting more forceful each time he comes in, Valley."

I snort. "You know there is only so much that he can do, Lulu. You and I both know that Ivan doesn't care how handsy the clients get. As long as his pocket is full of green."

I know her returning grumble is at both my nickname for her as well as the fact that our boss is a fucking asshole.

The Alpha and his pack are fucking heathens. Their hands are as dirty as their money. This club is just a front for their dealings. Particular customers come in for much more than a lap dance.

We make small talk while we finish sorting and counting. One thousand dollars for a Friday night. Something settles in my chest at the number. Even with the club taking their cut, I know that Amity's daycare fees will be covered, a portion of rent will be covered as well as food for the week.

Stripping affords me that. Security in the fact that I can ensure my little girl is provided for. That she has a warm, safe bed to sleep in every night.

Because we have both known what it feels like to not have that.

If I have to sacrifice this part of myself for her, I will.

I wave goodbye to the rest of the girls as I make my way out of the club. The streets still crawl with half-cut club-goers that attempt to make their way home. I wrap my wool coat around myself tighter. I keep the knife in my hand hidden in the layers but still at the ready.

At times like this, I wish I had a car of my own.

Little good that would do me though considering I still don't know how to drive.

Even if I wanted to, *they* never would have allowed me to learn. They liked being able to keep me locked up and ready for what they wanted from me. Or more so: my body.

That's always the way isn't it?

A pack of Alpha's find an Omega that has a scent that appeals to them and they don't stop until they own them.

There is no choice for the Omega.

There was no choice for me.

I was at their mercy.

I was too young to fight back.

I was filled with too much grief to do anything apart from succumb.

There was no way for me to say no. Not when I was an impressionable young Omega whose parental pack was killed. When the four Alphas who had been after me for years stormed my home and took everything from me.

My family. My innocence. And at times, almost my life.

Alphas are monsters.

A designation that is lost to their primal instincts. They are cruel, abusive and cunning.

I refuse to allow myself to ever be caught in one of their snares ever again.

Being an Omega has felt like a death sentence since the day I emerged. Seeing as it was the same day that saw me catch the interest of them.

Which is why I now do everything in my power to hide what I really am.

To everyone, I am a Beta.

Double doses of heat suppressants, a can of scent-neutralizing spray a day, a lifetime subscription of slick-absorbent panties and the refusal to have a nest, are what see me hiding who I really am.

For four years, I have refused to be anything else but a Beta.

For four years I have been on the run terrified of receiving backlash for killing the Alphas that almost succeeded in killing *me*.

What they weren't expecting that night was for me to turn into the reaper, ridding the world of the Alphas that tortured me since my sixteenth birthday.

The sound of footsteps behind me pulls me from my downward spiral thoughts. I instantly stiffen, tightening my hold on the knife still in my hand.

I take a calming breath in an attempt to slow down my heartrate even though I know it is pointless.

The footsteps get louder as whoever is behind me sees the opportunity the now deserted street affords them.

The moment the offender grabs hold of my waist, I am already turning, my knife now visible to the Alpha who reeks of cigarette smoke and olives. It's a revolting combination that I have to force myself to not empty the contents of my stomach over.

I swing my knife, aiming straight for his shoulder, but come up short as he sees the glint of the metal coming, knocking it from my hand.

I hear the clank of metal against concrete and know that I am done for.

The knife was my only line of defence.

While I have spent a good portion of the last four years learning hand to hand combat, I am still useless when it comes to a surprise attack no matter how much I will myself to not freeze.

The moment their hands are on me, it's like all survival instincts leave me and in its stead is the scared girl I have been running from.

"Nice try, bitch. You think you can get away with teasing me all night long and not follow through?"

It takes me a moment to realize who has me.

Mr. CEO.

I should have known my run from him earlier wasn't the last I saw of him tonight. I know that I am not that naive to think that men like him are ever content with being told no. It's a word that just isn't in their vocabulary.

"You are a cock tease aren't you, Cherry? You like getting me worked up. I can tell how much you want my knot in that tight Beta pussy."

I feel a whimper threaten to escape me. I know that if he gets a hint of my real pheromones, I am done for. Presenting as a Beta is the only thing saving me.

He slams me up against the brick wall of the dark alley he managed to push us into during the struggle. The Alpha pushes his body against mine, this weight keeping me trapped. Not like it matters. I can't move, no matter how much my brain screams at me to get the fuck out of here, to actually implement everything I have learned.

He chuckles and leans in closer towards me, his nose pressing against my neck. The Alpha groans and I feel him stiffen through his clothes.

"Sometimes during our time together, I have convinced myself that you are actually an Omega. But you are a filthy little slut, aren't you? You want me to split open that Beta pussy. To force my knot inside of you."

He rolls his body into mine. My stomach clenches in revolution.

"No."

My voice is a harsh whisper but I know he hears me loud and clear. He freezes before pulling his face from my neck, his dark eyes finding mine.

"What did you say to me?" he mutters through gritted teeth.

With a little bit more conviction, I put everything I can into my next words. "I said no."

He pauses for a moment before he descends into laughter. I look upon him in shock, unable to understand what's happening. Out of all the reactions that I was preparing myself for, this wasn't on the list.

Eventually he calms down enough to look back at me. Instead of the humor you would think would be on his face, I find an undeniable rage.

"You think that you can tease me and just tell me no? That's not how this works, Cherry." His upper lip raises as he sneers at me. "I paid for a service and I expect to be paid."

"I don't do full service work." I shake my head, proud that I don't stutter.

He snorts. "You don't do full service for anyone but me. I fucking own you."

"No," I whisper again. Dread washes over me in a wave. I already know where this is going. I thought I would have been one of the lucky ones. I never signed myself up for anything but dancing.

Guess my luck ran out.

"After months of begging, Ivan finally decided he was ready to sell you to me. It might just be for the night but I don't plan on letting you get far from me, Cherry."

"No. No. No," I murmur the words over and over again.

I feel a tear drip down my cheek. I knew that Ivan was a pig but I didn't expect this. Everything I have been running from is catching up to me again.

No.

This Alpha will take me. Mrs. Perry will eventually call Child Protection and Amity will be put into the system. My baby will be taken from me.

No.

I feel myself begin to hyperventilate. My breathing comes in ragged breaths that hardly reach my lungs before they are drawn back again.

The man pressed against me doesn't seem to notice my freak out. If he does, he doesn't pay it any mind. Instead he continues to mumble on, talking about everything he will do to me once I am his.

The words are drowned out, replaced by ringing that threatens to deafen me.

That anger that I had called when I was first attacked slowly returns to the forefront like some kind of flight-or-fight mechanism.

I thrash my body against the tight hold on me. The once murmured words quickly turn into shouting.

I feel like we are caught in the fight for hours but it must only be seconds before the body pinning me is pulled away from mine.

I go to fall to the ground but instead of the broken pieces of the alley catching me, a hard body does.

I go to fight them, refusing to relax, but I pause as a calming voice shushes me.

"Shh, it's okay. You are safe." A gruff voice makes me jolt, pausing the panic, if only for a moment.

Lifting my head, I look up to find captivating dark blue eyes beaming down at me. The man's graying hair is combed back from his face. While it is clear he is a good twenty years older than my twenty-eight, that does nothing to deny just how attractive he is.

He has this rough, stern look about him. Like he has seen plenty of shit in his life.

Three frown lines sit between his dark brows. They seem highlighted even more thanks to the concerned look he is giving me.

A short beard covers the lower half of his face. Something inside of me is desperate to run my fingers through it but I refuse to move my hand from where it grips the front of his suit jacket.

Letting go of him, I scramble from his arms, doing my best to find my feet again as I stand up.

The man stands to his full height and I gulp taking in his sheer size. I know I am not tall by any means. My five-foot-five being stood over by the taller population regularly, but damn.

He has a good foot on me, most likely more if I was to break out a tape measure.

We both stand rooted in spot for a moment looking at each other, waiting for the other to do or say something.

He seems to take the lead, dropping his shoulders as if an attempt to look less threatening.

"You are safe now, sweetheart. He won't bother you any longer."

At his words, I finally allow my eyes to leave his as I look in the direction of the grunting and occasional muffled yell.

Two men stand over Mr. CEO, beating him within an inch of his life. Blood sprays through the alleyway, adding the already foul decor.

I know that I should be terrified. That I should be pulling out my already busted cell and call 911.

But I can't.

Instead, I turn back to the man in front of me. I nod at him once before turning and making a run for the exit of the alleyway.

The guy shouts after me telling me to wait but I don't listen.

Why would I when he and his friends are Alphas too?

CHAPTER TWO

VALENTINA

I finally slow down as I reach the front of my apartment building but I refuse to stop completely until the elevator doors open in front of me. It's a struggle to catch my breath but I eventually do, slumping against the elevator wall.

It's only seconds before the doors open, spilling out into the quiet corridor.

I quietly unlock the front door, unable to stop myself from checking behind myself a dozen times before stumbling inside.

"Valentina, are you okay?" The gentle voice of Mrs. Perry instantly settles my raised nerves.

I swallow down the panic that claws at me and nod, even though it is a lie.

"Yeah, Mrs. Perry. Sorry about banging around in here so late. I didn't mean to wake you."

She shakes her head, getting up from the couch and makes her way towards me. The older lady smiles at me and a piece of my heart shatters, the way it always does when she looks at me the way she does.

"Don't you be sorry, girl. Those silly TV show games always put me to sleep."

We both chuckle knowing it's true. The only thing that doesn't seem to put her to sleep are the late night telenovellas she is addicted to. I have to admit, there have been many nights I have turned them on and sobbed into a tub of caramel ice cream.

With a quick goodbye, Mrs. Perry takes the few steps back to her apartment, leaving me alone again.

Setting my bag down on my bed, I don't linger too long, instead I quietly open the door to my daughter's room.

The princess night-light casts shapes around her room, helping to lighten the dark corners like I know she likes. I thank myself that she is still so little that we are able to share a twin bed without much fuss.

I wrap my arms around my three-year-old, smiling at myself at the snore that escapes her.

I sigh, lowering my head to breathe in her floral and baby powder scent.

I came too close to losing her tonight. She would have been taken from me like she almost was all those years ago.

It's futile to even try and stop the tears that escape me then. So instead, I allow them to flow freely, crying myself to sleep wrapped around my tiny human.

A foot in my rib-cage jolts me awake. Opening eyes, I find Amity staring down at me. Her dark blonde hair sticks up from her head making me snort at her ethereal clown look she is serving.

"Mommy! What you doing?"

I chuckle at the sweet voice of my daughter, "Well, Mommy really missed you last night and your bed looked so much more comfortable than mine so I thought we could have a little sleepover."

She nods, the words processing for a moment before her green eyes brighten. "Pancakes for bek-fast?"

I nod, smiling as she cheers and does a little dance before pulling me out of her bed and rushing me towards the kitchen.

The both of us are covered in flour and pancake batter by the time we sit down to eat. Not once do I complain as I smile down at Amity.

She is worth the time it will take to clean up the mess that we made.

Seeing her smile makes everything worth it.

Amity chatters about everything and anything that she can think of. I nod along to her chatter as I finish off my short stack.

Eventually, she pauses enough to finish her breakfast before she is off playing with her dolls. Her being distracted gives me enough time to do my daily house chores.

And enough time to think about the events that unfolded last night.

It's not the first time that one of the patrons has been pissed off about their dance not going further. But it was the first time one has followed me home and proceeded to tell me that my sleazebag of a boss 'sold' me.

I can't believe that asshole! Who the fuck does he think he is selling us like we are objects to be bought?

I know that a few of the other girls regularly take part in more than just dancing. Crystal and Misty are regularly seen walking out of the club at the end of the night with their man of the night hanging off them. Diamond boasts about the men Ivan has introduced her to, telling us how good they are to her.

I now know that it is more than just an introduction.

We are being sold off to the highest bidder like we are some kind of show ponies.

My anger is disrupted at the sound of my phone buzzing on the bench.

Lulu:

I have coffee. Be there in 5

Me:

See you soon xx

Since the first night I started at the club, a morning after debrief has become a tradition for Luna and I. From moment one, she took me under her wing. Not only did she become a mentor of such but also someone that I grew to rely on.

While neither of us has ever taken a deep dive into our pasts, it was almost like we were able to sense a fellow victim in each other.

We didn't have to share our traumas to be there for the other person when memories resurface.

I never thought that I would have allowed myself to ever trust someone ever again, yet I have been able to with Luna.

Putting my phone down, I continue stacking the dishwasher. The mundane chore also allows me to dive back into the rest of the events of last night.

The men that saved me.

More to the point, the Alphas that saved me.

Putting saved and Alphas in the same sentence doesn't feel right after all of the trauma that designation has put me through.

Yet, here we are.

It also didn't get past me that the Alpha that spoke to me smelt delicious. I have never smelled anything like him. Even all of these hours later, I can still smell his warm and deep forest-like scent. There was also a hint of leather in there somewhere.

I choke on my own breath when I notice my Omega scent spike. Dropping what I am doing, I race into the bathroom, finding my scent-neutralizing spray and immediately douse my entire body.

I curse myself for forgetting it. That as well as my scent-blockers and suppressants.

The doctor I saw when I gave birth to Amity warned me to not double up on the pills but I had to do everything in my power to hide my Omega designation. Research had shown that doubling the tablets could cause heat and fertility issues.

Good thing neither of those issues bother me in the slightest. I refuse to allow my designation to make me vulnerable ever again.

Knocking at the front door of my apartment makes me startle. I drop the neutralizing spray on my foot and curse myself as another knock sounds at the door.

"Give me a minute," I yell as I jump around the cramped room.

Pushing all of my previous thoughts to the back of my mind, I quickly grab my pills, throwing them back before going to the front door.

The moment the door is open a crack, Luna already pushes through the gap.

"Ugh, finally! What were you doing in here? Did you forget where your front door was?"

I roll my eyes at my best friend before closing the door behind her.

"So dramatic, Lulu. It was like a minute."

She waves her hands in the air before setting her bags down on the bench. Everything else is forgotten when she hands me my coffee.

I sigh as I sip the liquid gold before making my way over to the lounge. The breath I exhale is heavy enough that Luna is immediately able to catch on.

With a pointed look, she raises her eyebrow at me. "Come on, spill. It's been hours since I saw you last. What happened in all of that time to have you looking at me like that?"

I swallow thickly as I work up the courage to tell Luna exactly what happened. I already know that she is going to be pissed off.

Luna is absolutely the mother of the group even though she is a year older than me. She takes her role seriously too, regularly whipping the more immature girls into line.

She is the only one of us that Ivan doesn't walk all over.

I take another final breath before looking back up at my best friend.

"You know how I have been having issues with Mr. CEO being too pushy?"

She nods, so I continue.

"Well, last night as I was walking home, he followed me and ended up cornering me in one of the alleys down the road from the club."

I don't stop talking but I do notice Luna become increasingly irritated.

"He said that I have been teasing him. That I want him but I am just leading him on. When I told him no he informed me that I couldn't say no. That he finally *bought* me from Ivan."

The room is deathly silent for a moment. I don't look up at Luna, instead I pretend to find the hem of my shorts incredibly interesting.

I startle when Luna launches up from the lounge. "Are you fucking kidding me? That filthy old cunt *sold* you? Who the fuck does he think he is? King fucking Ding-a-ling?"

My eyes widen as I watch her continue to rant, calling our boss some of the most colorful names I have ever heard.

"That limp-dicked potato better just wait for when I see him next! Not only that but that pig of a client you have been seeing. He better not come into the club ever again. I don't care how big he is; I will beat a motherfucker for putting his hands on you!"

I chuckle, unable to help myself from smiling at the protective side of her. For a Beta, she has a ridiculous amount of Alpha qualities.

Honestly, it wouldn't surprise me if she is masking like I am.

"I don't think he will be much of a problem anymore..." I trail off, finally looking up at her.

She lifts an eyebrow, waiting for me to continue.

"The only reason that I was able to get away was because three guys jumped in and pulled him off me."

Luna's eyes widen with interest, her previous anger gone quicker than I can blink.

"Three guys you say..."

I roll my eyes at the suggestive undertone in her voice. "Yes, Lulu. Three Alphas stormed in and saved the day." She goes to speak but I stop her, holding up a finger. "Before you get too excited and say what I think you are going to say, no, I didn't stay around and wait for them to finish their beat down of the crusty foreskin."

"So they beat him up for you?"

She pretends to swoon, collapsing into a heap on the couch. "Oh, Valentina. Your knights in shining knots swooped in and protected your chastity. How incredibly noble of them! Oh, I just know they will call on you!"

I snort, slapping Luna on the thigh. "Fuck off. The last thing I need is a man in my life. They're too much drama."

I do my best to act nonchalant when on the inside, I am anything but.

She scoffs, "I don't mean you need to fall in love, have a litter of children and a white-picket fence. I mean, when was the last time you got any?"

"I..." I drift off with a shake of my head. She's got me there.

Luna gives me a pointed look. She already knows just how long it has been since I have been with anyone but my vibrator. The thought of sleeping with someone, even if that someone is just a Beta, gives me hives. It would be near impossible to not out myself there and then as an Omega. While I feel much more secure around Betas than Alphas, I don't need anybody in this new life of mine knowing my deepest secrets.

"I just ... I don't think I am ready to put myself out there again. I already feel bad enough missing out on so much time with Amity.

Adding someone else to that mix just feels like a disaster ready to happen."

It's Luna's turn to smack me then. "Stop that self-hate bullshit, Valley. I don't have to tell you that you are the best fucking mother on this entire planet. You live and breathe for that precious little girl. You don't make a single move without thinking about her." She straightens her posture and grabs my hands, bringing my full attention to her. "It's okay to be selfish. It's okay to be a mom but still prioritize you and the things that make you happy. It's okay to have a day off. To just be Valentina and not be Mama."

"But, I just..." I trail off again, unable to really find the words. I know part of what Luna is saying is true but I still can't stop those negative thoughts from surfacing.

"I am the only person that Amity has. She relies on me to be there for her. To be stable and to provide. If I am off with some guy, I can't do that."

"Stop," Luna pauses, her face scrunching. "Amity doesn't only have you. She has me as well. I love that girl just as much as I do any of my nieces. I also know for a fact that even if you didn't need the help, Mrs. Perry would demand to spend time with Amity."

Luna is right. Like she normally always is.

Mrs. Perry has adored my daughter since the moment she heard her cries in the hallway the day I brought her home.

While I had spoken to my elderly neighbour a few times up until that point, the moment she saw my little girl's face, it was like something in her changed.

Those first few weeks, Mrs. Perry was practically over every single day, helping to put us into a routine, allowing me to sleep after an entire night of being awake and ensuring that I also looked after myself.

She was the mother that I needed but didn't have.

I know without a shadow of doubt that I wouldn't have survived the newborn period if it wasn't for her.

"You have a village, Valley. It's okay to call on us. It's okay to put yourself first."

I deflate completely. There is no use fighting it. What Luna is saying is right. I do need to be selfish. I do need to put myself sometimes.

"I just don't know if I am ready yet."

"Will you at least consider it?" she questions.

I nod, knowing that I will. It has been years since everything went down. I need to move on from what happened. I can't allow myself to remain stagnant.

I deserve to find true happiness.

I deserve to love and be loved.

It just may take me a while.

CHAPTER THREE

VALENTINA

After Luna left, I followed the tiny chatter down the hallway, finding Amity in a sea of her dolls. It was impossible to not join her as I allowed myself to indulge in the childhood throwback.

The day seemed to fly by then as we went through our regular Saturday routine. I didn't notice it at first but as the sun began to set, a feeling of nervousness started to settle in my stomach.

I know I shouldn't be anxious about returning to work.

I have no doubt in my mind that those Alphas got rid of the CEO—the man's name something I never bothered to remember—but the unsettling feeling still lingers as I begin getting ready for work.

I try to replay my mantra over and over in my head.

I am okay. I am safe. No one can hurt me anymore.

Yet, it doesn't seem to give me that comforting edge that it normally does. I don't stop repeating it though. It took months for it to catch when I first escaped.

I hate thinking about that time.

The time where I was the most vulnerable.

Newly pregnant and on the run in a city that I had never been in before.

I startle when I hear the knock at the door, gasping and clutching at my chest. I give myself a moment to breathe through my panic before checking my watch. I berate myself as I realize that it's just Mrs. Perry coming to start looking after Amity.

I knew I shouldn't have gotten caught up in my head thinking about my old life. It has never done me any good before. But since Mr. CEO got too handsy, it has been creeping in on me more than I would like.

Maybe it's time to finally speak to a therapist. Yet, as the thought comes to mind, I banish it, knowing that I won't ever spend that kind of money on myself. I can barely buy myself new clothes—even if they are only from the thrift store.

Putting down the mascara I am lucky I didn't stab my eye with, I take a breath, making my way to the front door and greet my babysitter.

Instantly, the older woman can see the stress on my face. She doesn't say a single word, folding me into her arms and holds me for a moment before letting me go.

"Is the rugrat in her room?" she questions, putting her bag down on the kitchen bench.

I nod, not able to say anything with the threat of tears spilling thanks to the motherly gesture.

Grabbing a hold of my shoulder, she gives me a slight squeeze. "Go finish getting ready, I've got her from here."

Swallowing back more tears that threaten to fall, I head back into my room. Rummaging through my draws I try to find the right outfit to wear. Just as I am about to pick the more modest set that I used to wear when I first started stripping, my phone buzzes.

Lulu:

You better not be wearing that granny set tonight, V. Fuck those creeps. They don't own you. Remember exactly who the fuck you are.

Me:

I swear you are a mind reader.

Lulu:

I FUCKING KNEW IT!!!!

If you wear that horrific shit that you should have burnt years ago, I will disown you.

I roll my eyes, snorting at the girl I consider my best friend. The worst part is, I know that she would do something extreme like that.

Me:

Fine. What should I wear?

Lulu:

The red set. You know the one.

Me:

Lu…

Lulu:

Do it, Val. It's the best fuck you to those fuckers!

Eyeing off said outfit I look at it for a minute before looking back down at the texts Luna sent.

She is right. I do need to give them a big fuck you. I need to remind myself of who the fuck I am. I shouldn't be hiding or cowering away from these men.

They want me to cower to them. To submit to them.

Its so fucking typical of Alphas. They see other designations as below them. That to not be an Alpha is a stain on humanity.

I feel my jaw tick, the anger I try to keep hidden day in and day out threatening to burst from me.

Fuck Alphas. Fuck men who think that they can get away with controlling others.

Grabbing the scraps of red lace from my drawer, I stuff them into my bag.

I won't cower.

I won't be that weak, whimpering Omega that I have withdrawn myself from.

Fuck that.

Pulling the scraps of red lace onto my body, I instantly feel more powerful. I know that we have another full house tonight, something that I am grateful for. Having what will no doubt be my choice in high-rollers and successful businessmen ready to throw their money around will give me the best opportunity to take back that bit of me that was stolen last night.

Not allowing myself to get dragged back down into those negative thoughts, I shake my head, grabbing up my belongings before making my way back to my station.

Whistles, hoots and hollers greet me from the girls in the room.

"Hot damn, Sweet Cherry Pie! Way to ensure none of us get paid tonight!"

I laugh at Candy who is looking at me with a proud glint in her smokey lined eyes. The blonde should know that is a lie, especially judging by the stack of cash she is already counting.

"Don't be jealous, C. Our girl needs to send a message tonight," Luna pipes up, walking over to me and taking my stuff from my arms and shoving it into my locker.

Crystal narrows her eyes. "What do you mean?"

My fiery best friend turns towards the other girl, "Did you know that slime bag Ivan sold Cherry last night without her knowledge?"

Not a single noise apart from the distant thump of the club music is muttered. The girls all look at me with a mixture of horror and anger. The latter are the ones that I know have also seen some shit in their lives.

"That motherfucker," Crystal finally mutters. Each of the girls echo their agreement with her.

"I know that some of you girls are okay being a part of the extra deals that Ivan offers, but not all of us have signed up for that."

Both Misty and Diamond at least have the audacity to look sheepish.

"Just because we are apart of the sex work industry, does not mean that we have consented to everything," Luna continues as more of the girls agree with her. "So tonight, our girl is going to say fuck you to those that can't take the word no as final."

Cheers from the girls instantly boost me as I brace myself to talk out the door.

I pull each of my walls up, cementing them as best as I can.

It's the same ritual that I do every night.

Taking a final breath in, I open my eyes.

I am ready.

The sounds of rowdy men celebrating the end of the current dancer's set are near-deafening. It's hardly a surprise considering not a single scrap of fabric is currently covering her body. She is a newer dancer—one that I haven't had the chance to get to know yet— so it's no surprise to me to see her grinning at the attention she is receiving.

It is a little bit like that at the start. The attention becomes addicting. The thrill of men lusting after you is an amazing boost to the ego.

And having them throw their entire paycheck at you just to see a bit of extra skin? Yeah, that keeps you coming back for more.

But once all of that wears off, it simply just becomes a job.

The new girl beams at me carrying her overflowing money bag in her arms. "They are hungry out there tonight! Have fun out there!"

I give her a small smile and a nod before turning back to the runway.

The Cherry persona that I have perfected over the years slides easily into place as the DJ introduces me with his regular speech.

The sounds of the guitar riff from the late eighties hit causes an uproar of the patrons just like I knew it would. I can't help the devious smile that brightens my face knowing that I already have these men in the palm of my hand. They are begging for it and I haven't even stepped on stage.

Turning my head, I find Luna grinning at me. Giving her a wink, I turn and walk out onto the stage.

I don't know how, but the roaring gets impossibly louder. I swing my hips to the beat, taking slow steps towards the pole.

Dollar bills are thrown at me with each step that I take. I have to be careful to not slip on any of the bills. While the black strappy heels are comfortable to walk in, I refuse to make a fool of myself; especially when I am on my redemption dance.

I slide my hands up my body, teasing my fingers over the straps of the top. I spot an Alpha gripping his crotch as he hollers at me. I wink at him, giving him a saucy smile that he goes wild over. My false bravado wins in the end as I watch him throw me a fifty dollar note.

I turn away from him quickly, as I continue to eye off the rest of the crowd gathered around the stage. Reaching out, I grab onto the pole, taking slow steps around it before hooking my leg and giving a slow spin. It gives me another perfect chance to work the crowd over.

The smile remains on my face as I spin a second time. That is until a familiar set of eyes catch mine.

I gasp, my smile drops as the eyes of the man that all but saved me last night look back at me.

His piercing blue eyes feel like they can see straight through me, able to analyze every single one of my secrets from a single glance. The orbs are filled with a hunger that makes the single hand gripping the pole, shake. My stomach does flips as I finally lose eye contact, having spun past the Alpha.

Never in my life have I reacted this way to anyone. Never has a single glance both unsettled and aroused me.

Even though my back is now to him, I can still feel his eyes on me as I come to a stop.

With my back to both the crowd and the pole, I am able to give myself a moment to regather myself. With one hand above my head gripping the pole, I slowly slide down until I am on my knees on the stage.

Whipping my loose curls, I slowly begin to crawl and to the front of the stage. I don't allow myself to meet the eyes of the Alpha again. Instead, I find a younger guy at least a few years younger than my twenty-eight. He is sitting amongst a few of his friends who are nudging and teasing him. Judging by his attire and demeanor, he is clearly on his bachelor night.

His eyes meet mine from where they were locked on my tits that are threatening to spill out of the skimpy bra. His smile widens as I make my way over to him. The moment I reach the end of the stage, I slowly throw my legs off the end of the catwalk. Money from each of his friends is quickly slapped to the man's chest.

He doesn't lose eye contact with me as I reach him and sit down on his lap. It's a much bolder move from what I thought I would be able to manage tonight but I don't dare stop. Especially not when I get a hit of his scent.

Beta.

Thank fuck.

Getting the extra dose of confidence that I need, I spend a good majority of my first song giving the groom-to-be the best lap dance of my career. Once I have well and truly earnt the money safely tucked under my garter, I slip off his lap, giving him one last grin.

The guys around him cheer and I hear slaps on the back and plenty of 'fuck yeah, that was so hot' remarks as I step back onto the stage.

The rest of my set goes off without a hitch. With only a glance, I know that I have well and truly made more money than I ever have in a single night.

Ben helps me to collect my earnings with the help of a velvet sack. It is practically a pillow case, not that anyone seems to care. He hands it over, along with my discarded bra.

Making my way back to the dressing room, I can't wipe the smile off my face. Tonight was exactly what I needed. I feel like I am me again.

Well, the new me at least. The me that I want to be. Even with that Alpha from last night's presence that unnerved me for a moment, I feel more powerful. More in control.

After stuffing my money into my locker, I redress and finish reapplying my makeup just as Ben comes through the door of the dressing room.

"Hey, Cherry. You have been booked for a private. Are you ready?"

I snicker under my breath. Hook, line and sinker.

"Sure am." I fix a final strand of my hair before following him into the private rooms.

Ben is one of the only guys I have been able to give an ounce of my trust to since working here. I know it has a lot to do with the fact that not only is Ben a Beta, but also the fact that he is in a very committed marriage. It was a comfort that was cemented even further when I watched the pair get married to each other a few months after I started here.

With a smile and a promise of a catch up when the night is over, Ben opens the door to room five.

CHAPTER FOUR

VALENTINA

Before I can even step into the room fully, the scent of oakmoss and amber hits me like a ton of bricks.

Snapping my head up, I find the source of the smell.

It's him.

The Alpha from last night who stepped in to stop the creep from succeeding in his threats.

I close my eyes and take a calming breath. A decision that was not one of my finest as the tantalizing smell overcomes my senses.

Instead, I open my eyes and smile at him, just like I do every single private room guest. If I treat this like any other booking, I will make it through ... right?

"Hi." My voice has a sensual edge that I pray isn't laced with the nervousness that I feel.

"Hi."

Just like last night, the deep rumble has an immediate effect on me. My knees wobble as I close the distance between us even though I wish that I was currently anywhere but here. I wonder if that groom wants a private dance. Fuck, I would take any of his friends right now just to get out of here.

But I don't run.

Omegas run.

I am not an Omega.

Making my way to the pole in front of the couches, I slowly begin one of my favorite routines. It distracts me enough that I am able to actually do my job.

Once my feet are back on the ground, I crawl over to him and onto his lap.

An electric shock tingles my fingers the moment they lace around his neck. I'm unable to hide the hitch in my breath as I settle onto his lap. My core tightens and it takes all of my willpower to not moan in pleasure.

What the fuck was that?

It's clear I am not the only one affected judging by the hardness I feel tenting his slacks. I don't give it any attention though. It's not the first guy who has got a hard-on while I have been in his lap and it certainly won't be the last.

Instead, I smile and grind against him before slowly dragging my hands down his suit-clad body. Even with the fabric in the way, I can tell that he is well built.

It doesn't do me any favors at all.

I should not find this man as attractive as I do.

He is everything that I am rebelling against.

Yet, I am like putty in his hands. A fact I will never make him aware of.

Up this close, I am able to take in the face that haunts me. It's clear that there is an obvious age gap between us. Enough of one that his hair is majority gray. There are fine-lines around his eyes only visible because I am sitting on his lap. They are slight though, not giving me any more of an indicator of how old he is.

I would die to know his skincare routine though.

What I wouldn't do to be able to bat off my impending thirties just a little bit longer.

Eventually I break the silence between us. "What is your name?"

"Victor. And yours, *bellisima?*"

The Italian makes my entire body shiver—the words my near undoing—but I still manage to grit out, "Cherry."

"*Hai infestato i miei sogni, dolce ciliegia.*"

Goosebumps spread over my skin as he continues to speak in what I am assuming is his native tongue.

"*Però ti piace, vero? Vuoi che io sia infatuato di te. Incapace di respirare se non sei vicino.*"

Unable to voice any kind of appropriate response, I instead nod my head. It was clearly the right thing to say as his eyes heat impossibly so.

Ever so slowly, I begin to move my hands from his neck, back down his body and to where ours meet. Victor's breath hitches as I continue moving my hands over my body and to the clasp behind my back.

"*Sei una tentatrice mandata dalle profondità dell'inferno per torturarmi.*"

Unclipping my bra, I let the fabric fall between us.

"*Non vedo l'ora di essere bruciato.*"

He gulps and I can't help but chuckle at the reaction to my bare chest. I continue to move against him, teasing both him and I.

I thank my earlier self for making sure to take my suppressants. I don't know how well I would have been able to keep my secret a secret with this guy teasing me the way he is

While my whole goal of tonight was to say fuck you to Alphas, there's no harm in getting a little bit of pleasure from one... Is there?

Besides, like Luna so graciously pointed out today, it's been years. Everytime I have been out with Luna and have found someone remotely attractive, the thought of going any further breaks me out in a cold sweat.

Yet here I am, topless and dry humping a complete stranger.

I try to convince myself that I am just simply doing my job. Being half naked, dancing on men is literally how I pay my bills. But it doesn't feel quite like work right now.

Why does it feel *right*?

It shouldn't.

I should be repulsed by him.

I shouldn't be picturing what it would be like if he bent me over this couch.

No.

I shake my head and immediately put my walls back up.

Victor must be able to sense something off as I feel him stiffen beneath me. This time, it's not his cock.

"Hey, where did you go, *dolce ciliegia?*"

He lifts a hand up to my cheek but I push myself up out of his lap before he can touch me.

"Um, I think your time is up. I hope you have a great night."

I don't bother to pick up my bra from wherever it fell.

It can stay there for all I care.

I need to leave.

Before I can take a step further towards the door, a hand on my arm stops me from going any further.

I stiffen under his touch. Whipping around, I find Victor towering over me.

"Don't leave."

It's not an Alpha bark but it is close enough to one that I freeze. Scenes of deja vu begin to flash before my eyes before I can stop them.

I see those Alphas on top of me. The way they used to grab me. Force me to present for them. Next comes the hits they would rain down on my flesh every single time they saw fit.

Torturing me was their favorite part of the day. They got off on my pain. On my screams. Of my begging and pleading for them to stop.

But no matter how hoarse my voice would get, they never stopped.

Not until I stopped them. Permanently.

"Get your fucking hand off me."

My tone gives no room for play as I grit out the demand. Immediately, Victor lifts his hand from my arm, raising both so I can see them.

"I..."

He goes to speak but I cut him off.

"No. I don't know who the fuck you think you are, but no. Thank you for stepping in last night but if you think that thank you is going to extend to anything past a few polite words; you are wrong."

Not giving him a chance to say anything else, I turn tail and race out of the private room.

Fuck Alphas.

Fuck every single one of them.

CHAPTER FIVE

VICTOR

I stare at the door of the private room after my *dolce ciliegia* gave me the dressing down of my life.

I haven't been this drawn to someone in a long time.

After my world was torn to pieces years ago, I gave up on ever finding love again. I had come to the conclusion that my pack would be alone for the rest of our lives.

Because I didn't think that anyone would ever compare to her.

Until *her*.

Initially, I didn't know what to think when I heard the scuffling coming from the dark alleyway last night. This area of Vadena is sketchy at the best of times.

But coming face to face with that fuckwit Gerald with that sweet girl in his arms was not on my bingo card for the night after meeting with the Angels.

It was like a red haze came over my vision.

Women getting hurt is not something I tolerate. Not in my fucking city.

I know that both my packmates Conall and Olis feel the same.

We didn't even have to communicate verbally. Having worked alongside both my brother and best friend since we formed our pack in high school, we don't need to. We automatically know what the other is thinking before we act. Which is why Conall and Olis pulled Gerald off her while I helped to comfort the girl.

Cherry.

God, it suits her. Even though I know that isn't her real name.

Her scent doesn't give me anything. Her being a Beta makes it more neutral.

She looked so breakable looking up at me, cowered in fear. Something in my heart snapped when her eyes met mine.

There is only one other time that I felt that feeling.

It doesn't make sense though. How could that Beta be mine? Alphas have always been destined to mate with Omegas. I know of many Betas that are a part of packs—having relationships with both the Alphas and Omega—but it is rare that they would form without an Omega.

Yet here I am, stalking the woman that I have quickly become obsessed with.

All it took was one look.

After she ran off on me, I followed closely behind her in the shadows, vowing to protect what I know is mine. She didn't run for long before she entered an apartment building that has seen better days.

I don't know how long I stood outside of the building before I eventually left before returning first thing the next morning.

Color me shocked when she finally left after making me wait all day to see her, only to follow her into The Throbbing Knot.

I couldn't help but cringe at the thought of her in there. I know Ivan relatively well. The weasel loves sucking up to me in the hopes that I will help to further his business in the underground.

Jokes on him because I refuse to have anything to do with the skin trade. I have no issues with prostitution, as long as there is consent. Something Ivan doesn't care about.

He wants to dip his toes in depravity.

I have heard a magnitude of whispers about the shading dealings in his club. Dealings that he knows I don't appreciate.

As I sat in the corner of the club, nursing my whiskey on the rocks, I already made up my mind that I was going to 'buy' the club from Ivan. A decision that became affirmative when my angel graced me with her presence.

It was impossible to take my eyes off the way she sensually moved her body to the music. It is clear that this isn't just a job for her.

It seems that my girl genuinely likes to dance.

I knew that I had to see more once her set ended.

Having her dance for me and me alone was like a fever dream. Having her sit on my lap as she moved against my aching cock made me feel pubescent again.

And having her put me in my place? Fuck, if that didn't nearly take me to my knees.

I shake my head before downing the rest of my drink. It shouldn't surprise me that Ivan is rebottling cheap whiskey to make it appear expensive. It's a low-baller move, one he will answer for.

No one fucks with my whiskey.

It's not hard to find Ivan. It doesn't surprise me that he is surrounded by a few low-level goons that I recognise. What does is his current conversation with them.

"...I finally sold that Cherry bitch to Gerald. He has been after her for years. The stupid slut has always told me no to any of the ... extracurricular activities if you know what I mean."

He nudges one of the men next to him and they all descend into laughter.

He fucking sold her?

My hand twitches uncontrollably as It takes every ounce of willpower that I possess to not shoot him between the eyes in the middle of his friends.

Instead, I remain as level-headed as I possibly can as I walk over to the group.

"Gentlemen."

It's impossible to control my growl as I step into the gap. Each of the men immediately stiffen before exposing their necks in submission.

I doubt they even know they are doing it. The move pleases something inside of me knowing that they know there is a predator amongst them.

"V-Victor, I d-didn't know that y-you would be h-here tonight. I-I would have or-organized my best girls for y-you."

Ivan stumbles over his words as he straightens and attempts to straighten his crumpled button down.

"Thank you, but it seems I have already found myself a gem. Care to take this somewhere private?" I ask, raising my eyebrow at him in a silent gesture of telling him to fuck these goons off.

"Oh yes, absolutely. Gentlemen." He gives them a nod before holding a hand out. "Victor, please follow me."

I struggle to hide my snort as I follow Ivan through his club and into the backrooms. I feel a slight hint of disappointment that I don't see my *dolce ciliegia* again.

That's okay though. She will be seeing a lot more of me soon.

Ivan's office is exactly what I expected. Run down and cheap, just like the rest of the establishment.

Maybe if he spent more of his earnings on the club rather than fueling his drug and gambling addictions, this place might actually be worth something.

"How can I help you, Victor? It's a surprise to see you here," Ivan says once he is seated at the desk that seems to be ready to fall apart.

"I am buying you out."

Ivan's mouth drops and he stutters over his words. I raise a single finger and he immediately shuts his mouth. Pulling out my phone, I press a few buttons before putting it away again.

At the same time, a ping sounds on Ivan's open laptop.

"Open it," I demand.

Ivan rushes to open the document and I watch as he reads through it.

"Sign it."

I would laugh if I wasn't so furious at the man before me. Ivan is a disgrace to the Alpha designation. He doesn't fight me like the many of my brethren have done in the past.

The man before me is weak. It's a pitiful sight, watching as he shakes and signs the contract handing me over complete control over the club. Over *her.*

Once the document has been sent back, I pull the glock and silencer from the back of my pants. I take my time screwing it on as I stare at

Ivan, transfixed on the way the sweat pours off his greasy forehead. There is a bitter resignation in his eyes that I revel in.

After letting him stew in his fate for longer than I need to, I lift the weapon and aim it between his eyes.

"It was a pleasure doing business with you."

CHAPTER SIX

VALENTINA

I'm still shaking with fury the next day as I stuff my washing machine full of dirty clothes from the week.

These fucking Alphas thinking that they rule the word just because they have a bark and a knot.

Fuck that.

And then for them to just think that because they helped you once that they are entitled to suddenly know everything about you.

No. Absolutely not.

I don't care how attractive and good Victor smells. He could be a goddamn chocolate cake for all I care and I still wouldn't take a bite.

I slam the door of the machine closed before standing up with a huff. I drop my head between my shoulders and give myself a chance to take a deep breath.

I had prided myself in doing so good. I hadn't had a single slip up in a long time. But this man all but stumbles into my life and I am now a blubbering mess.

"Okay, Mommy?"

The quiet voice of my daughter has me snapping my head up. Amity is looking up at me with concern written all over her fair features.

I bend down and hold my arms out. “Mommy is okay, baby. Just a little bit frustrated.”

Amity steps back from me after giving me a tight squeeze and raises her eyebrow.

“You need ice-cream! Make you feel alllllll better!”

The excitement on her face has me chuckling. My three-year-old knows me way too well.

“Ice-cream and the park?”

My daughter's eyes light with an elation that lets me know I said the magic words.

I can’t help but snort out a chuckle as I clean the chocolate ice-cream off my vibrating toddler’s face. From the moment her cup was empty, she has been beside herself with desperation to go play on the playground.

With one last wipe, I give her a nod before she takes off with a squeal.

A deep snicker behind me has me whipping around with a gasp.

“I don’t think I have ever seen someone so excited to be at the park before.”

I grab my chest at where my heart is thudding out of my chest. “Holy fuck! You scared the shit out of me.”

He grimaces, having the decency to look embarrassed. "Sorry. I just couldn't help but stop when I heard that laugh. It reminds me of my sons when they were younger."

I shake my head as I fix myself slightly, cursing myself internally for being so surprised that someone might have been behind me. I'm in a park for god's sake.

"It's okay. How old are your boys?"

He smirks at me and rubs his hand over the stubble on his chin. "My boys are twenty-five."

My eyes widen in shock as I look the guy up and down. There is no fucking way that this guy is old enough to be my father.

I don't know what is in the water of Vadena lately, but the few men that I have come across in the last few days have been breathtaking; this one is no different.

His dark brown skin is emphasized by his biceps that stretch the fabric of his almost too tight T-shirt. His black hair is kept short and cropped much like his beard. Looking closely, I can see a few strands of gray hairs that give more of an indication of his older age.

He might be older but damn if he isn't the most beautiful man I have ever seen in my life. The hint of a smile on his face only seems to add to his attractiveness.

Would he be mad if I licked him?

No, bad Valentina. You can't just go around licking random men.

I shake my head before my eyes return to his. He is already smiling at me, having noticed how I was checking him out.

"There is no way you are old enough to have a son that age." I shake my head. "I need to know your skin care routine."

He laughs at me before rubbing a hand over his head. "Yeah, I get that a lot. I definitely feel my age though."

I shake my head but snap around as I hear Amity yelling out to me.

"Mommy! Look!"

I smile and wave at Amity as I watch her slide down the slide.

"She is precious. How old is she?" he asks, coming to stand beside me.

"She is three."

"Ooft." I turn to look at the guy who is now cringing. "I remember that age vividly. Threenagers are real."

I can't help but laugh at the accurate description of this age. I thought two was challenging but it has nothing on three. I just thank my lucky stars that Amity is a good kid.

"Shit, I completely forgot to introduce myself. My name is Olis Duran."

Olis holds his hand out for me to shake. Reaching my hand out, I smile at him. "I'm Valentina."

The moment our hands connect, a spark of electricity zaps up my arm and through my entire body. I gasp at the same moment the wind changes at Olis' scent hits me like a freight train. The scent of cinnamon apples—the kind that your grandma would use in her secret apple pie recipe—has a whimper threatening to crawl from my throat.

Alpha.

Another motherfucking Alpha.

Just my luck.

Pulling my hand from his, I take a few steps back.

"It was great to meet you Olis but Amity and I should get going."

I pray that he can't hear the panic rising in the tone of my voice.

Why now? Why are these Alphas strolling into my life and flipping everything upside down? Why does Olis have to be an Alpha and be so fucking *nice*? There is just no way that he can be both. Alphas aren't biologically programmed to be *nice*.

They are brutes. A designation that can't control their aggression.

I turn my back on the predator who tries to stop me with my name and a few pleas to wait but I don't listen.

I need to get the fuck out of here and back to the safety of my tiny apartment.

"Valentina, wait!"

I can hear footsteps that slowly begin to quicken behind me but I don't stop. Not even once I have Amity in my arms. Not until the front door of my apartment shuts behind me and I know that I am finally safe.

Fuck this week.

After wasting away the rest of the day trying to distract my mind with trash TV, I begin getting ready for work again.

Sunday is the final day of my work week until Thursday rolls around again.

I feel an edge of disappointment when I have to say goodbye to Amity again. I know why it is so important that I go to work every night that I can but it doesn't stop the mom guilt. That evil little voice in my head telling me that I shouldn't be working and instead staying at home with my daughter every night.

Yet the other voice in my head is telling me that if I miss one night of work, we will lose everything that I have worked so hard for. That we will end up on the street and at the mercy of Alphas that will control us; again.

It feels like I won't win no matter what I do. I just know that I can't let the latter happen ever again. Especially not now that I have someone else that I need to think about. Someone else that I need to protect.

My best friend's face is the first to greet me as I make my way into the dressing room. Her smile is wide, her face bright with an excitement that I could never feel being in these walls.

"What has you all happy, Lulu?"

Instead of giving me shit for using her nickname, Luna grins even wider, bouncing over towards me and enveloping me in her arms.

"You will never believe what happened, Cherry. Ivan sold his club to some billionaire! The new owners came in earlier to introduce themselves to us. Apparently, over the next few days, they are going to shut the club and remodel it for a reopening on Friday!"

It takes me a moment to catch on to what exactly Luna is saying.

"Ivan's gone?"

She grabs me by the shoulders and shakes me. "Ivan is fucking gone!"

My breath exhales in a broken shudder. Relief deflates my entire body. Even though I despised my now old boss, I held onto this job with both hands. Now that he is gone, it might actually be enjoyable to come to work each day.

Maybe the new owners will ensure that nothing shady goes down behind closed doors. Maybe the next time a client shows a bit too much interest, instead of selling them a dancer, they will get kicked out.

A slight grin remains on my face as I get dressed for my shift. I have a stage set first up followed by privates with two of my regulars.

I decided to keep my 'Fuck Alphas and Men' theme going for this weekend. My metallic silver set was too good of an option to pass up. I swipe a final layer of red lipstick over my lips, smacking them as I look over myself.

Not to toot my own horn but damn, I look fucking good.

I keep my smile on until I hit what feels like a brick wall as I walk out into the hallway that leads to the main stage. A chuckle and hands on my shoulder that cause sparks to fly through my body from the brick wall has me stepping back.

I can't help holding back my gasp as I come face to face with Victor.

"Are you stalking me now?" I accuse, unable to stop a growl forming in my throat.

"Me? Stalking you? Baby, I would prefer for you to know just how obsessed I am with you." His chuckle has my stomach twisting up in knots but I ignore it.

"You aren't fucking funny, Victor. I told you to leave me alone."

Victor's eyes widen as he looks down at me. His salt and pepper hair seems lighter tonight than it did last. He is also missing his glasses.

Maybe he has contacts in...

Victor shakes his head, chuckling under his breath, "Ah, so you have met my brother. It doesn't surprise me that he has already managed to piss you off. He has a tendency to do that." He raises his eyebrow as he does his best smolder—one that works on me as my knees threaten to collapse beneath me—before taking a step closer into my space. "My name is Conall. It's a pleasure to meet you."

Conall lifts my hand up to his lips, keeping his eyes locked on mine and places a delicate kiss to my slowly heating skin.

I'm shocked out of my trance-like state as shouts from the other end of the hallway startle me.

The man before me isn't the man that has been following me around.

No, he is in fact that same man's twin brother.

Another mother fucking Alpha if I am to go off his tobacco and vanilla scent that has me tightly in its clutches.

I want to bottle the scent and douse myself in it.

No.

No.

I can't allow another one of these Alphas to have this kind of power over me. Fucking again.

Snatching my hand out of Conall's, I bless him with the most uninterested look I can, one he grins at like it is a challenge he wants to concur.

"Well, it was delightful to run into you Conall but I have a job to do."

I don't bother with any other pleasantries as I hit my shoulder into his which I know hurts me more than him, as I continue heading down the hallway. I can already hear the end of Misty's set and I don't plan on being late, especially not when I know the new owners are in tonight. I don't need to add being fired to my fucked up week.

I decide to add a little bit of salt to the wound that will no doubt be Conall's freshly shredded ego as I swing my hips with a little more vigor. His sounding pained groan behind me has me snickering under my breath as I walk up onto the stage.

CHAPTER SEVEN

CONALL

I know that my mother would be cursing my name if she could see the way I stare at the little devil's ass as she walks away from me.

I couldn't hold back on my scepticism at my twin buying a strip club, especially one this rundown and derelict. But as the woman, who I now follow without question, makes her way up onto the stage for her set, I don't question Victor's choices.

In fact, I applaud his decisions.

I don't pay attention to any of my surroundings as I watch her walk up to the pole before performing tricks that have my eyes blowing wide in surprise.

It's impressive at just how much she trusts the tiny pieces of fabric that hide her most private parts from the world.

Her lush, curvy body has me transfixed.

This woman is an enigma.

Just by the single interaction with her, I want to know every single one of the secrets that she is so desperately clinging to.

I want to know everything about her.

What is her name?

What is her favorite color?

What does she like to do other than dance?

What does she taste when her head is thrown back in pleasure?

I shake my head, surprising myself at the dirty thoughts that begin to plague me. All of the new fantasies that I am desperate to try are filled with nothing but the striking brunette.

The only woman in years that has made me feel anything remotely special.

The day mine and my pack's Omega was murdered was single handedly the worst day of my life. Seeing her bloody lifeless body has haunted my dreams for years.

Getting her the justice that she deserved was the only thing that made the years of grief livable.

Yet, this little spitfire stumbles into my life and up turns it within minutes.

I don't know how long her set goes for but I watch every single second of it. How could I not? My little devil is spectacular. Not only is she drop dead fucking gorgeous, but the way she brushed me off like I was a spec of dust on her seven-inch heels had me wanting to get on my knees for her.

A hand slapping down onto my shoulder has me instantly on edge, ready to throttle whoever the fuck is disturbing me out of my new favorite show.

"Conall, I..." Olis trails off as he finally gets a proper look at my new obsession. "Valentina," he growls.

Valentina.

I groan as I turn back to her. Her name suits her so fucking perfect-ly.

My beautiful new little obsession.

Both of us remain motionless, hardly able to breath as we watch Valentina finish her set.

I stiffen as I watch her slowly begin to remove her bra, exposing her perfect chest to the entire room.

The only thing stopping me from storming the stage and covering her is the hand that grips my shoulder.

"Sit, brother. Let her finish her set."

The sound of Victor's voice doesn't calm me, instead it has me stiffening as I watch my girl tease the Alphas and Betas going wild for her. How fucking dare they look at her with lust! How dare they look at the utter perfection that is mine!

Because that's exactly what she is. Fucking *mine*.

If I have to cause a scene, putting bullets into the skulls of every single person in this room, I will.

She eventually finishes her set and I feel a pang of relief as she covers her chest with the almost overflowing garbage bag full of money.

There is this look of relief on her face that is quickly covered up as she smiles sweetly at the security guard.

Valentina clutches the bag to her chest like it is a lifeline.

Is it?

Does my girl really need this job? Because if she does, I don't have a single issue booking her for a private session every single night, laying blue strips at her feet as she dances for me.

Fuck, she doesn't even have to dance for me. I would just pay for her to be in my presence.

"She is spectacular, isn't she?" my brother asks. He appears breathless as I turn around. He looks towards the door that Valentina just walked through as if he keeps watch, she might grace him with her presence again.

Although, judging by the way she spoke to me when she thought I was Vic, I highly doubt it would be a pleasant interaction.

"How do *you* know her?" Olis questions, his arms crossing over his chest as he frowns at our packmate. The inner Capo is never far from the surface. Since the family business was handed down from Victor and my fathers not long after we graduated university, the three of us have been permanently tuned into our work, hardly ever taking a single day off.

"She was the girl that we pulled Gerald off the other night," Victor murmurs before taking a sip of his whiskey. Judging by the perfect color of the liquid, I'd assume that he ensured that we no longer serve the cheap shit Ivan insisted on.

I feel shocked as I look back towards the door that Valentina escapes through. I had wondered what had happened to that girl, not seeing her after Gerald was finally in pieces at my feet. To know that it was her that he was harassing has me wanting to pour another vat of acid over his corpse.

Maybe we should have put his still alive body through a woodchipper before putting him in acid.

I shake my head out of my deranged thoughts. I'm not surprised that they went in that direction though.

My Alpha has already claimed Valentina as his. He made his decision the moment that she stumbled into us.

I don't utter a single complaint though. I want her just as badly as he does.

"How do you know her, Olis?" Vic utters, snapping me out of my stupor.

"I was walking Kye through the park when I noticed her and her daughter."

Both Vic and I freeze.

She has a daughter? Fuck, that probably means that she already has a partner.

Disappointment floods me at the thought of my obsession being even further out of my reach.

"I...I didn't know that she had a daughter," Vic mutters almost under his breath.

Ha, so the fucker has been stalking her.

Not a surprise.

The moment Victor becomes intrigued by something, he doesn't stop until he gets it. Valentina will be another one of his obsessions.

At the mere thought of one day not being able to claim her as mine, my Alpha rebels inside of me.

Mine.

Mine

Mine.

He keeps repeating in my head over and over.

Yeah buddy, she is fucking ours and I will make sure of it.

For the rest of the night, I sit in a dark corner of the club, watching each time Valentina comes out of the dressing room and back down to one of the private rooms.

The thought of her being alone in those room with those men sets me on edge. I know that my girl has fight in her but the thought of her being vulnerable is too much to handle.

The time doesn't go quickly enough until her next stage set.

My pack mates remain just as quiet as I do, each of us in our heads as we come to terms with what we know about the one person that has each of us by our balls.

As the night progresses and the more I think about the possible objects that are in my way, I decide that I am actually not bothered by them at all.

She is pissed off at Victor and doesn't want him? Fine, more for me.

She has a partner at home already? Not for long she doesn't.

She has a daughter. Cute. I already class my daughter-in-law as mine so adding another to the mix is no big deal.

She is a stripper. I will be in the front row of every single one of her sets, watching her get her bag.

Yeah, none of those things are a deterrent. If anything, it makes me even hungrier for her.

The three of us remain seated in our area of the club as we watch security kick out all of the drunk seedy men who are still clinging onto hopes that one of the girls will take them home.

Even if we allowed that, I doubt that those limp-dick fucks could even get it up, no matter how much ass was shook in their face.

My heart skips a beat as I watch my little brunette come out of the backroom. She looks so different now, dressed in her street wear. It does nothing but make her even more beautiful.

The makeup has been completely removed from her face, leaving her bare for us to see her flawless skin underneath. Her hair is pulled back into a messy bun that seems to still be perfect.

Maybe it is just her.

It makes me question for a moment why I am so obsessed with a woman that is obviously a Beta. While I have nothing against the designation—one of my fathers being an incredible Beta—it is still surprising.

Alphas aren't meant to be drawn to them like this.

Yet here the three of us are. Completely and utterly taken with her.

The moment she is out of sight, the three of us stand up in sync and follow her home.

I hate watching our girl walking down the street this late at night completely on her own. Why doesn't she have a car?

I mentally write myself a note to ensure that I buy her a car. Something practical obviously. She has a daughter after all. Maybe more once I worm my way in.

Even though I am not a young Alpha by any means, I can't help the thought of pumping her full of cum and seeing her round with my baby.

I can't hold back the growl that escapes me. Yeah, I like the thought of that way too much.

Once we reach her apartment, I ensure to pin the location on my phone. The three of us stiffen as we watch an older man stumble out of the building, startling Valentina. She squeals, clutching her chest before laughing at the man who bows before her then proceeds to turn and fall into the bushes.

I already know without a shadow of a doubt that this woman is too good for me as I watch her smile down at the drunk she is clearly familiar with. She grabs him around the shoulders, helping him to stand and shakingly bringing him over to the entry of the complex before sitting him down against a wall. Judging by the look on her face, she hates the idea of leaving him outside at night but I am glad she slowly walks away.

I already told my girl that she would know if I was stalking her but I want to keep it a secret for a little bit longer. Admire her from a distance while I sort the obstacles stopping us from wooing her.

Because she is mine and I won't stop until she is in my bed, swollen with my pup.

My breeding kink is locked and loaded.

Hold on, Little Devil, because I am coming for you.

CHAPTER EIGHT

VALENTINA

The week passes by way too quickly and before I know it, it is already Friday night: reopening night.

The bosses who brought The Throbbing Knot still remain a mystery to me. They did, however, send out a group message letting us know the ins and outs of the new runnings of the club.

When Ivan oversaw the club, he demanded a nightly fee be taken. After speaking to a few of the other girls, we quickly found out that he was taking well above the regular going club fee.

It was a shock to be informed that no fee will be taken under the new management. That every single cent that we earn will be ours.

The relief I felt was immense. Never again will I allow myself to stress out about bills being paid on time. Maybe I might even be able to spend some of my earnings on spoiling myself for once. Maybe get my hair and nails done. Maybe even a new outfit.

The possibilities feel endless.

The biggest one is the knowledge that I won't need to live week-to-week anymore. That I will be able to actually open a savings account.

That one day, I could move Amity and I out into a bigger home. One where we don't have to deal with Joe, the resident drunk. Even though he is harmless—unless you are a bush—I still want better for my daughter. I don't want her to ever be burdened by the evil of this world.

Not like I was subject to.

After receiving the good news from my new bosses, it felt like I was actually able to enjoy my few days off with Amity.

It was impossible to not treat her to a new princess dress that she has been eyeing off for what she tells me has been forever.

What I didn't expect was the delivery man knocking on my door the next morning with boxes and boxes filled with princess dresses and an array of toys that I know Amity had begged me for the day before.

The delivery company didn't seem to care that I didn't order the haul that would have cost thousands. To them, the boxes had my name and address on them. They were delivered to me and that is where their job was done. No matter how much I tried to backtrack to try and find whoever sent this stuff, I was met with brick wall after brick wall.

In the end, I decided to just narrow it down to some kind of miracle. Or maybe we won some kind of mystery raffle.

The surprise packages aren't the only different thing I noticed that week.

Every single time I walked outside, it felt like someone was watching me. Following me even.

It didn't matter if it's the grocery store or if it's the park, I couldn't help but constantly checking over my shoulder to see if anyone was there.

Each time I came up empty.

My knife has become my new best friend. I haven't let it out of my sight since the eerie feeling first began.

While the eyes watching me don't necessarily make me feel uncomfortable, I can't allow my guard to slip.

There is too much at stake.

I just want to know who it is and why they are following me.

A part of me suspects that it is Victor.

Yet, that doesn't feel possible.

He wouldn't have followed me all the way to my home would he?

Surely not.

My jaw drops the second I walk into The Throbbing Knot.

Gone is the tacky red carpet that had been nearly devoured by carpet worms (it's a real thing, I googled it) and in its place is a black wooden flooring that elevates the look of the room.

The worn leather couches have been replaced with couches that look ridiculously comfortable. The main stage remains in the same spot but it is clear it has been renovated, making it actually look inviting.

Two new poles on smaller platforms have been added to either side of the main stage. Low lying leather couches surround each pole making it the perfect spot for us to dance while we are waiting for a private or stage set.

The bar has also received an impressive face lift. Rows and rows of shelves behind the bar are completely stocked with some of the best alcohol that money can buy. I have never been a big drinker but I know that some of those bottles of whiskey are priced in the hundreds.

What also comes as a shock is the fact that Ben isn't the only security guard on the floor. Four more men, equally as big as each other stand around the room, watching each of us as we stand in a mixture of shock, awe and excitement.

I step further in the room, walking over to the stage that is clear of gouges and scrapes from years of high heel abuse.

It is a dream to work in a club like this. For the club to not make us feel like our job is dirty. To have a space to work that is clean and elevated. Where we can be respected for our work versus criticized.

"Afternoon, ladies. Thank you so much for coming in early. Welcome back to The Throbbing Knot. I hope you guys like the changes that we have made over the past few days."

The familiar voice has me shooting around to where I hear it behind me. My mouth drops in shock as I stare in disbelief at the three men that have been haunting me for the past few days.

Victor, Conall and Olis.

The three Alphas that have consumed my every waking thought are my new bosses.

Fuck. Fuck. Fuck.

It all makes sense now as to why I stumbled into Conall in the hallway on Sunday night. I was too flustered to have given it a second thought but now I know better.

What is even more surprising is the fact that Olis is standing with Conall and Victor. It's clear that they are a pack. They have this air about them that makes it clear they formed while they were younger. Like each of the men knows what the other is going to do before they even do it.

That kind of relationship is both fascinating and fucking insane to me.

I couldn't imagine becoming that accustomed to having known someone that long that I would know each of their tells.

Although, there is a small part of my brain that wishes that I could have that. Even once.

I disregard the thought before I even allow it to blossom.

Pack life isn't for me.

Those motherfuckers ensured that.

Victor continues to talk to the group as I continue to stare daggers into the side of his head.

The asshole knows that I am staring at him too yet he doesn't give me the time of day, unlike his twin who is smiling at me, near begging for my attention.

I don't give him it though. My focus is completely locked on the Alpha that can't take a hint.

I told him to leave me the fuck alone and this is what he did instead? Bought my place of work out from under me, firmly solidifying a place in my life. A place that I don't want him or any other Alpha anywhere near.

Letting in my best friend was hard enough. Ben and his partner felt like I was stepping out of my skin.

But this?

Yeah, no. No fucking way.

The instinct to run is strong but I can't allow myself to do what my suppressed Omega wants me to do.

Beta's don't run.

Beta's face their shit head-on and don't cower, so that is exactly what I will do.

Even if I would prefer to shit in my hands and clap.

Maybe even stab forks into my eyes.

Honestly, I would rather be doing anything other than what I know I will now have to.

I drown out everything the silver-haired Alpha is saying, unable to focus through my anger.

Eventually he smiles at the group of us, nodding before turning to Olis and Conall who also nod before dismissing everyone so they are able to get ready.

I don't move from where I am white-knuckle gripping the side of the main stage.

I don't want to see the aftermath of a furious Valentina.

The club doesn't need that kind of disaster; not when it looks so fucking stunning.

"Valentina." My name rolls off Olis' tongue like it has been dipped in chocolate. My knees threaten to weaken at the sound but I don't allow them to.

Instead, I give the Alpha a pointed stare. "Olis."

"I promise you right now that I had no idea that you worked here before we brought your old boss out."

He seems so sincere, standing with us arms awkwardly at his sides like he doesn't know what to do with them.

I almost feel bad for him but I can't.

He is an Alpha.

That is enough for me to know that he is a big fuck no.

I hum quietly but just enough that the sound reaches the three of them.

"He is telling the truth, *dolce ciliegia.*"

My head snaps towards Victor, my eyes instantly narrow on him.

"So what, you are the only one that is stalking me? The only one that can't take the hint that I'm not fucking interested?"

I raise an accusing eyebrow, hardly surprised when he remains silent; as do his other two packmates.

I scoff, "Just as I thought. Take the hint, boys, because I would hate to have to repeat myself."

Hitching my bag up on my shoulder, I storm past the three men and make my way to the dressing room. Enough time has already been wasted and I refuse to get up on that stage flustered.

"Fuck, did she just threaten us? God, that's hot. Come back, Little Devil. I want to know more about your devious plans for us."

Conall has a smile threatening to curl my lips, even more so when I hear a hand slap his stomach and his responding grunt.

Is that one to Valley, zero to the Alphas?

It feels as though every exposed bit of skin on my body burns as I spin around the pole. I know exactly who the sets of eyes belong to.

Victor, Conall and Olis.

I make sure to add a little extra spice to my dance knowing that they are watching me as intently as they are.

I try to not let their focus disrupt me though, instead keeping my attention purely on the way my body moves and contorts as I work the stage.

The vibe tonight is completely different.

Gone are the men that used to hoot and holler at us as we danced. In their place are Alphas and Betas in suits, brown liquid on the rocks and stacks of cash in their hands.

Instead of throwing dollars, they are throwing big bills.

I don't have to count what is currently sitting on the stage waiting for me to know that I have already exceeded what I would normally earn in a day. Well past last week's takings.

I have to hold back the tears. Breaking down and crying on this stage in a skimpy outfit would do terrible things for my night.

Instead, I work myself to the bone, spinning, dipping and shaking my ass like my life depends on it.

If these guys are going to pay this well, I don't mind going the extra mile.

By the end of my stage set, I am exhausted. Not only is my money sack completely full, but so is the garter I am wearing around my leg that is full of hundred dollar bills.

I all but collapse into the brand new chair at my dressing room station.

It wasn't only the front of house that the new owners renovated. They also completely transformed the back area. Instead of the dancers having to fight to get a station, we were each given one of our own. Our stage names have been engraved into plaques above the mirrors. Lockers with actual working locks sit behind us well stocked with makeup, toiletries and all the hair tools that we could possibly need.

No matter how much I despise our three new owners, I have to cut them a bit of slack for how thoughtful they have been towards us. Ivan didn't give a single fuck about us apart from how much money we could make him earn.

There is a small whisper in my head that maybe not all Alphas are the same. It's only small and quick, a fleeting thought, but it was there.

I can't be that wrong about them can I?

All of the Alphas that I have dealt with, especially since I emerged as the 'inferior designation have been exactly the same. Aggressive, abusive assholes who think way too highly of themselves. Which is why the doubt has slowly begun to creep in. Because as far as I can tell, these three Alphas are nothing like that.

If anything, they are the complete opposite.

While they have shown me that they do have some stalkerish tendencies, they haven't forced my hand at anything.

When I feel their eyes on my skin, I don't get that icky feeling that I normally do. It's the polar opposite.

I instead feel safe. Like nothing in this world could hurt me ever again.

I know that is just the Omega side of me that refuses to stay suppressed. Which is why I can't trust it.

I can't trust anybody.

Because the moment I do, the script will be flipped and I will be back to where I was four years ago.

Trapped and hopeless.

CHAPTER NINE

OLIS

Never in my life have I been so utterly captivated with a single woman.

I know that I wasn't even this obsessed with my son's mother when I first met her, and she was my scent match.

Yes, I was completely and utterly in love with her—my soul ached when she was taken from me—but I was never obsessed. I never wanted to follow her to the ends of the earth. To pull back every single layer of skin until I understood the very core of her.

I loved my Omega but I wasn't like this.

For the past week I have been over analyzing every single thing that I thought I knew.

To me, scent matches were the pinnacle of love. That once you had found that one person, nothing else mattered to you anymore.

While there is a part of me that will forever hold onto her, not only as my first love but the mother of my children, it feels freeing in a way to finally have something else consuming me.

Since that night, my grief has consumed me in a way that I didn't think was possible. It was my first thought in the morning and my last at night. I became angry, someone that people were terrified of. I made a name for myself in our family, helping to solidify our name as being one of the most powerful in the country.

But since meeting Valentina at the park, my thoughts have been dominated by a certain brunette.

That and her precious daughter. Both her and her mother had my protective instincts spiking. I want to be there for them. To provide for them. To ensure that they are safe.

It's abundantly clear that Valentina has trust issues. A blind man could see the way she assesses everyone she interacts with.

It's surprising to me that she chose stripping as her job. Especially when you are left so vulnerable up on that stage.

Watching the way that Valley moves her body is an experience like no other. I never knew that someone could be so fucking perfect.

She has this aura about her. One that seems to be magnified the moment she steps into her heels.

I'm completely and utterly addicted to her.

It's a shame that she has zero interest in any of us.

I'm embarrassed to say just how hard I got when she told the three of us off. It was magnificent watching just how little she cared about hurting our feelings. A lot of other Alphas would have been pissed being spoken to like that, but not us. If anything, I want to encourage that defiance in her.

From Conall's reaction to her attitude, I know that he will do anything to help motivate that ire.

He is a fucking masochist.

I can hardly taste whatever the bartender has been pouring me; too focused on the vision on the stage. I clutch my glass tighter in my hand.

If I don't hold myself back, I will storm the stage, throw her over my shoulder and take her for my own.

My Alpha is riding at me hard to claim her. To rut her and mark her with my bite.

She isn't an Omega. She is a Beta.

The knowledge of that also doesn't make sense to me. How is she, a Beta, able to pull such primal needs from the three of us?

The thought makes me suspicious.

What is our girl hiding from us?

It is clear that it is something. No one is that steadfast in rejecting someone unless they are already in a committed relationship.

Judging by what little of her I have seen, I doubt that is the case.

No, my girl is unattached.

There is more to this than meets the eye.

Going back to our first interaction, Valentina was fine until the wind changed and she caught a whiff of my scent. Is that her problem?

Does she hate Alphas?

If so, that's going to prove to be a bit of a problem.

While I would never choose to be another designation, I can understand the reasons why she might not be all that interested. Some of the Alphas I have had to deal with through my life have made me question their choices more than once.

But that also isn't fair to put all of us in the same box.

On the other hand, I get it.

Sometimes it's better to just remain cautious. There are too many men that would be more than happy to push someone that is too trusting.

Eventually, Valentina's final set of the night ends. I feel a stab of disappointment as she collects her earnings and walks off the stage.

How can I already miss someone I have barely met?

I mourn her loss either way as I turn back to my packmates. Judging by the looks on their faces, they are feeling the same way.

Cal sits up straighter and places his now empty glass onto the table.

"How the fuck are we going to win her over?"

Both of us are looking at Vic already. As the unofficial leader of our pack and the Don to our Syndicate, we always turn to him.

It's a lot of pressure to put on a single person but Vic seems to be able to handle it. It's why we have been so successful.

"I don't know."

My eyes blow wide at the dejected sound in his voice. For the first time in thirty years, Vic looks lost. I turn to look at Cal who looks like he could currently catch flies with the way his jaw is dropped.

"What the fuck do you mean you don't know?"

Vic's head snaps up to his twin's. A frown forms on his face for a moment before he shakes his head and runs his hand through his hair.

"It's exactly that, Cal. I don't fucking know how to win her over. She isn't like any one else I have ever met. Just when I thought I had her worked out, she goes and turns it completely on its head."

I nod, agreeing with him wholeheartedly.

"She is an enigma. A fucking perfect one at that." Conall picks up his drink but shakes his head when he finds it bone dry. "I don't understand it but there is this pull in my guts. This desperate need to make her mine."

"I feel the same," I murmur.

Vic nods but remains silent for a moment as he stares in the direction of the backrooms before turning back to us.

"She is ours."

There is no room for play in Vic's voice. This is the man that hundreds of men cower in front of. The man that has made powerful men weep at his feet. The man that I would follow into any situation blindfolded.

"If we have to tie that cute ass up in our fucking basement just to show her that, we will. Now that I have had the slightest taste of her fire, I need more."

I chuckle but nod. While the delivery leaves much to be desired, I know that I will do exactly that just to make her mine.

I never said I was a good man after all.

CHAPTER TEN

VALENTINA

The minute my back hits the other side of my front door, I sigh in relief. While I have zero complaints about the money I was able to bring home tonight—considering it's the most I have ever made—the eyes that penetrated my body were enough to set me on edge.

Every single moment I was out on the floor, whether that be during my stage set or speaking with a potential customer, I could feel them watching me.

It was unnerving.

I have never felt that way before. Not even when I have drawn big crowds.

It was like they still undressed me even when I had nothing on. Like they were peeling back every single inch of my flesh until they got to the core of me.

Strangely enough, the moment I was out of their sight, I found that I missed the feeling of them watching me.

Because while it was unsettling, it also gave me this feeling of comfort. Of safety. A feeling that could be dangerous if I was to get used to it.

I am under no delusions that these three Alphas are after more than one thing. Isn't that what they all want while they are waiting for the one?

I'm not interested in being someone for them to just pass some time with. Maybe younger me might have been, but older me knows better.

I know that Alphas are a trap. Delicious and tantalizing traps that will suck you in and spit out just as fast.

While their interest is flattering, I don't want it. I have enough on my plate. The biggest being Amity.

Having three dangerous looking Alphas lingering around isn't good for her. I want to set her a better example.

I don't want her to hold the same traumas that I do.

I want her to want a pack of her own. To safely find her scent matches. To be able to be loved and to love in return.

I want everything for her that has been stolen from me.

Once upon a time, I dreamed about having a pack. Of finding that group of Alphas that scent called to me. I want so desperately to have what my mother had with my four fathers.

But it was a dream that was stolen from me when I caught the attention of Pack Andrews.

If I could go back in time and not attend that dinner my parents and I were invited to, I would have.

I would have run as far from that pack as I possibly could.

The moment their eyes were set on me, I was already doomed. They were persistent from that night on. They did everything they possibly could to court me.

Even though I denied them at every turn, they didn't care.

That should have been enough of a red flag for the authorities to be called in. But my fathers thought they would be able to handle it on their own.

Unlike many other parents in the circles that my family used to interact with, arranged matings with packs was a common practice.

These hoity-toity packs couldn't have their sons and daughters mating with trash could they?

Their words, not mine.

Thankfully, my parents didn't share the same sentiment. Especially not when their background was the 'trash' the other packs turned their nose up at.

My parents worked their way from the bottom to the top.

They built an empire that saw their success soar for years. They were able to become a part of high society with their success.

But all of that work was for nothing when Pack Andrews stole it from them.

That night is still burnt into my brain.

The sounds of distant gun shots had me shooting out of bed. I could feel my heart pumping in my chest as my eyes remained glued on my bedroom door.

Each shot had my entire body jolting.

Tears ran down my face as pure, unfiltered terror ran through my blood.

The gun shots slowly got closer and I knew I couldn't just sit on my bed frozen, waiting for the inevitable.

Even though hiding under my bed was the first spot I knew they would look, I had to do something.

The minute I finally slid under my bed, my door shot open, hitting the wall with a bang.

I slapped my hands to my mouth, holding back a scream that wanted to desperately escape.

Dark chuckles that sent a chill down my spine seemed to echo through the room.

I knew that I was done for.

That I was only biding myself some time.

But I prayed to every God that they would leave. That they would decide that I was too hard for them to deal with and they just left.

My luck ran out when rough calloused hands gripped my ankles and ripped me from my hiding space.

No matter how much I kicked and screamed—yelling as many obscene curses as I could—the grip never faltered as I was dragged down the hall to my parents' room.

The scene that welcomed me has my earlier dinner rising up in my stomach.

My mother and papa lay on the floor with bullet holes in both of their heads. Their eyes were blown wide, shock on their features even in death.

Puddles of blood surrounded them where their bodies had fallen after more bullets had peppered their flesh.

"Ah, finally. Our Omega has arrived just in time."

The hands that had been dragging me, finally let my legs drop, allowing me to sit up and get my bearings enough to try to escape them.

I was stopped by a force behind my back before I could get too far.

With a whimper, I turned my head to find the hard glare of Trey behind me.

"Not so fast, Omega."

The sound of his slimy voice had chills running over my entire body. A sick feeling clenched my stomach as Trey caught the reaction. His eyes heated with pleasure at seeing my reaction.

No.

No. This can't be happening.

In a lightning fast motion, Trey bends down, grips my ponytail in his fist and yanks my head back to where my dad and pa are sitting on the bed.

Their hands have been tied behind their backs. Gags have been secured around their heads.

Their eyes are what kills me the most.

Grief has already taken hold as they look from me to my mother and papa in horror.

"No. Please no," I whimper, even though I don't mean to.

"Too late for begging, little girl. You should have allowed us to court you that first time. But like the brat you are, you denied us time and time again," Scott, one of the Alphas, says as he slowly steps towards us.

Out of all four of these Alphas, he is the one I despise the most.

Since the moment I saw him, his attention sparked caution in my chest. His scent of rotten apples turns my stomach even more now as his slimy hand grips my chin.

I swallow roughly as both of the Alphas hold me tightly between them.

"The chase was fun for a while. What wasn't so fun is when you allowed other packs your attention. Didn't you know that you are all ours, Omega?"

I shake my head as best as I can. "I will never be yours."

A slap across my face has me yelping out in pain. The skin burns as I bring my hand up to clutch the area that I know will bruise.

"Wrong. You are ours. Tonight, we have made sure of that," Scott chuckles darkly as he steps away.

My cheek throbs but I look up at my two remaining parents with so much regret.

The fire that had started to burn inside of me has been snuffed out.

I should have known that it was a mistake saying no to these Alphas.

I should have been thankful to have their attention.

I should have said yes to them courting me.

Maybe if I didn't fuck up, my parents wouldn't have met their maker.

Maybe my life would have been peaceful in whatever way I could have made it.

Maybe I wouldn't have watched as Jason and Matt held pistols up to my dad and papa's foreheads.

Maybe I wouldn't have watched the light being taken from their eyes.

Maybe I wouldn't have been taken from the pack that raped me for the next six years.

Maybe I wouldn't have had to kill the four men that held me captive.

Maybe I wouldn't feel the need to constantly look over my shoulder, terrified that I didn't do it right. That they still haunt the shadows, waiting for me.

A hand on my shoulder has me startling out of my flashback.

Gripping my chest, I can feel just how fast my heart is racing. That familiar sickness that claws my insides everytime I think back to that night, turns my stomach contents.

"Valentina, it's okay. You are safe honey. You are at home. No one is going to hurt you."

The sound of Mrs. Perry's voice has me slowly calming down.

I look up at her motherly face and attempt the best smile I can imagine.

"Thank you. I'm sorry for freaking out like that," I apologize but the older woman is already shaking her head.

"Don't you dare apologize for something you can't control, Valentina. You should know me better than that by now," she berates me just like I knew she would.

I sigh, shaking my head as I push up off the door that has been holding me up.

"Do you need me to stay for a while?"

I look towards the hallway that leads to both mine and Amity's bedrooms.

"How did she go down tonight?" I question, trying to divert the attention away from me. Amity is a very predictable sleeper. If she goes to sleep early, she will be up early. If she goes to bed later, she will give me a sleep in.

The fates seem to be on my side when Mrs. Perry replies with, "She went down late tonight. Little Miss was a bit hyper."

She laughs and I smile even though my heart clenches at just how much I miss her.

"I will be okay. You should go home and get some rest. I know just how exhausting looking after her can be."

Mrs. Perry waves her hand in the air, collecting her bag from the bench.

"Nonsense. That beautiful little girl keeps me young. You know just how much I wanted kids and grandkids of my own. You both help to fill that hole I have been missing all of my life."

Tears well in my eyes as I walk over to the older Beta woman and wrap my arms around her tightly. She chuckles, returning the embrace but I don't miss the sniffle as she does.

"You have no idea how much you fill that mother and grandmotherly hole for both of us too," I murmur into her warm jacket, unable to say anything more. It would be a sobbing fest if I did.

"I love you, Valentina. I hope you know just how proud your mother would be of you."

I nod as we eventually separate. Mrs. Perry smiles at me as I see her out the door, silently watching as she steps inside her apartment and locks the door behind her.

It gives me a bit of peace of mind that she is safe as I close my door and lock it behind me.

I don't know what I would do if I was to lose her as well.

The distraction that Amity brings me is welcome. After a visit from Luna who can't stop gushing at how good our night was, along with a Beta client that she saw who has become her new fascination and in turn obsessed with her, I feel at least partially ready for my night.

As I step into the club, I thank my lucky stars that I don't see any of the three Alphas that seem to be popping up everywhere I am.

I know they are here though. Judging by the sweet and earthy scents that I am able to identify as theirs, I know that they won't stay hidden for long.

That isn't their thing.

Especially not Conall's.

From the limited reaction that we have had with each other, I already want to tease him. To really play with the Alpha that seems hell bent on not listening to my warnings that I am not interested.

Even though I have swarn off the entire designation, that doesn't mean I can't have a little fun and fuck with them, can I?

My outfit tonight is a simple bikini set. The fabric is a gorgeous purple holographic color that helps to make the more basic outfit pop.

It also does wonders against my lightly tanned skin.

My hair hangs in curled cascades down my back and I make sure to fluff it before I walk out the door.

Tonight, I have a little bit of time on the floor before I have to be up and ready for my stage set.

Even though I have been mostly distracted with my three year old, it hasn't stopped me from running tonight's routine over in my head.

Much like last week's revenge dance, this routine is one of my favorites. I have been savoring it for a night that I felt like I needed to give a little extra something.

Tonight feels like that night.

The club is already packed with suited businessmen and I know that this shift will be much like the last.

A hand gripping my wrist has me stopping with a jolt.

Panic grips me, making me want to turn around and slap the hand away to escape. But I don't.

Instead, I plaster a fake smile on my face and turn around to the Beta who is smiling at me. Once he has my attention, he quickly drops my hand, his smile now shy.

"Hi, I um... I was... Ah. You are...um," he stumbles over his words, a blush forming on his cheeks as he fights for his life to speak to me.

It's clear that this is this guy's first time in a strip club. Surprisingly, he is here alone, clearly not wanting his friends to make a big fuss out of it.

I have seen a lot of situations like that and I refuse for this guy to feel as uncomfortable as the others have seemed.

"Dance?" I ask simply. The Beta exhales and nods, that nervous look still on his face, before picking up his drink and downing a good portion of it.

I smile sweetly at him as I grip his hand in mine. It doesn't take any convincing to get the guy to follow me. His willingness is actually quite flattering.

I smile at Ben who stands at the front of the private rooms, another bouncer who I haven't met yet beside him.

"You only have an hour until your set, Cherry. Is that good with you, bro?"

I turn to the Beta who is already nodding, his cheeks just a little bit redder now.

I chuckle as I drag him through the curtain and to one of the available rooms.

Somedays, having the senses of an Omega can be helpful, like right now when the door closes behind us and I can instantly sense the shift in the Beta.

If I thought he was nervous earlier, it has nothing on the way his body shakes now.

Instead of allowing him to drown in his nerves, I grip the front of his shirt and gently push him onto the couch.

His eyes blow wide as he looks up at me. His mouth is slightly agape as the leather under him creaks with the adjustment of his seat.

His jeans are already tented just like I expected.

The poor guy is probably only seconds away from unloading in his briefs.

I guess I just have to give him the best over the clothes five seconds of his life.

As expected, a groan is ripped from his throat within seconds of me moving over his crotch.

I don't stop there though like I know a lot of the other girls would have. In a way, I feel sorry for this guy. He is clearly inexperienced and it's my job to blow his mind for the next hour.

Figuratively, that is.

There is a look of wonder on the Beta's face as I dance. It is the best confidence boost; one I didn't know I needed.

I soak up the attention, not feeling a single ounce of shame in doing so.

After all, this is my body and I deserve to use it however I want. If that's dancing on stage naked for a heap of men, then so be it.

Eventually, the timer I set before the dance began goes off. With a final dip and swing of my hips, I straighten, reaching out for the Beta's hand who takes it willingly.

There is a dazed look on his face that Ben chuckles at as we get back to the main room.

Feeling bad for the poor guy who made a mess of himself, I give him a quick kiss on the cheek and a seductive smile that only goes surface level.

Three growls from behind me has me rolling my eyes as the guy straightens with a look of horror on his face. I don't even need to turn around to know who the owners will be.

I'm not surprised in the slightest that they are exerting this kind of dominance. It's such typical Alpha postering bullshit.

"I would greatly appreciate it if you didn't scare away my potential customers," I mutter with a hint of snark in my tone as I turn to face the three people I know are standing behind me. I didn't even have to get a whiff of their scent; it was just like I could sense their presence.

"Do you kiss all of your clients, *dolce ciliegra?"* Victor says, stepping up into me. I have to reinforce my walls so I don't shiver at the nick-name he has dubbed me.

I should hate it. I should demand that he calls me by my name and not some pet name.

But I don't.

Instead, I roll my eyes at him, pop my hip as I cross my arms over my chest. It doesn't give the desired effect I was after though as all three Alphas look down at my tits that are now pushed together.

"What I do with my clients is none of your business, Victor. He paid for a service that I delivered *professionally."*

I put as much emphasis on the word as I can as a little extra dig.

I know for a fact there is no way that these three men are carrying on with the other dancers the way they are with me.

It seems I have caught a catch I never wanted.

Victor just huffs but remains silent as he stands over me. It's dom-inating in a way that I want to push back on. I want to show him that I'm not some little 'Beta' that he can just push around. That just because he is naturally more dominant, doesn't mean he needs to control everyone and everything.

"Well, this conversation was riveting but I have a stage set to get to."

I glance down at my naked wrist, holding it up just for that extra edge of drama before I walk through the group of men, shouldering past them.

I don't get far before a hand is capturing me in its hold. I pause but don't turn.

I can't when a body presses itself against my back.

A low rumble and a deep inhale and exhale has a shiver running over my entire body. My nipples rub uncomfortably against the material of my shirt and I know I will have to douse myself in scent-neutralizing spray after this.

"Such a stubborn brat, Little Devil. Just know that I see you. I see those secrets you are so desperate to hide from us," Conall's low, sensual voice has me struggling to hold back a moan as his breath continues to drive me wild.

"You can run, but you can't hide."

I swallow roughly and against my better judgement do exactly what he knows I will.

I run.

CHAPTER ELEVEN

VICTOR

I never knew that I possessed the kind of restraint that I have had to practice tonight.

For a woman that I have only just met, I feel jealous over that Beta in a way that I know I shouldn't.

Seeing her walk out of the private rooms with him and then kiss him had me seeing red.

I wanted to tear that little cunt's head off his fucking shoulders. Rip every single one of his finger nails off. Burn the pads of his fingers so he knows the consequences of touching what is mine.

I thought that I would be okay with Valentina being a dancer until tonight.

She may not know that she is mine but she will soon.

I know that both Cal and Olis have been just as impatient with wanting to get their hands on her too.

It's not a want anymore. It's a need.

I need Valentina just as much as I need my next breath of air.

I haven't allowed myself to dive into the feelings of betrayal that have stirred when I have been alone with my thoughts.

I can't.

I have to believe that my Omega sent this woman to us to help us with moving on.

But the nagging thoughts are still there.

I brush them away just as quickly as they come. I can't allow them to infiltrate my thoughts. Especially not when my girl needs my complete attention as I follow her home.

We didn't even bother asking her to allow us to drop her home. Not when we could feel the daggers she shot us during her entire stage set.

The message she was delivering was loud and clear.

But I have never been one for listening. My parents had always said that that was the difference between Cal and I.

He is a people pleaser through and through. Whereas I like the challenge. I love to work people down until I get what I want.

Probably not the best trait to have when trying to win this girl over, but I never claimed to be perfect.

I mean, I'm currently stalking the poor woman. That certainly puts me on some kind of list as some kind of weirdo.

But I can't stop myself.

I know morally it's wrong, but I know that I will hate myself if I don't.

If she insists on pushing us away, following her everywhere she goes is the only way I know that she will be safe.

I refuse to allow anything to happen to her. Hence why I am sticking to the shadows the best that I can.

For over a week now, it has bugged me that she doesn't seem to have a car. It's almost unbearable to think that she is walking home with no protection with the amount of cash that I know she earned tonight.

What if she got robbed?

What if someone followed her home from the club and stole all of her money?

I curse myself, knowing that I am at least one of those things.

But I would never hurt her.

Fuck, just the thought alone of something like what happened that first night we met happening again makes me want to steal her away and keep her protected.

There is just one little hump in the road that I hadn't expected.

My girl has a daughter.

The thought brings a smile to my face, surprisingly.

I relish at the idea of being able to help our girl raise her daughter. To be able to take care of both of them. To spoil them like they deserve.

What it makes me want even more is to see that beautiful body of hers rounded with my baby. To have our cells merge in the most spectacular way.

How could I not?

Valentina is perfect in a way that it is hard for words to even describe.

And after seeing my boys be brought into the world, it's impossible to not want to feel just a second of that love again.

I know without a shadow of a doubt that I want that with her.

I wonder how obliged she will be to giving her daughter another sibling.

Piccolo, will already be gaining three older brothers and an older sister. What's a few more siblings?

I shake any thoughts of Valentina swollen with my child as I creep up closer behind her as her apartment comes into view.

I'm lucky that I do as a figure just ahead of me steps out of his shadows and begins following her.

Instantly, I am on edge. Even more so when the dark figure pulls out what looks to be a switch blade.

I immediately see red.

How dare this scum pull a blade on my girl!

On light feet, I hasten my pace up behind him until I am right behind him.

Before he can even know what is happening, my hand is already covering his mouth to muffle his shout of surprise. With the other hand, a knife, very similar to the one he still holds in his hand is pressed against his throat.

I keep my eye on Valentina as I disappear again back into the shadows.

I hate the thought of leaving my girl vulnerable but I know that she will be fine. She has a fire in her eye that I know won't let her down if she really needs it.

The darkness of the alleyway surrounds us as I drag the struggling man. He tries to break out of my hold but I keep a hold of him.

My anger has given me a strength that I didn't know that I possessed.

"What did you think you were going to do, huh? You were going to sneak up behind that girl and rob her, weren't you? Steal her hard earned cash that she is going to use to feed her baby."

The guy's head bounces off the brick wall that I slam him up against. He shouts in pain but I don't give him any sympathy.

No, I laugh like a fucking psychopath.

"See, the thing you should have known is that woman is *mine,"* I growl, tightening my grip on his shoulders.

He whimpers like the pussy ass bitch I know that he is.

I chuckle darkly as I step in further into him.

"Not so tough now are you, *segaiolo."*

It gives me some kind of sick satisfaction calling this *scemo* an Italian curse. It's childish and ridiculously petty but I don't care.

Pulling my blade from his neck, I slowly begin to drag the sharp tip over his scruffy jacket. I can almost hear the way his heart is trying to beat out of his chest. His body shakes beneath my hold like he is some kind of small whimpering dog.

It's pitiful.

Even more so when I get a whiff of this scent; rotting flesh.

It's appropriate, considering he will soon be rotting six feet under.

Although, now that I give it thought, maybe his death needs to be a little bit more ... creative.

Deciding to go with the latter option, I pull my cell out of my pocket and dial one of the higher up soldiers.

Only minutes pass before the sound of one of our vans pulls up out the front of the street.

I turn back towards the Alpha, plastering a sinister smile on my face. "It's play time, *testa de cazzo."*

The dank scent of the torture room penetrates my senses. The rich copper scent of blood and tang of piss is almost unbearable but I put up with it anyway.

It makes it easier to know I am about to exact my first lot of karma for my girl.

It's my first time doing this so the nerves are feeling a little bit real.

I need to do this right. This piece of shit needs to feel the hurt he planned on donning on my *dolce ciligera.*

She may never know what I have done for her tonight, but I need to make sure it's done properly. I can't let her down.

My dark chuckle reverberates off the walls of the room. The man's body tenses before he starts struggling. There is no use in him pulling against his restraints. He will die where he hangs.

I plan on having a little fun while I am at it.

"Not so tough now are you?"

"Why the fuck are you doing this to me? I'm innocent!"

I feel my face redden in anger. It feels as though my body boils as I stare down the whimpering man. He looks fucking pathetic trembling under my gaze.

"Innocent? Do you think it is innocent to follow a young woman on her way home from work? Do you think an innocent man would pull a fucking knife and hurt someone?"

I chuckle as I step toward him.

"No, *segaiolo.* There is nothing innocent about you."

He continues to try and plead his case but there is no point. Nothing he says holds any kind of merit anyway. I know what his intentions were and that's enough for me.

I pick up a set of spiked knuckle dusters that I have altered to be a little more ... lethal. I turn as I fix them on my fingers.

The guy's face pales as he whimpers. A wet spot darkens the front of his jeans and I sneer at him. Typical that he pissed himself.

He is fucking weak Alpha. He was brave when he thought he had my girl on her own and vulnerable, yet faced in front of a real threat, he cowers.

I don't bother wasting a single second of my breath again on him. There is no point. He will die no matter what he or I say.

The first hit of the sharp metal on flesh has satisfaction thumping through my body. Blood splatters across the room, some dots of crimson splatter my suit jacket.

I cringe as I look down at the mess he has made on me.

He will pay for that too.

I get lost in my anger as I rain down hit after hit on his body.

By the time I am done, I am panting and exhausted but am still not completely satisfied. Even in his current state, which is far from pretty—his face now completely unrecognizable—it still hasn't satisfied the beast inside of me.

Discarding the knuckle dusters, I pick up the pliers. He groans as I lift his hand, his head rolling to the side. His eyes are mostly bloody and closed over, the swelling blinding him.

The sound of his nail being ripped from his nail bed would curl the most sensitive of stomachs.

Yet, I just get sick pleasure out of it.

His cries of pain are like a sweet symphony to my ears.

Once each digit's nail beds are exposed and bleeding, his cries turned into moans of pain, I become bored.

Simply beating the man and ripping off his nails doesn't feel like enough.

The door to the torture room slams open and the face of Olis and Cal greet me. Cal's eyebrows raise as he looks between me and the Alpha.

He snorts as both of my pack brothers move further into the room.

"What'd he do?"

Standing to full height, I throw the pliers I was using at the Alpha's feet. Blood splatters but I don't flinch. I am already a mess.

"Followed our girl home tonight. This *testa di minchia* thought he could jump out behind our girl with a knife."

I don't have to say anything more. Cal and Olis already knew where it was going.

Anger overcomes both of their faces and I watch as their bodies tense. Olis' fists clench beside him as he takes a step towards the range of implements on the table. There isn't a second of hesitation when he picks up the blowtorch.

The flame explodes out from the nozzle before colliding with the broken flesh of the hanging man.

His screams are ear-piercing.

He writhes and struggles against the chains in an attempt to get away but Olis is relentless.

There is a reason why he is my Capo. He is brutal. His torture techniques are renowned in the Underworld. There has never been a person that he couldn't crack.

I've seen powerful men piss themselves the moment he walked in the room. Men who have spilled every single one of their secrets without having to say a single word.

It's fucking impressive.

Even more so when those same skills are being passed onto our sons. Namingly, Ledger. I have a strong feeling he is going to outdo his predecessor.

Abruptly, the screams die out and so do the flames bubbling his skin.

Cal walks over to where Olis is just standing, looking at the Alpha in confusion. He presses two fingers to a pulse point.

We wait for a moment before he steps away and shakes his head. "Couldn't handle the heat."

Cal predictably snorts at his pun. It's certainly not the first time he has made a joke like that and neither will it be the last. He seems to have a particular love for them when we are in more precarious situations.

It helps to brighten the mood in the room.

Cal doesn't waste any more time with his jokes as he sends off a text to the clean-up crew. Either that or he is organizing clean-up with whoever needs to be pulled into line.

It was a particularly good way to discipline the boys when they got old enough to handle the horrors of this world.

He puts his phone back before pinning me with a look.

"It seems our little cherry pop has more than our attention. Good thing we decided to keep an eye on her."

I nod, agreeing whole heartedly. "Me too. It still doesn't ease my nerves though. I still hate the idea that she is in that house all alone with her *piccola.* I want to have eyes on her every moment of the day."

I run an exhausted hand over my face before looking back up at my brothers. There is a mischievous look on Cal's face and I already know that whatever he is about to suggest will likely age me years.

"We could always kidnap her and hide her away in the house. No one would be able to get to her then."

I quirk a brow at him as I mull over what he just said. For the first time in our lives, I think my twin just suggested something I am not completely opposed to.

CHAPTER TWELVE

CONALL

There is a strange anticipation built up in my stomach with each turn of the clock. I tried to busy myself with contracts for some of our bigger upcoming deals. When that didn't work, I tried going down to train. Taking sexual frustration out on a new soldier in the form of my fists just didn't quite hit right.

What I need is my little devil.

Watching her run away from me had my primal side screaming to chase after her. It was a good thing Olis held me back.

The idea of going into rut and hurting my girl that way is unthinkable. I don't know if Olis and Vic have seen it but I can see her underlying trauma. It's unthinkable to me that she has suffered in her life. I want to take it all from her. To take that burden off her shoulders and wear it for her.

But I also want to dissect it. To learn every single thing I can about her. To know what makes her tick. To find my place in her life because there is no other option for me.

It's her or it's no one.

Sitting at my desk, I watch as each minute ticks by. Every second feels as though it is stretched out longer and longer.

After what feels like a lifetime of waiting, I shoot up from my desk. Pushing my responsibilities to the side, I instead go in search of the one thing that I know will make it better.

My Valentina.

Finding a car park on the street outside of Valley's apartment, I walk along the path, keeping a close eye on the windows I know are hers.

Silently, I beg to get a glimpse of her even if it is just through the glass. One look will be enough. It has to be.

I'm not beyond knocking on her door and demanding she let me in but I know that if I want more with her I have to act like some kind of civilized human.

Unfortunately.

A high-pitched giggle draws my gaze down the road and I instantly straighten, my heart beats rapidly in my chest.

The way the sun hits Valley's hair makes her glow in a way that is ethereal. Like she was sent straight down from the angels tailor-made just for me and my pack.

I revel in the moments I have before she notices me. She is looking down at the little girl who is holding her hand and skipping as they make their way home. Based on the bags in my girl's hand, I assume they just went grocery shopping.

It pisses me off, yet again, that she doesn't have a car to drive her home. I make a mental note to bug Vic about making sure we get her one. We can just make it a company write-off.

Considering we are now her bosses.

There is an easy kind of smile on Valley's face, one that I haven't seen before. Which makes sense considering she frowns at me every-time she has seen me recently.

Although, that look disappears from her face when she looks up and spots me. That familiar frown that seems to be her go-to quickly appears.

I can't help but feel disappointed. I want her to look at me the way she does her daughter. The precious little blonde that still skips alongside her mother, not taking any notice of the shift in her energy.

"Conall, what are you doing here? How do you know where I live?"

I struggle to not reach up and rub away the frown lines between her dazzling emerald eyes. I want to ease her tension in any way that I can. Unfortunately, removing the stress that I cause her just isn't an option. She just needs to learn how to deal with me.

I shrug my shoulders as I take a step towards her. "I was just in the neighbourhood. Wanted to know a bit more about the community here."

She raises an eyebrow, suspicious of me and my half-assed explanation. " You wanted to know more about Sloburn?"

I shrug again, knowing that she is dangerously close to catching my bluff. "There is a bit more to marketing a club than putting up flyers. Got to get to know the people here and what they want."

She looks at me for a few moments skeptically. I tense, hoping that she won't notice the shift in my body and my lack of candor.

Eventually she nods as she continues walking. I step in, following her as she makes her way to her apartment.

"Hello!"

The little voice and the tapping on my pants has me looking down at the little girl. Getting down to her height, I smile at her and hold out to my hand.

"Hi, little firefly. My name is Cal. What's your name?"

Her smile brightens at the use of my nickname for her. It is way too fitting for the little light that she so clearly is.

"My name is Amity."

I nearly melt at just how sweet her voice is. Why are these tiny humans so precious and why won't my sons hurry up and give me some grandkids already? I know that Kennedy is all but begging them.

"Such a beautiful name for such a beautiful little girl."

She squeals and grabs my hand. "Come play, Cal!"

Almost tripping over my own feet, I right myself as I follow after Firefly who has a death grip on me. Valley protests behind me. I turn, holding up my spare hand in surrender as I follow after the little girl who leads me into their apartment building.

Amity finally stops at 1A. She rocks back and forth on her heels as she patiently waits for her mother to open the door.

Valley comes to stand beside us with the keys in her hand. Turning slightly to me, she holds up a single finger, her voice low enough that her daughter can't hear. "Don't think that just because my three year old is inviting you in, this means that you get some kind of special treatment. Just because you are one of my new bosses doesn't mean I trust you or your pack."

I nod, obeying her demands. My girl could have asked me to scrub her entire bathroom with my toothbrush, then brush my teeth with it, and I still would have agreed with her. Whatever she demands of me, she will get.

It's her world after all. I am just living in it.

Amity pulls me along behind her as the front door is opened. I hardly get a chance to look around the simple apartment before I am being tugged into a bedroom that feels as though a can of pink paint has exploded inside of it.

It becomes perfectly clear to me the kind of parent Valentina is.

Everywhere I look, there seems to be some kind of toy or girly item that Amity fusses over, the sweet little three-year-old over the moon to show me her treasures.

It's clear to me that Valley would prefer to forego luxuries for herself and instead ensure her daughter has everything she could possibly want and more.

Fuck, if that doesn't make me want her even more. What is it about a parent being a good parent that is just so attractive?

It does also make me think about when my girl allows herself to receive luxuries. When does she take the time to spoil herself?

The lack of male energy lets me know the father clearly isn't in the picture. She obviously has someone watching Amity while she is at work but based on what I know, I can't see her taking the time out for her.

I write another mental note to organize a spa day for her. I need my girl to know that I will look after her and Amity. That these two women are now the most important people in my life, along with my own flesh and blood.

Time slips away from me as I play dolls with Amity. Hearing her laughter as I changed up voices for each of the characters was like a cleansing balm to the soul.

Valley watched us closely for a while. After a pointed look from me, she eventually backed off and disappeared into the apartment.

Although, with the feeling of eyes on me every so often, I know that she doesn't go far. I don't blame her. I am a strange Alpha. One that has been adopted by her daughter. She has every right to be cautious.

I just hope that one day it could eventually turn into trust.

The clearing of a throat has me turning towards Valley who is leaning against the door frame with her arms crossed.

"It's time to get ready for dinner, Amity. It's also time for *Cal,*" she says, putting emphasis on the name I introduced myself as, "to go home."

"No, Mom! I want Cal to stay! Don't go home!"

The breath is knocked out of me as Firefly jumps into my arms, her little limbs wrapping around me in a grip that is impressive for someone so small.

"Amity..." Valley says, a hint of exhaustion and something else I can't quite pin point in her tone.

"No! Cal stay for dinner!"

There is an edge of a bark that startles me as I look down at the little girl that is now glaring at her mother.

Valley's eyes widen, looking down at her daughter. Her arms have dropped from where they were held across her body. One hand now grips the door frame, almost as if it is anchoring her to her spot, the other hangs beside her, tensed.

No words escape her, instead she looks up at me for some kind of guidance. She's a mixture of emotions, none of them positive. She needs me.

Reaching up, I turn Amity so she is looking back at me. I give her a gentle smile so as to not startle her.

"It's okay, Firefly. If you want me to stay for dinner, I don't mind staying. I want you to know something though..." I trail off as I wait to make sure I have her full attention. She nods and I continue.

"That bark that you just used?" I raise my eyebrow as I wait for her next nod, "You need to promise me that you won't use that on your momma."

She nods her head almost dramatically, darting back around to her mom. Running to Valley, Amity jumps in her arms and apologizes, peppering her mother's face with kisses.

Val looks up at me, a strange look in her eyes as she nods her head towards the kitchen. "Come on, your presence at dinner has been demanded."

I chuckle but follow my girl anyways. There is no way that my answer was ever going to be no.

Not only was I demanded to stay but I now have more questions than I originally did.

Like how could a Beta have possibly birthed an incredibly rare Alpha female? And why am I more certain than ever that my little devil is hiding more than I could have thought.

It takes everything in me to not groan at just how delicious the bolognese Valley made is. I know that it would come with one hell of an ass whopping but I would stand in front of my nonna and tell her that my girls recipe is better.

It may be a death wish but it's one that I would suffer.

I'm sure that Nonna would understand, especially after explaining why.

Every chance that I get, I watch Valley. Since the little mishap earlier with a surprised bark from Amity, I have started to draw some wild conclusions.

Female Alphas, along with male Omegas, are incredibly rare designations. I have only ever met four female Alphas and one male Omega in my almost forty-five years. Each of them came from an Alpha father and an Omega mother. As far as I can tell, a Beta can't birth an Alpha or an Omega. They only ever have Betas. So how is it that I am sitting in front of a Beta with an Alpha daughter? One that is showing signs of her impending designation far earlier than she should.

Normally we designate at sixteen. I have heard of a few cases of Alphas and Omegas designating earlier but it is rare.

Yet, here my little Firefly sits showing very obvious signs of her designation.

Which could only mean one thing.

Valley isn't a Beta.

I should be surprised. I should be reeling-freaking the fuck out because my girl is an Omega.

But I'm not.

I knew she was hiding something from me. It being her designation actually makes so much sense. Even more so as I mull over everything I know about her.

I understand now as to why she wouldn't give any of us the time of day. Why she has been butting heads with Vic every time they come face to face. Why she 'suddenly' had to leave when she met Olis in the park. Why I got a dressing down in the hallway of the Throbbing Knot.

Valley is an Omega. An Omega that is my mate.

I have to hold back a growl that threatens to escape. The woman before me was made to be mine. I know it without even smelling her scent.

Her being my mate explains why there is this strange connection between her and our pack. Why the thought of having her between us just feels so right.

It also explains why every single one of my more primal instincts is screaming at me.

Rut. Breed. Mine.

I should be applauded for my self control. I am a fucking saint right now.

Little does my sweet Cherry know but after today, I am going to be embedded in her life.

From this day on, everywhere my girl turns, I will be right there beside her. Or behind her.

CHAPTER THIRTEEN

VALENTINA

I'm on edge every second of the drive to work. After Conall had dinner with us, Amity again demanded that he stay with us until she went to bed. It was a request I didn't bother denying her.

Not after she Alpha-barked at me.

I am thankful that Conall was here to help diffuse the situation. Even on suppressants, denying an Alpha-bark is a near impossible feat.

I haven't even had time to process the fact that at the age of three, my daughter is already showing signs and of her designation.

It should be impossible. Especially this young.

I don't allow myself to think anymore of everything that it means and the fact Conall was there to witness it. There is a bottle of wine at home with my name on it that I have every intention of popping the minute I get home.

So as I sit here in by far one of the most expensive cars that I have ever seen, it's fair to say that this night is going to be an interesting one.

Conall—or should I say Cal—has a look on his face that is setting my nerves even further on edge. It is a look that tells me that my ruse is up.

He knows.

This fucking *Alpha* knows that I am not who I say I am. That the persona that I have had in place for years is just a smoke-screen now for him.

I still plan on holding on to it for as long as I can.

Admitting to him that I am actually an Omega isn't an option. Clubs don't hire Omegas and for very good reason. It would be armageddon if someone was to go in heat during a dance. Especially if they were dancing for an unmated Alpha.

I internally cringe at the image that paints.

"Are you okay, Little Devil?"

Cal's voice shocks me out of my thoughts. He chuckles as I turn to him.

"I'm fine," I mutter but nothing about the tone of my voice is remotely convincing.

He rolls his eyes as he turns away from me.

"You clearly aren't okay, Valentina." He reaches his hand over and grabs mine. I'm surprised that I don't jump but there is something about his tobacco and vanilla scent that is calming.

"I want you to know that I will be here for you and Amity every step of this journey."

The sincerity and honesty in his voice has tears coming to my eyes but I refuse to allow them to fall. I can't. Instead I whisper a quiet 'thank you'.

The thought of Cal being there for me for whatever the next few years with Amity is almost like a weight lifted off my shoulders.

But, I also want to rebel. I want to yell and scream that I don't need an Alpha. That I can do life by myself.

But I have never wanted to do life on my own. I was forced into a life of solitude.

Forced to rebel against every single thing that makes me who I am.

All because a man didn't like being told no.

It feels as though I have a bodyguard with me as I walk into work. Cal refused to allow me to open my own door which was a surprise gesture. I didn't allow that part of me—that wanted to melt over the chivalry—get too hopeful.

I have to distance myself from the part of myself that is wanting what he can offer. If I allow myself to become hopeful that maybe he is different, I know it will only end in heartbreak.

I will allow him to help me with Amity and help her to understand the new things her body is telling her. But when it comes to him and I, that relationship needs to remain strictly professional. Not only is he my boss but he is also an Alpha. One that I know I could easily let my guard down around. But one that I will just have to appreciate from afar.

I can't be the person that he needs me to be.

I need to remain strong for Amity.

The thought of my little girl being an Alpha is enough to send me into another tail-spin.

No matter what these three delicious Alphas promise, they will be denied at every turn. Because I refuse to let my guard down to only be hurt again.

Work goes by at an annoyingly slow pace. The smile that is plastered on my face is terribly fake. It's clear that Cal can tell, considering the look he has been giving me the past hour.

I wish that I could take him up on what I know is an unsaid offer. His emotions are clear as day. He is hating me being here right now as much as I am.

But every time I think about going home ‘sick’, the reminder of who is at home keeps me going for another hour.

I sigh in relief as I finally take the pleasers off my feet at the end of the night. Over the years, I have become used to the feeling of wearing them but every now and then, they play up on me.

Luna likes to joke that it is just our age showing. A joke that is only funny to her. I groan as I rub the ache in the arch of my foot.

“Damn girl, any louder and you will start turning us on with those noises you are making,” Candy laughs, putting her things in her bag. The other girls all laugh and I roll my eyes.

“It has never taken you much to get turned on, Candy. A mullet and moe combo makes your kitty wetter than the Pacific Ocean.”

I snort a laugh as Luna hits the girl back with a line that runs true. We all know that the girl is easy. She even knows that.

Whatever floats her boat though. At least one of us has a healthy relationship with sex.

It has been years since I was with my old pack. Not like any of what they did to me was remotely enjoyable. Not even when I would fall into the mindlessness of a heat.

By the time I have got undressed and have packed my bag, all the girls have left for the night. The time alone gives me a moment to decompress.

A moment to think of all the insanity of my day.

Cal met my daughter.

Amity Alpha-barked at me.

Cal promised to be there for me and Amity.

Fuck, my little girl.

Putting my head into my hands, I breathe through the panic I can feel rising in my chest.

What the fuck am I meant to do? I have only heard of a few cases of female Alphas and none of them have ever been pleasant. Those women fight every single day due to the rarity of their designation. There is a need for them to prove who they are in a world they shouldn't have to.

The thought of my daughter having to go through that, and at such a young age, is horrific.

I shouldn't have expected any less. With her fathers being Alphas and along with my designation, I was only ever destined for to have either or.

Omegas and Alphas just don't birth Betas. That is as rare as a female Alpha.

The next thought that enters the forefront of my mind just as brutally, is the fact that Conall knows what she is.

Shooting up straight, a cold sweat floods my body. My eyes dart to my bag and I stagger towards it. My breathing comes out in a harsh panic as the overwhelming need to protect my baby inundates my thoughts.

I need to get home. To bundle my little girl in my nest. To protect her.

Nest? Wait? What?

I pause at the exit of the dressing room to collect my thoughts. It has been years since the desire for a nest has nudged at me.

During the time the Andrews pack held me captive, my nest was my only source of comfort. And that was only when they weren't in there tainting it with their scents.

But the need for one now is so strong that it is impossible to ignore.

Shit, I don't even have any good blankets or pillows to make a nest. My bed has two flat and worn out pillows on it. I don't even allow myself decorative pillows.

I had that much desire to push everything Omega out of my life that any kind of 'comfort' item was an immediate no.

But now? All I want is a fluffy blanket to curl up in with my daughter. To hide out amongst fabrics that will feel like silk against my skin and protect what is mine.

To have my Alphas surrounding us and providing that extra level of care.

Alphas?

No. No. No. No.

I don't have Alphas. I'm not a fucking Omega. I am a goddamn Beta.

Shaking my head, I continue out the building until I run into a body. I grunt, stumbling back but another wall at my back steadies me.

"Hey, where are you going, Little Devil?"

The soothing voice of Cal has me swallowing thickly. A whimper threatens to escape but I refuse to allow it.

Judging by the scent behind me, I know that there is no way that I can allow myself to slip right now. It may be the worst thing that I could do.

"I...I...I'm going home," I manage to stutter out, fooling absolutely nobody.

Cal scoffs and shakes his head. "Not a chance, sweetheart. My mother, rest her soul, would be mortified if I let you walk home alone at this time of the night."

"I agree with Cal, Valley. Get in his car and he will drive you home."

The deep timbre of Olis' voice sends a shiver running down my spine.

I begin shaking my head but a growl from behind me stops me immediately.

"Stop arguing with us, Valentina. You will get your ass in the car and say thank you like a good fucking girl."

I am already nodding my head even before Vic has finished his sentence.

"And, you will message me the moment that you are tucked in bed with your front door locked."

Again, I nod but Victor just shakes his head.

"No, *dolce ciliegra*, I need your words."

I swallow thickly before replying, "Yes, Alpha."

Vic's eyes heat and I know that if Olis' hand wasn't on his shoulder, he would have done something that I'm not even remotely close to being ready for.

Judging by the look in his eyes, I know that I need to choose my stance with them and quickly. There is a promise in his eyes that makes anticipation swirl in my stomach. Vic wants more. They want more.

And I need to decide what I want.

Before it's too late.

Cal allows me to process my feelings on the drive home from work. I know that he has questions. Ones that I don't even know how I would be able to answer.

Ones that fucking terrify me.

But, if I was to be stuck in a car with anyone right now, I'm glad it's him.

Since he entered my home this morning—or yesterday morning seeing the stupid time on the clock—he has given me this sense of safety I haven't felt before. It's strange and uncomfortable after years of pushing people away.

It makes me wish that I could have met this Alpha first. Maybe I wouldn't have put them all into such a secure box. Maybe their advances would have been well received.

But that is not what I was destined for.

Cal finds a park outside of my apartment building. He pins me with a look as he exits the car. I wait as he opens my door and takes my bag from me.

I don't even bother protesting it.

If the guy really wants to be a gentleman, I will let him. I have no energy to fight him on it.

Neither of us says anything as we walk in the door. Mrs. Perry gives us a quick hello and goodbye before she also leaves. She does side eye Cal though, murmuring quiet words to the Alpha before making her exit.

As Cal is saying goodbye to the older lady, I take a moment to go check in on Amity.

Opening her door as quietly as I can, I make sure to keep my footsteps light as I walk over to her bed and sit down on the edge.

Tears spring to my eyes as I look down at her precious face.The chubby cheeks that have refused to disappear. The way her mouth is open as she lightly snores.

The peaceful innocence on her face.

She is too young to have to learn the realities of our world. She is too young to have that innocence of hers threatened.

The thought terrifies me enough that a sob gets caught in my throat. I slap my hand over my mouth to not wake up Amity just as Cal reaches the door.

His scent spikes in panic as he makes the few strides to me in the blink of an eye. He doesn't waste a second to pick me up from where I was sitting and makes his way back out of the room.

The moment he closes the door behind us, the flood waters break, as does the sob I was trying to hide.

I bury my face into the curve of Conall's neck as I let it all out.

I don't realize until he lays me down on my bed that we are in my room. I should feel some sense of embarrassment or maybe terror at the fact that I am alone with an Alpha.

But I don't.

All I can feel is the overwhelming sadness for not only my daughter, but also myself.

I cry for everything that has been stolen from me. All the opportunities to be me were taken by the pack that couldn't be told no.

I cry for my daughter who one day I will have to tell how vile her fathers were. Why she will never get to meet them and why I will always have to look over my shoulder.

I cry for my daughter who will have to face her own troubles with her designation. A female that will have to fight for her strength in a world where other men will be determined to tear it from her.

I don't know how long my face remains buried in Conall's chest. All I hear are his reassuring words of comfort and the overwhelming feeling of safety being in his arms makes me feel.

Eventually my sobs dissipate and the darkness of sleep steals me under.

CHAPTER FOURTEEN

VALENTINA

I wake with the start. The all too real dream causing a bead of sweat to roll down my temple.

"Shh, Little Devil. It was just a dream."

The comforting voice has me settling for a moment before reality hits me and I squeal, my fist flying around and connecting with the side of Conall's face.

He grunts, slumping back onto the bed beneath us.

"Fuck! Cal! What the fuck are you doing here?" I shout, bringing my fist to my chest, clutching it in pain. Motherfucker has a hard face.

"Good morning to you too, baby. I would have expected a kiss on the cheek or even a sneer but a right hook was certainly a surprise," he chuckles,opening his eyes to look up at me. "When are you going to understand that you are the woman of my dreams?"

I roll my eyes before I fling back the sheets. We are both still covered in the clothes we were wearing last night and I thank myself for small miracles.

I then allow myself to remember just what happened before I fell asleep.

I sigh as I cross my legs, looking down at my hands as they twist in nervousness before I look up at Cal.

"Thank you for being there for me, Cal."

He smiles sweetly as he sits up and grabs my hands to hold them in his own.

"You never have to thank me for being there to support you, Valley. It was my honor to be there for you when you needed someone."

I nod and drop my eyes to where he holds me.

"I know that yesterday was a lot for you. I have questions and I know that you have a million of your own. But there is one thing that I need you to understand before we get into any of that..." He trails off for a moment longer than I expected. I look up to find him looking at me with a strange look on his face. "No matter what happens, no matter what you tell me, I will be here for you, Valentina. I know that may terrify you but there is something about you that has me hooked and I can't stop."

I go to talk but he cuts me off. "I know that is a lot right now for you to process but I just want you to know that I'm not going anywhere. I will be here for both you and Amity in whatever capacity you will let me."

There is a part of me that wants to tell him no. To push him away. To demand that he leave right now and never speak to me again. It's small but it's there.

The other part of me though—the much louder part—screams to let this man in. To allow myself to have someone for the first time in my life.

Someone that actually seems to give a fuck about me and what I want.

Maybe just this once, I could allow myself to have just that.

Without having to say anything between us, I know that he knows the truth. I also think he knows that I know. He should be mad. He should be ripping shreds off me for lying to him.

But he isn't.

Instead, he is in my bed, fully clothed—jacket and all—and is asking for my permission to be in my life.

So, instead of saying no, for the first time in my life, I say yes to an Alpha.

I already am dreading my stupidity but I need to change my thought process. I can't allow myself to be terrified for the rest of my life.

The smile that Conall gives me lights up the entire room. He chuckles, bringing my hands up to his lips and places a delicate kiss on my fingers.

"Thank you, Little Devil. Now, we better go check on our little firefly. I heard giggles before and I have a feeling she may be up to mischief.

The squeal of excitement from my three-year-old as both Cal and I make our way out into the lounge room helps ease any kind of lingering sadness.

Instead of beelining straight for me like she normally would, Amity launches herself into Cal's waiting arms.

"Cal! You had a sleepover! Are you going to have another sleep-over?"

The excitement in her voice has me chuckling, "It's only just the morning, baby. Let's see how the rest of our day goes before we ask Cal to stay again tonight."

Amity nods before she wiggles out of Cal's arms. "Okay! But you have to play dolls with me again!"

Cal chuckles but nods. "Anything for you, Firefly."

I smile as I head over and begin making breakfast for us. Cal doesn't leave me waiting long before he is right beside me helping to prepare bacon and eggs.

It's strange doing such a mundane task with him.

To be honest, it feels unnatural even to have an Alpha in the kitchen with me.

My old pack refused to step foot in the kitchen while I lived with them. Every single meal they ate was prepared by me. If they wanted something to drink, even a glass of water, I still had to bring it to them.

To them, Omegas belonged in the kitchen.

But as Cal works along beside me, it's clear that he doesn't feel that way. Even as I shake my head, so used to doing this job alone, he refuses and finds something for him to do.

It seems at every single turn, Conall proves me wrong.

In a way, it's refreshing. In another, its scaring the living fuck out of me.

Why does he have to be so goddamn perfect? Why has this man steam rolled into my life and completely turned it upside down?

Why the fuck am I falling for an Alpha I have no business falling for?

I keep trying to tell myself that he is my boss. That he is forbidden. Though, if it was meant to be so wrong, why did it feel so good having him beside me last night?

A boss doesn't hold their employee in their arms like that.

A boss wouldn't have stayed the night at their employees house only to promise them forever and stand beside them in the kitchen preparing a meal for her daughter.

I know that my delusions of keeping our relationship strictly professional are just that; unrealistic.

A man like Conall won't stop at the word no, but not in a way that terrifies me. It's obvious that when he sees something that he wants, he will do anything and everything in his power to get it.

And right now, his sights seem to be set on me.

We eat and clear up breakfast all together. The entire time we laugh and joke around, poking fun at each other.

By the time we are done, both my cheeks and stomach are sore from laughing so much.

I know that it's only a matter of time before this feeling disappears. The conversation that we need to have lingers over our heads like a dark cloud.

Conall follows Amity into her room, setting her up with her toys before he comes out to where I am huddled up on my couch.

I wish that I had some blankets and pillows that I could cuddle into but alas.

Cal's smile is almost sad as he collapses into the seat beside me.

I sigh as I look up at him. "Where do you want me to start?"

"Wherever you feel comfortable, Little Devil. I don't want to push you into telling me anything you aren't ready for."

I nod, a sick feeling curdling my stomach at the thought of telling my inner-most secrets to Cal but I know that I need to.

If I want to stay true to who I am and potentially see where this thing with Cal could go, I need to be honest. I need to tell him the whole truth.

Taking a deep breath, I brace myself as I meet Conall's eyes.

"I designated as an Omega on my sixteenth birthday." I pause, allowing that information to sink in. Cal nods, allowing me to continue.

"Do you remember the Rossi family?" I question. He ponders it for a moment, as if sifting through a filing cabinet before he nods.

"Yeah, I remember them. Denzel, Roberto, Giovanni and their Omega Caterina."

I nod, my throat feeling tight as I attempt to swallow down the pain that comes along every time I think about my parents and that night.

"My mother, Caterina, was beside herself leading up to my sixteenth birthday. She knew that I was going to designate as an Omega like her. She wanted to shout it from the rooftops. So, like any mother in high society, she threw me a massive birthday."

Cal's eyes blow wide as he connects the dots. His mouth drops, looking me over. A mix of emotions running over his face.

"We were there that night."

It's now my time to be shocked. I gape at him as he continues.

"I can't believe I never connected the dots." He shakes his head, rubbing a hand over his face before he looks back up at me, "You look exactly like your father, Gio."

A lone tear trails down my cheek. For years I had thought that the memory of my parents had been lost to me forever. That as their only surviving relative, I was the only thing that kept even a part of them alive.

"Vic, Olis and I did a lot of business with your parents. It would have been impossible for us to have got to where we are today without their knowledge in tech."

I make a note to come back to what it is exactly that these three men do apart from owning a strip club. For now though, I just continue my story while I still can.

"I started to show signs of my designation just before the party started. So when the time came for us to greet the guests, I was essentially put on display for all of the unmated packs. I know that may not have been my parents' intention, but that is what happened.

"The Andrews pack was one of the last groups that I met that night. From the moment Scott, Matt, Jason and Trey walked through the door, their eyes were set on me. No matter how hard I tried to avoid them, they seemed to be everywhere I would be. The day after my party, Pack Andrews put in an official bid to 'court me'."

A spark of anger lights in Conall's eyes. I don't let it derail me as I continue on.

"My fathers, of course, turned them away. They wanted me to find my pack naturally. To find my scent matches. To find love just like they had with Mom. It took two years for the Andrews to be sick of waiting around for my parents or myself to give in."

I inhale, working up the courage for the next bit. "On the night of my eighteenth birthday, I woke up to the sound of gunshots. I tried to hide but it was useless. Trey found me and dragged me to my parents room where they had killed my mom and papa. My pa and dad were both bound and gagged."

A numb feeling comes over me as I recite the living nightmare. Tears stream down my face as the words continue to pour from me.

"I watched as they put a bullet in both of their heads before they took me."

My eyes drop, unable to continue looking at the tortured look on Cal's face. Seeing the devastation is almost too much to handle.

I jump as he reaches over to hold my hands. Unintentionally, he gives me the strength to continue.

"For the next six years, I was under Pack Andrews' control. For six years, I was tortured, raped and treated like I was a slave. For six years, I was their toy to use and play with whenever it suited them. For six fucking years I despised the day I emerged as an Omega."

At the last word, the tears that were slowly trickling down my cheeks turn into a downpour. A sob explodes from my chest as for the first time, I admit to what happened to me.

Cal gathers me into his arms and I cry into his chest just as I did last night.

By the time I eventually pull myself together, my throat is raw and Cal's shirt has well and truly soaked through with tears.

I half-assed cry and snort as I look at the wet patch. "I'm so sorry. I've ruined your shirt."

I go to get up to get him a towel or something but he stops me. Reaching up, he places his hands on both sides of my cheeks.

"Valentina, you do not need to be sorry for crying on me. Ever."

I go to argue but he doesn't allow it.

"No. You are allowed to cry on me whenever you like, baby. You have been through fucking hell. You have had your body and soul used and abused in ways that I will never understand. The fact that those men call themselves Alphas is a fucking disgrace to our desgination."

"Used to," I mutter as I wipe my face.

Cal looks down at me in confusion.

"Used to. As in past tense. As in they used to call themselves Alphas. They can't anymore because I killed them."

I brace for impact. If Conall thought my trauma was the pinnacle of my problems, he is sorely mistaken. I wait for the look of disgust. Of the yelling that should come with a confession of killing multiple people.

But it never comes. Instead, a smile brightens Cal's face.

"That's my fucking girl," he says, his voice holding a proud note to it before he leans in and presses a gentle kiss on my lips.

My breath stutters in my chest, my lungs hardly able to take the next breath as he pulls away.

I have never been kissed before.

Out of all the years I spent under four Alphas' control, never once did they kiss me. It was why I never fell into Stockholm Syndrome. I knew that they didn't love me. And I never could have returned the sentiment even if they were able to feel that kind of emotion.

But Conall just kissed me.

I struggle to catch my breath as he remains holding my face in his hands. His touch is so gentle that I can't help but melt into him.

"I am so fucking proud of you. Not only did you continue on for years even after dealing with the worst the world has to offer, but you also killed off those that took so much from you."

He shakes his head as he looks at me with wonder in his eyes. It's almost like he is seeing me for the first time but in a completely new light.

"You are utter perfection, Little Devil. I don't deserve to revel in the light that is you but I'm a greedy fucking man. I will take whatever dregs you decide to give me."

CHAPTER FIFTEEN

CONALL

I didn't think that I could possibly be more obsessed with this woman even if I tried but here she goes completely decimating everything I thought I knew about her.

My little devil is a fucking warrior.

While I am still looking upon my girl in awe, it's impossible to not be beside myself in anger. The thought of Valley having to go through those horrors, especially at such a young age has me seeing red.

If those motherfuckers weren't already dead, I would hunt them down and kill them myself.

No wonder why she has avoided our advances every step of the way.

How could she not? The very essence of our existence would be a reminder of everything she has lost.

The fact that she is even allowing me to sit with her in my arms right now speaks a lot about the kind of person Valentina Rossi is.

My girl had to hide herself away as a Beta just so she felt like she could be protected. She had to deny every single instinct that I have no doubt would be raging at her just so she could never be hurt again.

My girl had set herself up to spend the rest of her days packless as a person that needs to have others around her.

It's obvious to me that she is also on a cocktail of suppressants. The thought of what they could be doing to her body is unthinkable, especially right now as she remains curled in my arms.

Now that I have my girl, I don't ever want to let her go.

It's an honor for her to have trusted me with as much as she has. To know that I am most likely the only person to know has a strange emotion clogging my throat.

For now, I silently vow to protect her with everything I am. She will never have to walk this earth alone again while she has me.

She will never have to look over her shoulder in fear.

And the day that she finally decides to go off her suppressants, I will be there for her every step of the way.

We sit in silence together and I breathe in every single moment. My hands trail up and down the delicate skin of her arms. I'm unable to hide the smile from my face as I look at the way her flesh pebbles under my touch.

It makes me long for the scent that she is locking away from me. I want it just as much as my next breath.

It's selfish to want something like that from her but I never claimed to be a good man. Rather the opposite in fact.

Because if it is what I am suspecting, Valentina's scent will indicate that she is mine. More so than I already know.

And not in the way of me just declaring it to the world.

No, it will be on a whole other level.

A scent-matched level.

I never thought I'd want that kind of connection with someone ever again. After losing Gwen, the idea of falling in love again after her was unthinkable.

In a way, finding happiness while she was dead almost felt like a stain to her memory in a way.

But now that I have allowed myself to actually think back to her and who she was to her core, I know that she never would have wanted us to be unhappy.

I know that she would have wanted us to find love.

And to find that kind of love with someone that has the potential to be my second chance at a mate is a blessing from the heavens. One I know Gwen would have had a part in.

She always loved looking after us in little ways like that.

I know that she would have loved Valentina. That they would have hit it off from the start.

Valley must be able to sense my subtle shift in mood as she sits up and turns to me.

"Whats wrong? Are you okay? Was I overstepping?"

Placing a hand on top of hers I smile at her. My inner thoughts are cheering at the preciousness in front of us. Even after pouring her trauma out to me, her own bleeding heart still laying in her hands, she is already thinking about me and how to make me feel better.

"No, baby. There is nothing wrong. I was just thinking about Gwen and how much she would have loved you."

She gives me a puzzled look for a moment so I continue without giving her the time to make assumptions.

"Vic, Olis and I became a pack in high school. Vic and I knew that we were going to emerge as Alphas long before our sixteenth birthdays. Our fathers used to joke that it was because of their good breeding."

I roll my eyes at the joke and Valley laughs.

"When Olis finally turned sixteen, we formed a pack that same day. It wasn't long before we met Gwen."

I smile sadly as I think back all those years ago.

"We had never put much thought into our Omega. We were so caught up in our parents demands for us that anything more than forming a pack was too much for our then pea sized brains.

"But the day Gwen walked into the classroom, everything changed. It's like those moments you see in movies where the princes meet the princess and they live happily ever after."

I chuckle and shake my head, knowing that reality is never like that.

"We were bonded in a week and pregnant with twins just after we graduated high school."

There is an almost sweet but sad smile on her face as I continue.

"Around the same time we found out that we were going to have sons, mine and Vic's parents died in a mass shooting."

I look down almost debating my next words before I continue. If Valley was brave enough to share her trauma with me, I can be brave enough to share this part of our life with her.

"Being the first born son of the Mafia Don, Vic had to step up straight away and take over from our fathers. There was no transition period. No lengthy discussions on daily runnings. Nothing."

I shake my head, thinking back to some of the darkest days we had following the deaths of our entire parental pack.

The war that we had to continue to fight without even knowing why we were fighting. The worry each and every day at the thought of not being able to protect what was ours. The horror as we learnt what we were bringing our unborn sons into.

It was a lot of hard work but now as I stand back and look at what Vic, Olis and I have created, I know that if the worse was to happen tomorrow and Theo had to step in, our legacy would be left in capable and safe hands.

Valley's eyes are blown wide, looking at me in shock.

"Damn."

I nod at her lack of words. I prepare myself for the inevitable. The screaming and shouting. The 'how fucking dare you' and 'you are a psycho' statements that are always thrown in my face whenever I have mentioned this side of my life before.

It's exactly how Gwen reacted when she discovered this side of our life. To say she was unhappy is an understatement.

If our previous Omega was capable of murdering someone, she would have had our three heads on a chopping block quicker then you can say, *bada-bing, bada-boom.*

I should have expected the unexpected though as my little devil's reply shocks me to my core.

"I couldn't imagine having gone through all of that, especially with an Omega and twins on the way."

I nod my head almost dumbly. The fact that I haven't smelled this girl's scent doesn't even matter to me anymore. She could smell like rotting fruit and I would still want her.

Because biology aside, this girl fucking sees me. She sees me clearer than any other person ever has.

She could clearly see just how deep my feelings towards our unchosen birthright and all she did was validate me.

My little devil is perfection.

“So what happened to Gwen?” Valley questions. I feel my stomach fall. I have to steal myself. It’s not like I have Vic or Olis here to back me up on this one when it gets hard. It’s been years since Gwen died but it doesn’t get easier.

That grief has never faded. I have just learned how to deal with it. How to make the days go by easier until I am able to see her again.

Taking a deep breath, I grip Valley’s hands tighter, needing to hold onto her for some kind of emotional support.

“Things were good after a few years. We fell into a good thing in the Syndicate and Underworld. We built a strong standing and became feared. Rivals didn’t mess with us because we were ruthless. We had a family to protect.”

Valley nods so I continue.

“All of that came crashing down as the boys got older. I don’t know if we just got sloppy or our routines just became too familiar but one night, the three of us went to a standard meeting with one of the motorcycle gangs in Vadena. It was seen as a low threat as we had quite a good relationship with them so we didn’t bother to take extra soldiers with us.

“Everything was going good until our phones started to blow up with calls. Olis answered the phone at the same time one of the worst pains shot through our bond to Gwen.”

Valley gasps just as the first tears roll down my face. The first tears I've cried since the funeral. But I don’t stop. Because if I do, I know I won’t be able to continue.

“We didn’t think about sticking around. Instead we stormed out of the clubhouse and raced home.”

I choke on my words and shake my head, wishing I could unsee the horrors that flash before my eyes.

The blood. The bodies of our fallen men. The horrified looks on our son's faces as they described what happened to their mother.

I do my best to convey all of the pain from that night to Valley but it's hard. It's hard to relive the worst night of my life. To explain the horrors that we went through for almost a year until we finally got put out of our misery.

Tears stream down both of our faces as I come to the end of the journey.

"We found Gwen broken and beaten almost beyond recognition at our doorstep after we said good night to the boys one night over a year later. The coroner we hired was unable to list the true extent of the injuries she suffered both while she was alive and when she was dead."

"Oh, Cal. I'm so sorry." A sob breaks from Valley, launching herself at me. I catch her and bring her into my arms. Her legs rest either side of mine as she sits on my lap. I cling to her like my life depends on it. I need the comfort that I know only she can give me right now.

It's been eighteen years since I cried like this. The pain of reliving that time of my life feels almost as raw as it did then as it does now. The difference now is, I have someone that I can lean on. Someone that can help me work through the agony.

Back then, I had to be strong for my boys. I had to be there for Olis and Vic. I couldn't allow myself to break into a thousand pieces like I know I could do right now.

"Cal? You okay?"

The tiny voice has both Valley and I startling away from each other. I turn around and see Amity looking at both of us in concern.

"Why you crying?"

Wiping the tears away from my face, I smile sadly at my little firefly.

"I was just telling your mommy a really sad story. I got a little bit upset but I am okay now. You and your mommy make it all better."

Amity's smile is sweet as she launches at the both of us, pulling us into her tiny arms.

"You are all better now! We are a family and family makes us all better!"

Well, fuck. If I thought I had cried enough today, my little firefly has just gone and broke my heart again.

"I would be honored to be a part of your family, Firefly."

CHAPTER SIXTEEN

VALENTINA

After reliving the horrors of what both Conall and I have gone through, we decide to have a movie day.

Or more so, Amity decided that we were going to have a movie day.

"I hope you are okay with princess movies because that is all Amity will watch at the moment."

Cal chuckles, "Princess movies are my kryptonite, Little Devil." He turns to Amity and gets down to her level, something that should have sparks flying in my chest but inevitably does. "Now, should we let it go and build snowmen or should we have sleepovers with seven dwarfs."

Amity giggles, running over to the TV and selects her choice of film. I busy myself making a snack plate from the *DoorEats* order we made before we settle in as the opening credits start.

Cal grunts at the distance between us as immediately pulls me towards him. A tiny body jumps in between us, pulling one of the blankets from her bed over our lap.

We spend the entire movie laughing at our favorite parts, yelling at the bad guys and cheering when the hero gets the princess.

When Cal said that princess movies were his kryptonite, he wasn't kidding. It was a shock to the system to watch such a big burly Alpha sing along to the sound track.

All it did was put another tick in his favor.

I know not every male would sit on this couch and indulge in a three-year-old's wishes. Especially not one that didn't have some kind of familial connection.

Each moment that I spend in this Alpha's presence is another moment that I let my guard down. That I allow this person in.

For once, I actually want to. After trusting him with the dark secrets I hold close to me, I can see something more with him. A life that sees more days like today.

While there is still a large part of myself that holds fear, I know that I can't reduce every single Alpha down to the four that ruined everything for me.

At least for now, I am going to allow myself to open up to Conall. To at least see where things go.

Because I deserve to find out. To, for the first time in my adult life, have some kind of healthy interaction that involves a man.

I didn't realize I had fallen asleep until I jolt awake and instantly regret how fast I moved. I must have been laying in an awkward position as pain shoots up through my neck.

After taking a moment to rub out a spot that will no doubt have me needing Deep Heat and anti-inflammatories later, I gasp as I see just how dark it is outside my window.

My apartment is oddly quiet and I am completely alone.

No Conall. No Amity.

My first reaction is to panic.

I immediately jump to the worst conclusions. That I have finally let my guard down and in doing so, it has cost me my daughter.

I storm down the hallway, just about ready to barge into Amity's room to double check if she is in there but instead, come to an abrupt halt.

"...But where is the green sheep?"

I collapse against the wall as I hear the gentle words of the Alpha reading to Amity.

I shake my head as I clutch my chest. Slowly, my heartrate settles.

After a moment of berating myself for allowing my thoughts to drift to the worst, I step closer to the door and peek around the corner.

A smile brightens my face as I look at a half asleep Amity and a Conall who looks away too invested in finding where the green sheep is.

How is this man real? What have I done right in my life to ever deserve him?

Instead of walking in and breaking their moment, I silently walk away and return to the lounge room.

It's only a few minutes before I hear. "Goodnight, Firefly."

As Conall steps out into the lounge room, his eyes quickly find mine. That heartbreaking smile of his that I have become used to adorns his face. He comes to sit beside me and doesn't hesitate to pull me into his chest.

"Afternoon, Little Devil. I'm sorry that I didn't wake you but I could tell that you were exhausted after this morning. So when Firefly woke up from her nap, we decided to let you sleep."

I sigh, "Thank you, Cal. Seriously. I hope that she behaved for you."

He chuckles and rolls his eyes, "That little girl has me wrapped so tightly around her finger." He pauses for a moment, looking down at me and tucks a bit of hair that had fallen out of where I had tied my hair up into a bun that morning. "You both have me wrapped around your fingers. It's been a long time since I felt anything for anyone but I know that I am already falling in deep with you, Valentina Rossi."

It's almost a shock to the system to hear my full name on his lips. For years I have gone by some shitty last name that was one of the most generic names I could find.

Hearing him call me by my real name almost feels like he is giving me a stepping stool to allow me to be who I really am. To honor my parents in the way I should have been all of these years instead of hiding in the shadows.

It's as though he is giving me the opportunity to be the real Valentina. Not the Valentina that I thought was damaged beyond repair.

I don't say anything, instead I pull away from him. There is a look of hurt and rejection on his face for a moment before it is replaced with shock and a flicker of heat as I move, my thighs settling on either side of his.

Resting my hands on either side of Cal's neck, I smile down at him. "Thank you for seeing me. For allowing me to show you the real me. For trusting me with your own traumas. For just being you."

"Always, Valentina. Always."

I don't know who closes the distance between us as our lips touch softly. For a moment our kiss is gentle. I follow the motions of Conall's lips as they move against mine in a slow, sensual dance.

That is until I move my hips.

A growl is torn from Cal's throat moments before our once almost innocent kiss turns anything but.

This new Conall is hungry and he wants me.

Hands grip my hips tight as he pulls me into him, allowing me to feel just how hard he is beneath his jeans.

I groan into his lips as a spark of arousal shoots through my core.

It feels strange to feel such a pleasurable feeling with someone else. After my fear of sex had worn off a few years ago, I finally allowed myself to get off but it never felt anything like this.

I grip onto the gray strands of Conall's hair as I pull him impossibly closer to me.

I need him.

I need to feel his body against mine.

To feel the pleasure that I know he wants to give me.

Cal's answering groan has more pleasure shooting straight to my clit as I allow myself to move against the steel beneath me.

Stars spark behind my closed eyelids as I throw my head back.

Cal's kisses move from my chin to my throat.

A quiet voice inside my head begs him to sink his teeth into the exact spot but I push it away.

Now is not the time for any of that stupid Omega nonsense. Right now, I just want release.

I continue to grind over Cal's covered cock, wishing desperately that I could feel his naked skin move against mine.

Even though my mind is starting to feel fussy, I know that I am not ready for that right now. I need to stick to dry humping.

At least for tonight.

With each movement of my body against Conall's I feel my core becoming increasingly wetter. It's nothing like it was when I was still presenting as an Omega but it's more than a normal Beta would have.

"Use me, baby. Use me for your pleasure," Cal moans against my lips, inciting a guttural moan from my chest.

I do just as he says, continuing to rub myself against him.

The pleasure becomes unbearable. My stomach tightens before I scream against Cal's lips as an orgasm is torn from me.

"Fuck, Little Devil. Such a good girl," Cal grunts out as his body spasms beneath mine.

The jerking of his body along with the praise kicks up my orgasm a notch as a higher sensation overcomes me along with a rush of wetness from my core.

"Shit, Cal!" I yell as I grip tightly to the Alpha below me.

Once my orgasm subsides, I collapse into Cal's chest, unable to let go. He doesn't let go of me either as we both remain silent in an attempt to catch our breath.

After a while, one of Cal's hands moves up into my hair.

"Are you okay? That wasn't too far was it?"

The sincerity and concern in his voice has me smiling.

"It was perfect, Cal. I didn't realize being with someone else could ever feel that good."

It's impossible to miss the way that his body tenses. Cal pulls me in further into his body and leans in to whisper into my ear.

"When you are with me, there will be nothing but pleasure, Little Devil. Those fools have no fucking idea in what they gambled away when they treated you the way they did."

I sigh into him, allowing my body to melt as we stay on the couch.

It would be easy to drift back to sleep laying on his chest like this but the feeling of wet panties is far from pleasant.

I decide to further this bold persona that I have going on today as I break away from Cal. He allows me to stand but looks up at me with a questioning look on his face.

"Shower?"

I have never seen a single man move as fast as Cal does as he all but launches off the couch. In one swoop, he picks me up in his arms.

I squeal as I cling to him. He chuckles a low rumble that sends zings straight to my core, something I didn't think was possible after experiencing one of the best orgasms of my life.

Entering the bathroom, Cal sets me down on the sink before stepping away.

Slowly and way too sensually, he shrugs off his jacket allowing it to fall to the floor before he reaches a hand behind his head, grips his shirt and in one motion, pulls this shirt off.

My mouth drops, not only at just how smooth that action was but also at my first glimpse of Conall's body.

It had never occurred to me just how ripped this man could have been under his clothing. Sure, I had felt some of his hard edges from on top of his clothing but nothing could have prepared me for the spectacle that is this man.

The Alpha's body is all hard edges and smooth, tanned skin.

Shaking myself out of my stupor, with much less talent than Cal, I pull my shirt over my head, leaving me just in my bra.

Even though Cal has seen me in much less than this, it doesn't stop his eyes from heating, taking me in.

Slowly, just like I would during a dance at the club, I unclip my bra and allow it to drop on the floor with my shirt.

Cal's throat bobs, watching me with an intense look.

Sliding off the sink, I pull down my shorts, hooking my panties as I go. Once I reach my ankles, I kick them off, leaving me to stand completely naked in front of Cal.

Butterflies churn in my stomach as I wait for further reaction from him.

I have been naked in the club more times than I can count. In privates, I have danced with nothing but my heels for groups of Alphas and Betas and not once was I rattled.

But standing here in front of Cal is different. It's more intimate and far more intimidating than any kind of performance.

Because this one isn't for show. Because I want him and I know that he wants me. It's a sentiment I have never returned in a dance with any of my clients.

It was always going to be saved for a moment like this. A moment where being vulnerable in front of someone is more naked than any kind of lap dance.

"You are so beautiful, Valentina."

I smile shyly as Cal takes a step towards me. He lifts a hand but hesitates before he can touch me.

With a nod, he smirks before he drags the back of his hand from the top of my breast down my side and to my hip where he grips me.

I gasp as with that one hand, he pulls me towards him.

When our lips meet again, it's in another desperate kiss. My hands meet his chest and I feel as goosebumps break out over his skin.

I smile against his lips at the reaction I was able to cause.

He chuckles, able to tell just how proud of myself I am.

"You little minx. Now you know just what you do to me. How a single touch of your flesh against me has me ready to drop down to my knees before you and worship you for the queen you are."

With a cheeky smile, I look up at him.

"Well, what are you waiting for Cal? Get on your knees and praise me."

Cal doesn't hesitate, dropping to his knees on the tiled floor. Gripping my hips, he lifts me up so I am sitting back on the edge of the bench.

With a gasp, I grip the bench as he spreads my legs apart. All my earlier confidence instantly disappears as Cal looks at my bare pussy.

Ever so slowly he leans in, sticks his tongue out and swipes it through my folds.

I throw my head back and arch my back as pleasure zings through my body.

Cal doesn't stop at the one swipe. He continues to lick me until I begin writhing under his grip.

He moves his torture to my clit as he sucks and flicks his tongue. It's only seconds before my second orgasm of the night barrels over me. The slurping noises coming from Conall are near diabolical as he drinks up my release.

"Fuck, Cal," I moan as I collapse against the mirror behind me.

He chuckles, pulling away from me.

"Was that the kind of praise you had in mind, Little Devil?" he snickers, rising to his feet before shrugging off his jeans.

I get the perfect image of his toned ass as he reaches in and turns on the shower.

This man must be some kind of genius as steam quickly fills the room, the water scolding, just how I like it.

He turns back to me, allowing me to get a peek at what he is working with. My eyes blow wide as I take in the specimen that is jutting out from his body like it has something to prove.

The cock, which should be given some kind of powerful name like Thor or Adonis, twitches under my gaze.

"If you keep looking at it like that, Little Devil, you are going to embarrass me again," he laughs as he reaches for me.

I look up at Cal in shock.

"Does that thing come with some kind of warning label? That's not a cock, Cal. That's a weapon"

He snorts but I shake my head.

"No, I'm serious. You don't expect that thing to ever fit inside of me, do you? I know I am actually an Omega but that and a knot is just asking for trouble."

Cal groans, his head thrown back before he takes a deep breath. When he looks back down at me, his eyes are burning. He growls, shoving his head into my neck before sucking in the scent that I know won't be there.

"Fuck, Little Devil. When the time comes that you allow me into that cunt of yours, you will take every single fucking inch before I stuff my knot inside of you and you take that as well."

CHAPTER SEVENTEEN

VALENTINA

It's near impossible to focus on anything else other than each other's bodies as we stand under the spray of the shower.

Conall's touch is both gentle and teasing as he runs his soapy hands over my body. I know that I was well and truly clean ten passes ago but I don't stop him.

Because while he is teasing me, I am returning the favor.

I have become well and truly acquainted with the hard planes of his chest and biceps. If he wasn't covered in soap, I would have traced him with my tongue.

At least it gives me something to wait for the next time we do this, because there will be a next time. One time with Conall like this just isn't enough.

I need more.

Maybe next time I will have enough courage to work up to more with him. Although the thought of him putting that cock anywhere near me is terrifying. Especially after all of these years.

My body is desperate for it though. Even after two orgasms, I'm still desperate for more.

I would never tell Conall that. The man would be way too pleased with just how much he is able to wring out of my body.

Eventually, we stop teasing each other and rinse our bodies off. Cal gets out first and hands me a towel.

We smile like teenagers at one another as he follows me into my bedroom. Dropping my towel to the floor, I put an extra swing into my step as I walk to my dresser. Cal groans, the sound only heightening as I bend at the waist.

"You are a tease, Little Devil."

I chuckle as I sift through my draws. Remembering that Cal doesn't have anything clean to change into, I find my biggest pair of sweats and throw them to him.

"I know that they will probably be way too tight on you but they should do until I can get your clothes washed and dried."

Cal just shrugs his shoulders and drops his towel as he pulls the sweats on.

What would normally swim on me is ridiculously tight on Cal's much bigger body. I may have curves but it is nothing on the sheer size of the Alpha.

I am both slightly turned on and almost unable to hold back a laugh at the indecency of Cal's cock print.

No amount of adjusting fixes the issue and eventually he gives up right at the same time I burst out laughing.

His head shoots up at me and he hits me with a puzzled look that only makes me laugh even more. Finding my phone where I discarded it on my dresser, I quickly open the camera and snap a picture.

Cal's face turns from questioning to mischievous as he takes a menacing step towards me.

"My nickname is right for you. You are a little devil."

I go to run but Cal quickly catches me in his arms, lifting and spinning me as we both laugh.

We collapse on the bed in a heap, both still chuckling.

I sigh as I sink into Cal's arms. He positions me so I am half laying on him. Bringing a hand up, I trace my fingers over his chest drawing shapes in his skin causing the flesh to pebble yet again.

It's becoming dangerously addicting eliciting this kind of response from him.

Everything that seems to involve this Alpha is becoming addicting.

I want more. I want to know more about this man. Who he is at his core. How he likes his coffee in the mornings. What role he takes in the Syndicate.

It wasn't overly surprising to find out that not only is Conall a part of the mafia, but also Olis and Vic are.

The way that Vic dresses takes a lot of the guessing away. He looks the part of a Mafia Don.

The idea of these men doing something so illegal and frowned upon by society seems to be even more of a turn on.

There is no way that I could run from them. While some would be terrified, it makes me feel safer somehow.

Because the men that hurt me weren't like them. They were just business men with bank accounts big enough to destroy lives.

But these three men? Well, they are big enough to destroy lives with nothing but their bare hands.

Maybe I am delusional for thinking that I will be safer with them. That allowing both me and my daughter in their presence is a good idea.

My instincts have never led me astray so far. I mean they were screaming at me to run the night of my sixteenth birthday. But right now? They are telling me to trust them. That we will be okay.

"What are you thinking about, Little Devil?"

I smile at the nickname. At first I didn't know what to think of it but it has now grown on me.

"Just thinking about everything. What this is between us. Whether I can trust you three or not. If I am stupid to believe that I can actually get a happy ending."

Bringing a hand up to my chin, he lifts my head until we are face to face.

"No matter what is to happen between us, you deserve your happily ever after. You deserve it more than anyone."

I sigh as I continue to trace shapes in his skin.

"I'm trying to convince myself of that but it is hard. After years of denying myself any kind of happiness, it feels surreal to allow myself this. To open myself up to you, leaving me vulnerable and raw was one of the scariest things I have ever done."

He caresses his hand over my face.

"I'm so fucking thankful that you trusted your heart with me like that, Valley. Being the person that you open up to in that way is an honor. One I will treasure for the rest of my life."

I smile at him before bringing my hands up to hide my face. Why does this man know to say all of the right things? If my resolve wasn't already crumbling, he would have made a big step in getting closer.

"What do we do about telling Vic and Olis everything? They are your pack and I know that means they are a package deal."

Conall makes me find his eyes again. "Do you want them too?"

I pause for a moment and allow myself to really think instead of just jumping to agree. It's clear that there is something between both Vic and I as well as Olis and I. While I have had limited time with Olis, I know that there is something there. Something that I know I would kick myself over if I didn't.

It's a spark, one I refuse to not answer.

Eventually, I nod. Cal smiles down at me, pulling me into his body more, if that was even possible.

"We take it at your pace. When you are ready to tell them everything, I will be right there supporting you every step of the way."

I nod. "Do you think they will be mad?"

Cal ponders it over for a moment before he looks back at me. "They might take a moment to mull it over completely and everything that it means but I don't think they will be mad at you, no. At the situation? Absolutely."

I shiver as Cal continues, "We should be thankful that you killed those Alphas, Little Devil."

I quirk an eyebrow. "What do you mean?"

He chuckles and shakes his head. "Olis has never liked Alphas who hurt Omegas. It was only heightened when Gwen was killed. To say it would be a bloodbath is an understatement."

I shiver again but there is a hint of arousal there. An interested quirk of Cal's eyebrow lets me know he clocked that reaction, storing it away for a later date. I try to act casually but there is no denying the thought of an Alpha going to war for me like that.

"No matter what happens, I will be there for you," he murmurs, placing a kiss against my forehead.

We continue to talk before Cal eventually starts to drift off to sleep. Bringing a hand up, I thread my fingers through the gray strands, unable to hold back from teasing the slight curls that have been calling for me for days now.

It's only seconds before his eyes relax completely and his eyes shut.

I lose track of time as I continue to play with the strands and admire him as he slumbers.

Eventually, my own eyes begin to slowly shut and I fall into a dreamless sleep.

CHAPTER EIGHTEEN

OLIS

I frown down at the soldiers as I watch them train. I haven't been able to shake myself out of my mood since I watched Cal drive off with Val two nights ago.

How fucking fitting; Cal and Val.

I have no doubt that that motherfucker would love that both of their nicknames match in some way. He would get the biggest kick out of teasing us with it too.

He would also be getting a kick out of the fact that since that night that he has still clearly not left her apartment since taking her home.

Both Vic and I have called and messeged the fucker. The only response either of us receives is a short and sweet **With our girl.**

Vic has been on the edge since receiving the text. I have been in a similar state. It's been difficult trying to hold back the raw need that crawls through me every waking moment.

I need to see her.

This going a week without so much as seeing that beautiful face is grating at my nerves.

Everyone has been able to see just how unsettled I have been. Ledger has given me a wide berth, something I don't blame him for.

I know that the only solution would be to see her.

My phone vibrating has me pulling my phone out with a huff. My mood instantly brightens as a photo of Valentina sleeping on Cal's chest pops up on my phone.

I save the photo, crop the bits of my pack brother that are visible before saving it as my screensaver.

A smile quirks my lips as I keep looking at the photo.

God, she is just so fucking beautiful. It's impossible to understand how this woman has been able to awaken feelings in me that I thought I would never be able to feel again.

That with a single look and a quick smile, I have been hooked since that day in the park.

She is perfection and mystery all mixed up into one delectable Beta.

I tuck my phone away as shouts come from the mat in front of me. My frown reappears as I call the match and invite the next soldiers onto the mat.

It's the last round before I need to send them off to the gym. Keeping our soldiers fit is an important part of our regiment. We need them alert and ready for anything we throw at them.

Since our son's Omega was taken a few years ago, we partnered with the Omega Protection Agency. Normally, we would have stayed clear from something so deeply connected to the government but since both of our goals aligned, we decided to help them in some of their particularly difficult cases.

Jaiden, one of the Alphas that was undercover in Kennedy's case walks in through the side door. He nods in greeting to Ledger who hardly acknowledges him.

Even though Jaiden wasn't directly involved in what happened to Kennedy, he still holds some kind of grudge against him. Understandable, considering I murdered every person connected to the group that murdered Gwen.

Jaiden nods as he comes to stand beside me. "Olis. Morning."

I grunt and nod, not giving him anything further. He doesn't expect it either as he continues.

"I have a new case for you to look into. An Alpha has been going around the state murdering Omegas."

I turn to Jaiden, the Alpha finally getting my attention.

"Why wouldn't the cops be dealing with this one?" I question.

"They are dealing with it but they have called us in on this one. They don't think this is just some random killer. They think that this is targeted."

I nod and he continues, "Each of the Omega's has distinctive features. Each is raped, bound and gagged before they are strangled to death."

I sigh, shaking my head. Of course this is some kind of vengeful fucking Alpha. Surely this dickhead was turned down at some point and now he feels as though it's his right to take what he wants.

Fuck, when is it not like that. We see the same thing time and time again. Each case only seems to make me angrier and angrier.

"Send Conall through everything we need to know and we will look into it."

Jaiden nods and shakes my hand before he says his goodbyes.

Once the final fight is finished, I send Ledger off with this group to the gym before I head to the offices in search of Vic.

Even if I didn't know the warehouse like the back of my hand, Vic's office would be easy to find. The deep grumble of his voice as he growls out orders into his phone is a dead giveaway.

He is just sitting down with a sigh as I walk into the room. He removes his glasses and swipes a hand over his face before replacing them.

"Seen what that pesky little shit sent us?" I ask as I take a seat in front of the desk.

Vic finally looks up at me. Dark circles rim his eyes as he shakes his head and picks up his phone again.

"No, I only just ... that motherfucker!" Vic shouts, shooting up from his chair.

Slamming his hands on the table, he pins me with a look.

"I'm fucking sick of waiting around while our brother gets to spend all the time with our girl. Are you coming?"

I am already out of my chair and walking back towards the door before he is even finished.

"My car or yours?"

We pull up in front of Val's apartment ten minutes later. There will be numerous speeding fines that Conall will have to erase from the system but that is that last thing on either of our minds. Makes sense that something petty like that would be the punishment that Vic dolls out for stealing our girl away for the last few nights.

It's hard to not hate every single facet of the rundown building. I despise the idea of this being all that Valentina was able to afford. That she had to lower herself to rent this place just so she can put a roof over her daughter's head.

The moment she is mine, she will be taking up residence in our home. I already have bedrooms for both her and Amity picked out and ready for them to move into.

The thought of her being just down the hall from us settles something inside of me, almost more so than being able to actually see her.

I just want her safe.

Safe and away for creeps like this Alpha that is going around and killing Omegas. I guess that is at least one small thing that I don't have to worry about. Our girl is a Beta.

It doesn't surprise me that Vic knows just which apartment is our girls. His stalker tendencies are elite.

Knocking on the door, we only have to wait a few moments before a bleary eyed Valley is opening the door. She rubs a hand over her face but pauses when she sees us. Her eyes blow wide as she just stares at us in shock.

"Going to let us in, *dolce ciliegra?*" Vic questions and all but pushes Valley out of the road as he steps into the apartment without waiting for said invitation.

Unlike my pack brother, I wait until my girl looks back at me.

"You can come in," she mutters, her tone mixed with shock and sleep.

I smile at her as I step inside but come to a quick stop as I lean in, pressing a kiss to her forehead, "Good morning, sweetheart."

Her breath hitches as I continue inside and take in my surroundings.

Valley's apartment is just as small and barren as I thought it was going to be. It seems that she only picked the necessities versus styling her house as her own. It's simple and it works but it still makes a part of my chest ache.

The sound of pattering feet coming down the hallway has me turning. The spitting image of Valley turns the corner but stops as she sees both Vic and I in the hallway.

"Oh no! I'm going to catch a firefly!" Cal shouts, appearing from behind her. The little girl squeals as he grabs her, lifting, spinning and tickling her.

Both of them laugh together as he sets her down. Eventually he straightens like he is about to speak to Val but pauses when he sees the two of us standing with her.

A sheepish look appears on his face, bringing a hand up to ruffle his unkept hair, clearly having not long got out of bed. Judging by the lack of pillows and blankets on the couch; Valley's bed.

"Ah, hey guys. Um, Amity, these are my pack-brothers Vic and Olis."

Amity nods, grabbing ahold of Conall's pants leg and attempts to hide behind the Alpha's leg.

It's blatantly obvious that in the days he has been absent, he has been here developing something further not only with our girl but also with her daughter.

I can't stop the pang of jealousy that shoots through me. It's a foreign feeling, especially when it is aimed at someone that I consider a brother.

But here we are.

Valley steps up into us, breaking the now awkward tension in the room. “Ah, do you guys want a coffee?”

I nod and so does both Vic and Conall.

“How do you like it?”

“One sugar and milk please,” I reply just as Vic replies, “Black.”

Val turns a disgusted look Vic’s way. “Why am I not surprised that you take your coffee that way?”

He just shrugs his shoulders and turns, making himself familiar with what little there is in here. It wouldn’t surprise me if he had cameras that he was secretly stashing to keep a closer eye on our girl.

“Bitter like his soul,” Conall murmurs, eliciting a chuckle from our girl. The sound is like music to my ears.

“I don’t want coffee, Mommy,” a little voice grumbles. I turn to see Amity walk over to the bench separating the kitchen and the lounge room.

Valley chuckles again, opening the fridge and pulling out a juice box. Amity giggles and wriggles in her seat, patiently waiting for her version of liquid gold.

A smile turns the corners of my lips, unable to deny just how adorable she is.

Once our coffees are set out before us, Valley leans against the counter behind her, crossing her arms and pinning both Vic and I with a suspicious look.

“So, what brings you both to my home? I feel like this is overstepping the boss and employee work relationship.”

Vic scoffs, setting down his mug, “I think that was well and truly thrown out the window when you allowed one of your bosses to stay here for the last two nights and sleep in your bed, *dolce ciligera.*”

Valley's eyes narrow. "What I do in my house is none of your business, Victor."

I cringe at the use of Vic's name. He hates anyone using it after our father's overuse of it following demands as him and Conall were growing up. It's the same reason why Cal also prefers his nickname. Except he is much less anal about it.

To my surprise, he doesn't bark at her like I expected him to. Instead he just leans forward, his arms resting on the bench.

"The truth of why I am here is because I wanted to see you. A week without seeing your face would have been a catastrophe."

There is a slight tinge to her cheeks but she doesn't completely let go of the grumpy cat persona she is leaning on for obvious support.

"You having a school boy crush is no excuse for you to just barge into my apartment. Especially not when my daughter is here."

He shrugs his shoulders and straightens. "Fine, if you won't allow us to barge into your home, then pack a bag."

Valley's head tilts and she frowns in confusion, pulling her bottom lip into her mouth. A growl escapes my chest unwillingly as my eyes remain locked on that spot.

Cal chuckles from behind me, slapping a hand on my shoulder. I don't jolt or push him off, even as he leans against me.

"You biting your lip like that is Olis' Hail Mary, Little Devil," he snickers before he adds, "Keep tempting him like that and you will be getting more than you bargained for."

Immediately she lets go of her lip, aiming a not so innocent look at me. Little devil is right. Valentina knows exactly what she is doing.

She turns back to Vic after the small distraction. "What do you mean 'pack a bag'?"

Vic rolls his eyes. "Exactly those words. Pack your bags. Both you and Amity will come stay at our place for the week."

"Sleepover! Mommy, we get to go have a sleepover!"

Shooting up from her place on the couch, Amity races into what I assume is her room. Each of us remains silent as we wait for the little one to return. In a flurry, she comes barreling back out of her room, a bag stuffed with what I am assuming are clothes and her pillow tucked under her arm.

I chuckle, stepping around the bench and into her space, "I think Squirt has spoken, Valley."

She sighs, collapsing further into the bench. Reaching a hand up, I brush some stray hair behind her ear.

"Come on, sweetheart. What's the worst that could happen?"

She rolls her eyes, straightening, but there is a resigned look on her face.

"Famous last words, Olis."

CHAPTER NINETEEN

VALENTINA

I question every single one of my life choices as we drive up to the gate of the Alphas home. Cal had prepared me a little on the drive over but it's one thing to see it from his point of view and then mine.

An at least ten foot fence surrounds what I assume is the entire property. The gates welcoming us onto their land resemble something you would expect to see at the home of a royal, not some Mafia men. Then again, I guess they are royalty in their world.

I would never tell Cal that. The idea of him being a king would go straight to his head. I don't need to give his ego anymore encouragement.

Sprawling gardens seem to frame the house, adding something a little bit extra to the outside of the mansion.

Pulling up at the garage, I get out of the car and take in my surroundings. Both Olis and Vic come over to stand beside me just as a group of five soldiers come around the corner.

Nodding their heads at all three men they eventually look at me and Amity who looks at them curiously.

"Men, this is Valentina and Amity. They will be staying with us this week. Protection extends to them," Vic demands before dismissing them with a nod.

In sync, all five men nod before turning and disappearing to wherever they appeared from.

With wide eyes, I turn to Olis who looks at me with a similar expression on his face.

"Ah, that was um... We ah..." he attempts to find his words but can't seem to as a look of hopelessness clouds his features.

I chuckle and shake my head before placing a cautionary hand on his arm. "It's okay, Olis. Cal already explained everything to me."

He raises an eyebrow at me and is hesitant as he tilts his head. "Everything?"

"Yes, Capo," I chuckle with a wink. His eyes darken significantly and he goes to take a step towards me but stops as Vic clears his throat.

"If we are all comfortable now with the fact that we fucking kill people for a living, would we care to head inside for the grand tour or do we need to stand out here any longer?"

I snort at the brashness of Vic's words, the guy clearly having zero patience even now that I am here just like he wanted.

Vic doesn't bother standing around to entertain us any longer before he is walking up the staircase and into the house.

Cal shakes his head, as if already exhausted with his twin. "Sorry about the grumpy cat, Little Devil."

A giggle from beside me has me looking down at Amity who is trying to hold in a laugh.

"His name's Grumpy Cat?" she asks Cal.

He nods with a mischievous look on his face, making Amity descend into a full blown laugh.

Taking off in the direction Vic headed in, Amity yells, "Grumpy Cat, Grumpy Cat," on repeat as she follows after him.

Olis sighs, shaking his head, "You've done it now, Cal."

Conall just shrugs his shoulders. "Grumpy Cat needs to pull that stick out of his ass and lighten the fuck up."

I didn't know what to expect from three Alphas' bachelor pad but it certainly wasn't a house that looks like it has never seen a drop of color.

A bucket of beige paint looks like it was set off in the living room. While it has a lot more personality than the blandness of my apartment, it seems cold and unlived in. Like everything in here is just for show so there aren't a bunch of random empty rooms.

Conall can clearly see my thoughts written all over my face, "It's a blank canvas for right now but maybe you can help us make it a bit more homey?"

My eyebrows furrow as I look at the Alpha in confusion. He just smiles at me like this is all some kind of game to him.

"I mean, you will want to put your own touch on everything when you move in, right? This place needs a *female's* touch," he adds with an underlying double meaning to the word female.

I continue to gape at him, shocked at just how forward he is being. I shouldn't have expected anything less, especially when it comes to

Conall but I thought that maybe he would actually want to be official with me first before moving in.

Maybe even have waited until Olis and Vic knew the whole truth before booking a moving van.

But being patient is obviously not in Conall's vocabulary. In fact, I don't think that this man even has the capability of being able to wait. Not with the way he smiles like a Cheshire Cat, clearly proud of having shocked me.

I shake my head before we continue on with the tour. Much like the living room, the rest of the house has the same dull feeling to it.

It may seem strange to some but I always hated that every room apart from Amity's in my apartment also felt this same way.

Every single time we went into a home decor shop, I had to resist every single one of my urges to not pick up at least a few homely pieces. While I am no interior designer, the thought of being able to add that touch to a blank canvas is thrilling.

But in doing so, it would call to the part of me that I have been trying to deny.

Would it really be so terrible though if I was to indulge with that side of me that is so desperate to be let out?

I know that Conall has reassured me time and time again that I am safe with him but does that also translate to if I was to embrace my Omega?

I have a feeling it would.

Adding a mental note to the ever-growing list of shit that I need to remember to do, I follow Vic as he shows us the rooms we will be staying in while we are here.

His eyes don't stray very far from me the entire tour through the home. I know that there is something so obviously unspoken between us.

Vic is an intelligent man—much to my downfall—so I know that he knows there is more to me than meets the eye.

It's almost unsettling the way I can feel him watching me take everything in. I have never met someone that looked as though they wanted to dissect me. To work out what makes me tick.

The excitement as Amity is shown her room has me chuckling alongside her until I actually see her room.

Pink paint with a gorgeous floral wallpapered wall frames the bedroom. A twin canopy bed takes up the centre of the room adorned with linen of Amity's favorite princesses.

My mouth drops as I take in the exorbitant amount of toys that are spread out through the room. Amity squeals, jumping from toy to toy, oohing and ahhing with each new find.

Backing up a few steps, I come to an abrupt halt as I collide with a body. Hands grip my hips before turning me to face the man before me.

"This is too much, Vic. You... I..." I shake my head, trying to find the words that seem to evade me.

Vic reaches up, gripping the sides of my face in his hands.

"No, *dolce ciligera,* it's not enough. You and *piccola* deserve all of this and more."

I continue to shake my head as tears start to pool in my eyes.

With a growl, Vic pulls me flush to his body, gripping my tightly in his embrace.

"No. No tears," he murmurs, the tone holds a raspy sound to it.

I gasp as Vic lifts me completely in his arms, holding me close as he walks out of what I guess is now Amity's new room and into another room.

One that I assume is mine.

He doesn't set me down but he does pull away slightly, allowing me to lift off his chest.

Gone is the earlier facade of the big bad Alpha that acted like he didn't have a care in the world. In his place are soft gentle features that set my growing panic at ease.

"Knowing my brother, he has already wormed his way into your life," he says already knowing what happened but I nod anyway.

He sighs and holds eye contact with me, "From the moment I stumbled into that alleyway and saw your beautiful face, I have been addicted. It's like you are this beacon constantly calling to me."

He shakes his head and touches his forehead with mine. "I need to be in your orbit, *dolce ciligera.*"

A shiver rolls through my body and I nod, unable to speak. Nothing I could say right now would ever amount to what Vic just said to me.

I had been questioning myself, wondering if Vic even had this kind of side to him but I should never have doubted him.

It makes sense that the Don would have to have two sides to him. There is no way that he would be able to oversee a portion of the Underworld and not have hardened himself.

"The thought of having you here settles the beast inside of me. It's fast and I know that I have done nothing to warrant you even wanting to entertain me but I want to at least try. I can't deny what I feel for you."

There is so much raw emotion in Vic's voice that my own feelings threaten to clog my throat.

"Yes," I whisper, unable to say anything more.

With a jolt, Vic pulls away from me. His face is wide in shock as his eyes dart over my face. "What?"

I smile and clear my throat, pushing down my tears, "I said yes, Vic. Yes, I want to explore this thing with you."

I pause for a moment working up the dose of courage I need before speaking again.

"I feel it too, Vic."

He swallows roughly as a mixture of emotions pass across his face.

Shock, denial and relief.

"Fuck it," he grunts, surging towards me, his lips colliding with mine.

I remain frozen in place for a moment before I whimper against his lips as I return the kiss.

Vic groans into my mouth, a spark of pleasure shooting straight to my clit. He turns us abruptly, slamming me against the wall.

I don't register the pain, unable to feel anything but Vic and the way his body hungrily moves against mine.

The Alpha devours me like he has been starving for years and has finally gotten a taste of ambrosia.

I roll my body into his as the kiss deepens. Gripping his shoulders, I dig my nails into his flesh as his hardness that threatens to burst his zipper rolls against my core.

He chuckles against my lips, pulling back slightly and allowing my head to lean against the wall as he rolls his hips again.

"Fuck, you are so perfect as you moan for me. Do you want more, *il mio cuore?*"

I nod as desperation screams at me. I need more. I need more of this Alpha.

"Beg me," he growls.

My eyes open, finding the raw desperation on his face that mimics the one I can hear in his tone.

"What?"

"Beg me for more, *la mia puttana disperata. Lascia che te ne dia di più. Lasciami assaporare la tua dolce essenza.*"

My body writhes against Vic's as he mutters Italian to me. The words seem to increase my pleasure.

"Please, Alpha. Please give me more," I beg just as he asked.

He growls, his hold on me tightening a moment before he drops my legs. I groan, throwing my head back, disappointment flaring through me.

Vic doesn't keep me waiting for long, dropping to his knees in front of me. I gasp as he tugs down the front of my shorts.

"Such a good girl for your Daddy, *il mio cuore.* Now you get your reward."

CHAPTER TWENTY

VICTOR

I praise every single god I can think of as my knees hit the carpeted floor below me. It feels as though this day has been a long time coming.

I didn't think that my *dolce ciligera* would allow me this much so soon but I refuse to look a gift horse in the mouth.

Slowly, I tease the shorts off her hips, unable to hold back the groan at seeing the lacy panties she has been hiding from me.

It doesn't matter how many times in the past few weeks I have seen her in scraps of fabric or even bare, the sight is still as mouth watering as if it was the first time.

Sucking in a breath, I curse the designation that fate gave this beauty. While I have nothing against Betas, I long to smell a scent from her. I know it would be just as delicious as what my mind is conjuring up.

Whispering sweet nothings, I bring my hands back up to her waist, threading my fingers through the lace and tear them off her. She gasps, her eyes widening in surprise as I stuff the now ruined panties in my pocket.

"You better fucking replace them," she tries to grumble but it falls flat as she throws her head back as I swipe my tongue through her slit.

I growl as her taste explodes on my tongue. There is a hint of sweetness that I can't quite work out but I continue eating her like she is my last meal.

Her fingers thread into my hair, gripping the strands and pulling my face closer into her heat.

It feels like only seconds pass before her hold on me tightens. One of her legs wraps around my shoulder bringing me closer to her. Spearing her on my tongue, I guide a hand that isn't gripping her leg to her clit, flicking the nub gently.

With a scream, Valentina gushes all over my face. I groan, drinking down her release, refusing to allow any of it to go to waste. It would be a tragedy to wipe away such a gift on the back of my hand.

No, I want to taste my girl on my lips for the rest of the day. Maybe tonight she can give me a refresher of her essence.

Slowly, Valley's leg drops from my shoulder and she begins sliding down the wall, her legs too weak to hold her any longer. Collecting her on her way down, I bundle her up into my arms, holding her as the after shocks of her orgasm continue to pulse through her.

After all of these years having remained celibate, I chuckle at myself, proud of a job well done.

"What are you laughing at?" Valley asks breathlessly.

"Just that even after all these years, I still have it."

My girl pulls back and rolls her eyes at me, "Alright, Old Man. No need to get ahead of yourself. Wouldn't want you to pull a hip with all that postering."

She tries to hold a straight face but breaks seeing the stunned expression on my face.

Old.

My girl just fucking called me old.

What the fuck.

Never in my young forty-five years have I ever been this stunned.

I knew that my girl was wicked but I didn't think that she would go straight for the throat especially after I left her frazzled after an orgasm that I know blew her mind.

Yet here she is, fucking sassing me.

Someone has been spending way too much time with my brother.

She stands, giving me a final view of her pussy before moving away from me and collecting her shorts. There is a grimace on her face as she shrugs them on and I find a shred of delight knowing the rough fabric will be rubbing on her sensitive core for the rest of the day.

Perfect time to continue winding her up.

Getting back to my feet, I silently watch as she moves around her new room.

It's easy to see just how perfect she is in this space. It's as though we had it built with her in mind.

Her hands trail over a four poster bed that almost perfectly mirrors Amity's room. But where *piccolo's* room is filled with all things girly, we went for a much darker theme in this room.

The sheets on the bed are a dark green that seem to offset the black feature wall behind the bed. The rest of the walls are a warm off white, allowing the room to still feel breathable.

Decor was kept to a minimum, the room having nearly been forgotten about until the vision before me walked into our lives.

Scratching my head, suddenly feeling an odd nervousness, I clear my throat, "I know that it isn't much. Interior decorating isn't our thing but I want you to add your own touch. To make this room truly feel like yours."

She nods but keeps her back to me, looking out the window.

On quiet feet, I walk up behind her, hesitant as I wrap my arms around her waist. I pause as she tenses but continue wrapping my arms around her when she relaxes into my hold.

We are both silent for a moment as we look out over the property. The back of our property overlooks the city of Vadena. I know that Valley will be up here watching as the sun sets behind the skyscrapers.

Pointing at one of the buildings, I bring my head down to her ear, "See that building there?" She nods before I continue, "We own that."

"Wow," she murmurs with a hint of surprise in her voice. "What do you do there?"

I thank my brother again for skipping to the whole 'Mafia Don' speech so I didn't have to. It's never an easy conversation to have.

"The bottom half of the building we rent out to various companies for office space. A few floors above that are apartments where we house a lot of our single soldiers. Above that, each floor is dedicated to one of our businesses."

I cringe slightly as I leave that statement hanging between us.

"Do I even want to know how many of these businesses you have?" she questions, a hint of a smile in her tone.

"Ah, probably not. To be honest, I'm not as involved with them as I should be. Cal handless all of them while I handle the more..." I trail off trying to find the right word.

"Sinister side?" she adds, her tone laced with an edge of snark.

I nod with a chuckle, "Yeah, that sounds about right." I pause and squeeze her tight. "I know Cal told you about what we really do but I need to know... Are you really okay with it?"

I wait with bated breath as she thinks over what I just said.

There is a pit in my stomach. One that is fucking terrified that she will hate what we do, just like Gwen did.

I know that I wouldn't blame her if she did. It's not like the three of us have normal jobs. There is no nine-to-five here.

No, this job is a lifestyle. One that after all these years I don't know if I would be able to turn my back on, even for Valley.

I couldn't do it for Gwen.

But as I mull it over into my head, I know that I have been preparing Theo for the day that he will take over from me. Jax is already working closely with Conall. Olis has taken a backseat this last year as he has allowed Ledger to organize the soldiers under my command.

And Kennedy, well my *figlia* has fit in easily into the family business. I think all of us were surprised the night she took her life back.

I couldn't be any more proud of my kids.

Maybe handing things over to them, even just partially wouldn't be a bad idea. Maybe that makes me seem like some kind of helicopter Don but I don't see anyone telling me that I should do otherwise.

In fact, maybe it will be the answer to all of my problems.

After all, a life with Valley would be like balm to the soul.

"Honestly," my *dolce ciliegra* finally breaks the silence, turning towards me, "the idea of you three being able to protect Amity and I makes me feel at ease for the first time in a long time."

She sighs, looking down for a moment before meeting my eyes again. "I have been running for so long that it feels almost unnatural to now have the option to stop hiding. That maybe now that I know I will be safe, I can finally be the real me."

I don't know exactly what it is in her words that lets me know there is some kind of underlying to her statement but I brush it aside and focus on the words that have tears pooling in my eyes.

I haven't cried in what feels like forever but at a simple admission from my girl, I am nearly brought back to my knees.

Clearing my throat, I bring my hands up to rest on either side of her face. "I vow that both you and Amity will never know anything but true happiness ever again. That when you are here, your safety is paramount to us. That if it comes to it, I will put my life on the line just so you can sleep at night."

Tears stream down her cheeks but I quickly wipe them away, my heart aching seeing the raw emotion on her face.

It's unbearable seeing even an ounce of pain on her.

"I don't want you to put your life on the line for me," she says through her tears, her words choked.

Pulling her into my chest, I squeeze her tightly. "I'm sorry *il mio cuore,* but if it is between me and you, you will always be my first choice."

After Valley's tears settle, we move back through the house, finding Olis making lunch. There is an almost foreign smile on her face as she watches Amity dancing in front of the TV to a song I haven't heard before. Cal dances beside the three-year-old, but where *piccolo* is adorable, Cal just looks like a deranged chicken as he twerks.

Valley giggles at both of them but quickly, my slight annoyance at my brother dissolves.

If it is my brother that puts that smile on her face, I can deal with his antics for one more day.

It only takes moments for Olis to realize that we have walked into the room. He grabs a plate and dishes up lunch for our girl.

"Here sweetheart," he says quietly, placing the plate down at the table. The smile she aims at him is breathtaking, the look clenches something in my stomach.

I want her to look at me like that. Like her world starts and finishes with me. Very much the way I am starting to feel about her.

Piccolo uses that moment to turn and run towards Valley who collects her in her arms.

"Mommy, this house is so cool! Can we stay here forever?"

I chuckle at the sweet little girl as I bend down and get to her level, "The three of us would love to have both you and your momma here forever."

Her eyes lighten up even more. She surprises me as she launches herself into my arms, squeezing me tight with her little limbs.

"You are my new favorite, Grumpy Cat."

Well fuck if I don't just melt right there on the spot. Even including the nickname I know was encouraged by my brother.

CHAPTER TWENTY-ONE

VALENTINA

I hate the thought that Vic has given Amity false hope.

I want to berate him. To yell at him for letting my three year old think that this place could be our forever home because how could it?

While I have said to both Cal and now Vic that I want to see where this thing goes between us, I am still holding out reservations.

I haven't even had a proper conversation with Olis yet.

It feels like everything is moving too fast and I am still driving in the slow lane. I need it all just to stop for a moment.

A moment just to think about what the fuck I am doing with my life.

Am I really entertaining these Alphas for anything more than a lap dance when I have sworn off their entire designation for as long as I can remember?

I take a moment to question my sanity as I finish the meal in front of me.

It's impossible to not admit that Olis is a damn good cook. It's been a long time since I have had a meal that is as good as this.

While I have never let Amity or I go hungry, my cooking skills are far from that of even a diner chef.

I guess I do make a mean grilled sandwich if I am honest with myself.

Not like that's a necessarily hard thing to do.

A bit of ham, tomato and cheese on two slices of buttered bread. Maybe a bit of onion if you are feeling frisky and then you have a delicious savoury meal.

Well, Amity has never complained so I take it for the win that I think it is.

Once I finish my plate, I glance up to find Olis looking at me. There is this vulnerable but desperate expression on his face that surprises me.

I tilt my head to the side and give him a questioning look, one that earns an adorable smile in return.

God, he is fucking handsome.

"Did you enjoy your meal?"

The low timbre in his tone has a chill running down my spine. Instead of replying verbally, knowing that I can't fully trust myself to speak, I nod. That earns me another smile I can't help but savour.

Ugh, he isn't playing fair. The worst part is, I don't think he even realizes it.

None of them seem to.

A knock on the front door has Cal straightening, an excited look on his face. He doesn't say anything, pushing himself away from the table and makes his way to the front door.

I look up at Olis, his eyes already on me and ready to give me the explanation I need.

"I hope this isn't too soon but our sons and their Omega are here."

My eyes bug out of my head and I shoot out of my seat. I race over to the kitchen sink, turning on the tap and immediately bringing some water to my face to wash it, terrified that some of my lunch may still be on my face.

I roll off what feels like a ridiculous amount of paper towel as I dry my face and hands. Throwing the rubbish in the bin, I straighten my clothes, frowning as I look at them.

Are these clothes okay?

God, I can't believe they are springing me meeting their kids on me like this. These clothes are hardly suitable for meeting family. Especially now that I am sans panties.

Fuck, what am I doing here?

Hands land on my shoulders and I'm turned around to face one of the Alphas. Olis' face is a mask as he gazes down at me.

"Breathe, sweetheart. In and Out."

I nod and do what he says, the panic ebbing away from me before it can start.

"Olis, I'm not ready to meet your kids. Fuck, look at what I am wearing! I look like trash! I..."

Lips meet mine, cutting off anything I was about to say. My borderline hysteria is swallowed down as Olis claims me.

His cinnamon and apple scent invades my senses as though I had just stepped into a bakery. The warm and comforting taste has me melting further into his body, the hard planes of his chest welcoming me into him.

I groan as he pulls away from me, wishing I could just bring him back for more.

He doesn't deny me for long, resting his forehead against mine. I take shallow breaths as I allow myself to come back down to earth.

"I will only tell you this once, Valley. If I have to tell you twice, I will spank you until what I say sinks in."

My breath hitches and I feel my panties moisten at the threat of punishment. It shouldn't have elicited that kind of reaction out of me, but here we are I guess.

"You are so fucking beautiful, even the goddess of beauty herself is jealous of your perfection. Even if your clothes were threadbare and filth, you would still shine the brightest in the room."

He brings a hand up to my face and tucks a strand of hair behind my ear.

"So. Fucking. Beautiful."

His voice is a borderline growl as he accentuates each word. A shiver runs over my body as he continues to hold me against him.

"Do you hear me, Valentina? Or do I need to take you aside and punish you?"

I feel as my entire body reacts to yet another declaration from Olis. It feels as though my entire body lights up.

He steps away from me, chuckling quietly at my reaction to him.

I'm not given any kind of reprieve as Conall walks back in with three younger Alphas and a pretty little Omega with bright red hair. All four of them look around my age, maybe a year or two younger if I was to really guess. The Omegas eyes catch with mine, the beautiful green eyes seemingly to light, the kindness and excitement near-exploding as she walks towards me.

"Hi! I'm Kennedy. I'm so excited to meet you. Cal has told me so much about you." She smiles, pulling me into her arms.

I hesitate for a moment but quickly relax into the embrace. Although, I do find Cal and lock eyes with him. He just shrugs his shoulders and looks at me with a not so innocent look.

The little Omega eventually pulls away from me before she steps back from her Alphas. I startle as I look at the younger replicas of Cal, Vic and Olis. They must be able to read the surprise on my face as they chuckle before Cal and Vic's younger twin takes a step towards me. He holds his hand out in greeting.

"Hi Valentina, it's so lovely to meet you. I'm Theo and these are my pack brothers Jax and Ledger."

I shake his hand hesitantly before he steps away. Jax and Ledger nod their hands at me but remain beside their Omega, unable to keep their hands off her—or each other it seems.

There is an awkward silence for a moment but we are shocked out of it as Amity walks up to Theo and taps him on the leg.

"You look like my grumpy cat; just not as old."

I smack my hand over my mouth, a laugh threatens to break through my fingers. I look over at said 'Grumpy Cat' who just has an adoring look on his face looking down at my daughter.

It only lasts as long as the room is silent though as the once contained laughter overcomes us. Conall is bent over, clutching at his stomach as he looks up at his twin.

"Not only did Firefly call you grumpy, she also called you old," he snorts.

Vic levels his brother with a warning look. "I wouldn't hold any delusions that I am the only one that she thinks is old, Conall."

Conall stands up straighter then, an almost concerned look on his face ignoring his sons who are still laughing at Vic's expense.

"You don't think I am old do you, Firefly?"

Amity looks up at the Alpha, assessing him for a moment before shrugging her shoulders. "You are a little bit old."

Cal gapes at my three-year-old, a mixture of looks on his face. It only seems to set the younger pack off even more.

After each of us settle down, Vic leads us all to a sitting room where Amity squeals at an overflowing toy box one of the guys must have set up there for her.

I shake my head as I look at who I know is the offender.

"You know you don't need to buy all these toys for her. She has enough."

He just shrugs his shoulders, not bothering to answer me. I know that my complaints will just fall on deaf ears. That Alpha is stuck in his ways.

Even though the sitting room could easily fit my entire apartment inside of it, being the last one in the room, the only option to sit is right in between Olis and Vic.

I sigh as I make my way over to the spot on the couch and mentally brace myself as I sit between the two Alphas.

Even though I have slowly got used to being around Alphas, I still can't help the spike of terror in my chest at being surrounded by them.

I try to take a few calming breaths but curse as I get a whiff of both Alphas together.

A mixture of Vic's earthy scent with Olis' cinnamon apple is a dangerous combination that has the Omega I have tried to keep under wraps, threatening to come out.

I close my eyes as I continue to breathe them in, praying that my suppressants don't fail me now.

Eventually I reopen my eyes and come face to face with a concerned Cal.

"Are you okay, Little Devil?"

I nod but that doesn't seem to convince him. This man may come across as carefree and a joker but there is more to him than meets the eye.

He is able to see right through me. To see that I am freaking out for a magnitude of reasons. That my post traumatic stress is rearing its head violently, threatening to unravel any kind of progress that I had made.

I yelp in surprise as Conall lifts me out from between his two pack mates—who both quickly protest—and walks over to the chair he must have vacated.

With little care for the multiple eyes on us, he sits down in the arm chair, settling me in his lap.

Turning my head, I look at the Alpha in surprise. He just shrugs his shoulders and turns his attention towards his sons.

"So boys, you mentioned that there was something that you needed to tell us?"

The entire room is silent, mirroring the shock I feel after what was an out of character moment for Cal. Eventually one of the younger Alphas clears his throat, drawing my attention.

It seems that these primal urges aren't just limited to the man beneath me as I find Kennedy also sitting on her Alpha's lap. It does something to settle me, seeing just how comfortable and clearly in love this pack is with each other.

It makes me want to know more about them and their story.

Because even though brightness shines off the pretty Omega's face, I can see the fine lines of trauma still there. They may be faint, possibly dulled by the love she has been shown but it is still there. A wound that won't ever truly be healed, but one she will learn to live alongside. Just like mine.

Jax leans forward slightly, still holding Kennedy tightly in his embrace. My hands become drawn to where they move in a loving caress over her stomach.

My jaw drops as I look up at Kennedy who is smiling at her Alphas.

"We are having a baby," Jax says proudly.

Immediately, cheers erupt from Vic, Olis and Conall. The latter, while holding me tightly in his arms, shoots up out of his seat. I squeal as he spins us around.

His laughter is infectious as he holds me tightly before pulling away to look at me.

"I'm going to be a grandpa."

There are tears in his eyes as he looks at me, like the thrill is going to be taken away from him too soon.

"You are going to be a grandpa," I reiterate, reminding him that it's real.

Eventually, he places me down but hesitates for a moment, looking at where Olis and Vic are already hugging their sons and daughter-in-law.

I nudge him with my shoulder. “Go over there and celebrate with your family.”

He looks down at me, a small smile on his face. “You are our family as well, Little Devil.”

My breath hitches as Cal drags me over to the group.

As Kennedy pulls away from Olis’ embrace, her eyes catch mine. I feel like a deer in the headlights for a moment before her head tilts. There is an almost sad smile on her face as she takes a step towards me.

“I know things are really new with you guys but I could really use a mothers help with this journey.”

I don’t know how this woman was able to bring me to the point of tears with a single sentence, but here we are.

“I would love to be there for you,” I whisper, doing my best not to choke on the sob that threatens me.

I do lose though as Kennedy engulfs me in a tight embrace. The sound of her tears are the only comfort I have that it's not a ‘just me’ moment.

“Mommy, why is everyone crying?”

I pull away from the embrace and look down to find a very worried looking Amity. Her eyes dart between myself and Kennedy, the distress on her face evident.

It's obvious that her Alpha qualities are rearing their head. Alphas never cope well when Omegas are in distress. Their need to fix the situation overwhelms them. Their primal need to protect driving their instincts.

Bending down to my daughter's level, I reach out, grabbing her hands to hold them in mine.

"Do you know how sometimes you can get so happy about something that it makes you cry?"

She thinks for a moment before nodding.

"This is one of those moments. We are crying happy tears because Kennedy is going to be a mommy."

It takes a moment for my words to sink in but when they do, it makes my eyes tear up that little bit more.

"Do you mean I am going to have a little baby to play with?" she gasps and looks up at Olis who kneels down beside me.

I go to speak but I am cut off.

"It means that you are going to have a little niece or nephew to play with. You are going to be Aunty Amity."

My gasp of surprise has nothing on Amity's as she launches herself at Kennedy who quickly returns the excited three-year-old's embrace.

I stand to full height, continuing to gape at Olis who just smiles at me. There is an almost innocent look on his face, one that I call bullshit on. He knows exactly what he did.

"You can't just tell her things like that, Olis. Because if this doesn't work between us, she is going to have her heart broken. I…"

Olis cuts me off with a tug on my arm. I stumble into him, my hands land on his chest to help stabilize myself because my legs are sure as shit useless.

"Who ever said anything about this not working out between us? I don't know how clear the three of us need to be. You are ours. Amity is ours. There is no leaving. No 'things not working out'."

He holds up a hand between us and points between the both of us.

"This thing between us, it's real. It may be new but I am done with allowing what I want to slip through my fingers.

"From that first moment I saw you in the park, I knew I had to have you. Then when I found out my pack brothers were just as infatuated with you as I am, I knew that this thing was real."

This time, the tears that fall aren't led by one emotion. They drip down my face in heartbreak, fear, anger, terror, hope—and surprisingly—adoration.

"I know that you aren't there yet and that's okay. But just know that we have got you."

Olis raises an eyebrow waiting for me to answer. All I can manage through my tears is a whispered "okay" and a nod.

He seems happy enough with my response, pulling me into his chest, his scent flooding my senses and instantly calms the chaos running a muck in my brain.

After one too many tears—majority being from Cal surprisingly—we say our goodbyes to the younger Duran pack who seem eager to get Kennedy home.

Before her men can get her through the door, Kennedy hands me her phone.

"I already have a million and one questions to ask you about motherhood and parenting. Is it okay if we meet up one day for coffee? Maybe have just a girls day out?"

Her Alphas complain behind her, the men clearly overprotective.

"I would love to."

I hand back her phone after putting in my number and sending myself a message so I can also have her number.

We hug again before saying goodbye.

Once the doors close, I feel as though I can deflate.

The ringing of a phone makes me jump. My eyes dart up to Olis who is already frowning down at the offending device.

Gone is the gentle man that I was becoming to know. In his place is the Capo that Conall was telling me about. His entire demeanor becomes complete business as he answers the phone.

With a simple and straight to the point greeting, he answers the phone, listening for a moment before stiffening. His head shoots up and I know that his eyes lock on Vic's.

Turning to look at the other Alpha, I instantly get a feeling of dread wash over me.

After what feels like a lifetime, Olis eventually hangs up the phone.

"Some of the soldiers were doing security on Flame. They found the dead body of an Omega behind a dumpster."

I gasp, clutching my chest as I look at him in horror.

Immediately, the three Alphas jump into action. Conall grabs my hand and pulls me towards the door. I go to protest, trying to remind him that Amity is still inside. I find that I don't need to as I see Olis carrying her down the stairs in front of us before handing her off to a waiting Kennedy. The Omega nods at me and I breathe a little easier knowing that she is going to be well looked after. Something in me tells me I can trust Kennedy.

I do my best to keep up with the three Alphas but being five foot five, my shorter legs can't seem to keep up with them.

Conall must be able to tell my struggle as he abruptly stops. He doesn't give me a chance to ask him to slow down or even process what he is doing before my body is flung over his shoulder.

I squeal, gripping the waistband of his pants, trying to find some kind of grip on him.

"Let me down, Cal!"

The Alpha just laughs, a hand slapping down on my ass making me squeal again.

"There is a reason why I call you Little Devil, baby. While I am obsessed with those legs of yours, they are just a little short."

A growl rumbles in my throat and I bring my hand back, slapping it down on Conall's jean clad ass, paying him back for the snarky comment.

He just laughs, doing nothing but adding fuel to the fire.

I expected this kind of cave man bullshit from Vic. I am finding though that I should expect the unexpected. Especially with these three.

CHAPTER TWENTY-TWO

VICTOR

The scent of violence thrums in the air as I stalk towards the warehouse. It's not the first time that one of the soldiers has called us, informing us of issues regarding one of our clubs or properties.

It is the first time that a dead body has been left at one though.

It makes something in me tick.

Not only is whoever this is playing a dangerous game by leaving dead bodies near our businesses, they also murdered an Omega.

Old traumas begin to rear their head at this new revelation. I refuse to allow them to surface though. Not when I need to get to find who has decided to fuck with us.

The front door of the warehouse slams open, banging against the wall behind it. I cringe slightly, not realizing the force behind my push and the fact that my girl just saw an anger from me I never wished she would.

I should have known it was only a matter of time before they were dragged into this world with us. I just didn't expect it to be this quick.

I never would have been able to keep them away from it though. Business has always seemed to overflow into our personal lives. It's one of the reasons why our main residence is on the same property as our warehouse.

We could have lived in one of the other more inconspicuous houses or even in one of the apartments in the tower we own. But alas, city-living gives me hives. That and I refuse to allow Frankie to live in an apartment.

It is cruel to keep a breed like Frankie cooped up in an apartment. Dogs—especially border collies, need space to roam.

The statement 'speak of the devil and he will appear' runs true as the sound of nails hitting cement creep up behind us.

I don't bother slowing my pace as I continue making my way towards my office. I make sure to take a bit more care with my office door, not feeling like having to organize its replacement just because I am feeling pissed off.

As I turn to sit down at my desk, my eyes widen as Valley's ass walks in through the door.

What?

I shake my head, blinking my eyes open and closed a few times as I take in the scene before me. Valentina is hung over my brother's shoulder, my twin looking like a grinning fool as he stops in front of my desk. With a final slap on her ass, Cal slowly slides her down his body. I roll my eyes as I patiently wait for him to place her down on the floor.

I know she would punch me if I was to rip her out of his arms but the feeling is way too strong. After having a sliver of her earlier, the need to have her again is overwhelming.

When my brother finally puts down our girl, I snort as she smacks him on the shoulder with each word she grits out.

"Fucking. Cave. Man. Mother. Fucker."

After her miniature tantrum, she huffs before turning around to look at me.

"What do you need me to do?"

I stare at Valentina blankly, unable to utter a single word to the woman before me. If I wasn't already falling for her, that would have solidified it for me.

It feels as though all of my fears disperse when it comes to my *dolce ciliegra* and our more nefarious side of the Syndicate.

The fact that she is here right now speaks volumes to the kind of person she is.

I am fucking obsessed.

Looking at my packmates, it seems as though they also feel the same way.

Coming back to myself, I look back at Valley who is looking at me patiently.

"For right now, I want you to just sit tight and listen in. If there is anything that you can pick out, I need you to let us know."

She nods, crossing her arms over her chest. I turn to Olis, nodding slightly giving him the opportunity to fill us in on what else he knows.

"All the information I have is that there is a body near the dumpsters at the back of Flame. The body appears to be relatively fresh, around four hours old based on the rigor mortis that has begun to set in. The men have already cornered off the scene, waiting for us to give them further instructions."

I nod again before turning towards Conall who is just locking his phone.

"Cameras don't show us anything. I assume that the perp found one of the only blind spots in the surveillance at Flame," he sighs before shaking his head and whispering to himself, "An issue I will be rectifying immediately."

Looking down at Valley, I raise a single eyebrow.

"Are you sure you are ready to see everything this life entails?"

I should have known that my girl was as stubborn as an ox. The look on her face when I dared to question her decision to follow along with us on this journey was enough for me to learn that I will never be questioning her again.

I just had to make sure that she knew that if all of this was too much for her to deal with, that she didn't have to come along with us. That she had an out.

I don't think there would have been a single complaint between Olis, Conall and I if she wanted to stay behind.

Seeing a dead body, especially someone that has been brutally murdered turns even the hardest of soldiers into blubbering messes.

I know that mine and Conall's first dead body still haunts the both of us. Not hard when it was our mother.

Nudging the nose of my SUV into the alley behind Flame, the four of us climb out of the car.

Automatically, I go on high alert as I take in my surroundings. While it is mostly unheard of for the murderer to stick around the scene of a crime, I wouldn't dare put it past this one.

As we make our way further into the alleyway, I close in on where Valley walks between us. Bringing her here is a risk and I refuse to gamble with her safety.

I come to a stop in front of one of our higher ranking soldiers—Koby—who is standing guard of the body.

He nods at me, Conall and Olis before pausing on Valley briefly before giving her a nod of his head. Returning his attention back to me, he steps aside so I am able to see the body for myself.

There is no need to exchange words. It is near impossible to miss what has happened.

An Omega with the lingering scent of lavender lies haphazardly on the concrete. Her skirt has been hitched up to her waist to reveal bloody lace that is only barely covering her vagina. Her skirt has been slashed to pieces by what I am assuming is a knife, judging by the cuts in the material. Similar slashes cover her torso with the words 'mine' gouged through her midsection.

Her brown hair is matted with blood that has begun to dry. Bruises cover her throat, face, arms and legs. The worst are at her hips.

Rage boils inside of me as I stare down at the woman who would be somewhere in her mid-twenties.

I jolt as I feel a body brush past me. I watch as Valentina slowly drops down next to the deceased Omega.

With a grace that I know not a lot would be able to possess in a situation like this, she carefully pulls her skirt down, giving the Omega back some of her modesty.

Olis steps up beside me, shrugging himself out of his jacket before handing it to Valley. She smiles up at him, the look somehow brightening a situation so fucking dark and brutal.

Just like she did with the skirt, she covers the Omega's torso hiding the worst of her wounds.

For a moment, Valley stays still beside the woman. Whispered words too low for me to hear is the only sound in the quiet alley. Eventually she steps back to the three of us, her back coming flush with my chest. Snaking my hand around her waist, I hold her to me tightly as I say a silent prayer for the deceased.

Footsteps sound behind us. Without hesitation, I pull Valentina behind me, my weapon already out as I point it at the newcomer.

"Didn't realize you fancied yourself a fresh new 9mm sized hole in your chest, Jaiden," Conall snarks, tucking his gun back into the back of his pants.

Jaiden just laughs, closing the distance between us, "You know me, man. I like to live my life on the wild side occasionally."

I shake my head as the Alpha comes to stand in front of me.

It has been a bit of an adjustment getting used to working alongside a government organization. After Kennedy was taken, we were contacted by Jaiden, an investigator and undercover agent from Omega Protection Agency. Since then, we have been providing soldiers and intel that government agencies aren't able to get their hands on for the more difficult jobs.

It has been refreshing being able to provide assistance for something more than what I have created with my pack. Knowing that what we have been doing alongside OPA has been saving lives—lives of Omegas—has been rewarding in a way I didn't know I needed.

I shouldn't be surprised to see Jaiden here yet the lack of communication on his behalf is a red flag I want answers for.

"What are you doing here?" I question as I finally tuck my glock into the back of my pants. Even though I agreed to work alongside the Alpha, that doesn't mean that I trust him.

Jaiden just chuckles quietly to himself, putting his hands in his pockets.

"I was tipped off that an incident involving an Omega occurred at your club, Vic. I had to come see it for myself. Especially when this isn't the only body that has been dumped behind a club this week."

I nod my head, remembering Olis informing me of what Jaiden had come to him about.

Seems as though the murderer is rearing their head again.

"Over the past few weeks, we have received word from law enforcement about murders. Normally we are informed of when an Omega passes away by causes that appear unnatural so we can follow it up. When the third body was found in similar conditions, we knew that we had to step in."

Slowly, Jaiden bends down to assess the body closer. Pulling out a pair of gloves from his pocket, he pulls them on before returning his attention to the body.

With a careful hand, similar to that of Valley's, he pulls back the jacket covering the Omega's torso. He doesn't say anything, just nods and recovers the jagged words carved into her skin.

"Each of the Omegas murdered had the words 'mine' carved into their torsos. Each woman had been raped. Their throats, hips, legs and arms covered in bruises that only could have been given before they were killed."

I bristle as I take in the information. Jaiden eventually looks up at me after remaining silent for a moment.

"This is the eleventh body we have found."

I hear Valley gasp behind me. She latches onto my jacket at the confirmation of what I had feared.

That there is a murderer walking the streets of Vadena murdering innocent Omegas.

There is a fucking murderer on my turf.

Something that I refuse to stand for.

Because this? This means fucking war.

CHAPTER TWENTY-THREE

VALENTINA

The drive back home is eerily quiet. None of us have spoken. Not even small talk. I don't think any of us could stomach it. Not after what we witnessed.

The image of the murdered Omega is burned into my mind.

While it's not the first dead body I have been privy to seeing, it doesn't make it any easier.

Especially now that I know Omegas are being targeted.

Never have I been so grateful that I have kept my true designation hidden from the world.

While the more sane part of my brain knows that I should never have had to stoop to the measures I have, I am thankful that I had the opportunity to give myself a little extra edge of protection.

The thought of not being in this world anymore, to not be able to protect my daughter from the horrors of the world is unthinkable.

Because I have isolated myself so much, who would even take Amity if something was to happen to me?

I know that Luna would jump at the chance to take her. Her unofficial aunty status would be a fierce opponent for any child protection agency.

But would Luna even be able to handle her? Now that we know the inevitable label of her designation, a Beta just isn't equipped to handle the brutality of an Alpha.

My girl needs a pack.

I know that if I was to say any of that out loud, Vic, Conall and Olis would all assure me that I already have a pack.

Fuck, they have already declared that much. Yet there is still a hesitation in me that can't just allow myself to agree with them.

It's because they still don't know the truth.

Well, Cal knows most of it but Vic and Olis don't. And I think that is where the issue will be.

Vic is a hot head. A true to the bone Alpha and I know that he will believe that I'm not trust worthy, having lied to them for so long.

As for Olis, it's hard to know how he will react when he finds out I am an Omega. My hope is that they both react the same way that Cal did.

With acceptance and care.

Even though it has only been hours since I admitted out loud that I would give whatever this is between us a real shot, I don't know if I would be able to handle their anger or dismissal towards me.

The thought sends a sickening feeling to my stomach. I sigh heavily as I try to calm myself down. There is no point thinking about the what ifs and what could be.

A hand covers the top of mine. Turning my head, I find Conall looking at me with a concerned look on his face.

"Are you okay, Little Devil?"

I do my best to fake a happy smile as I nod my head but judging by the frown on his face, I can tell that he can read right through it.

I sigh, deflating a little.

"Not really. There is a lot running through my mind. So many what ifs and what the fucks that I can't even keep up."

He smiles slightly. "I know how you feel. I have so many questions myself."

Gripping my hand tighter, he pulls me towards him. I grunt as the seatbelt pulls at me. With a frown, he reaches over, unbuckling the strap before pulling me into his lap.

I suck in a sharp breath of surprise at the action but to my surprise, I don't fight it.

The comfort his touch provides actually seems to help. I try not to let myself over think the reasonings why all of a sudden an Alpha is able to provide me comfort in a situation like this. But, in typical me fashion, I do.

I can't decide whether it is the strange connection between Olis, Vic, Cal and I that admittedly, I have been feeling for a while now or if it's just Cal. Since meeting them, I can't deny any longer that something in my chest calls me to them. A part of me is terrified of what it could mean. Because deep down, I think I know exactly what it is. But, can it be? Can after so long of being terrified of Alphas and what a relationship with one can mean, could I truly have the one thing that I had longed so deeply for as a teenager?

Instead of continuing to haunt myself with the what ifs, I just soak it all in. Right now, I just want to feel the bit of peace that Conall's touch is giving me.

Pulling up to the mansion, we all remain quiet as we make our way inside. It's late enough that I am praying that Amity is already asleep.

A three-year-old fighting to go to bed is the last thing I want to deal with right now. My daughter may be my heart and soul but this threenager stage is insane. I wonder—and not for the first time—if there is some kind of parent handbook out there. One that specifies your three-year-old daughter showing early signs of Alpha tendencies would be fabulous. But alas, I don't think I am that lucky.

We find Kennedy and her Alphas in the living room, the TV on but the volume turned down low enough it is barely audible.

As they hear our footsteps approach, the four of them stand and make their way over to us. Kennedy makes a beeline for me, not bothering to hesitate to engulf me in her arms. I return the gesture straight away before pulling back.

"Where is Amity?" I question, noting the lack of pattering feet and never ending questions.

Kennedy smiles sweetly. "We put her down in her room around half an hour ago. We sat down to watch one of the princess movies she was speaking about and she was out like a light on Jax's lap before the movie was even half finished."

She holds up a baby monitor that someone must have set up in her room. A black and white image of my daughter sleeping in her bed greets me.

I thank the Omega and say a quick goodbye to her, Jax, Ledger and Theo before making my way upstairs to double check on Amity.

Carefully, I open her bedroom door, thanking my lucky stars that it doesn't squeak as I do so. Walking over to her bed, I smile down at her, carefully brushing a tendril of hair out of her face.

It's hard to remain frustrated at their antics when they look as sweet as she does right now. That no matter how much you want them to grow up, you also want to hold onto these moments. To protect their innocence for as long as you can before it is just gone and they are moving out of home.

The last three years have already felt like I have blinked and they have flown. It's terrifying to imagine my little girl grown up. The thought of her not needing me anymore. The thought of the dangers in this world breaking her like it did with me.

Damaging me beyond repair.

Yet, as I turn when I hear footsteps coming from the doorway, finding Victor standing there with a small smile on his face looking at my sleeping little girl, my heart flutters oddly in my chest. It's a strange feeling. One I have never felt before.

But maybe, just maybe, it's a feeling that I could very quickly become used to.

Vic doesn't take a step inside the room, instead, he nods his head, beckoning me to follow.

Quietly, I make my way towards him, unable to refrain from stepping into his space as I close the bedroom door behind me. It's a move that I know is one hundred percent intentional on the Alphas behalf.

Every fucking move this man makes is intentional. So carefully planned out I have no doubt he knows exactly how a conversation will go before he even utters a single word.

He remains quiet for a second as our eyes remain locked on each other. Eventually, he grips my hand gently—far more gentle than an Alpha like him should be capable of.

Silently, I follow behind him as he guides me towards my new bedroom.

He doesn't say anything, continuing through the space to the bathroom. Pulling me in further, he closes the door behind me before silently guiding me to lean against the vanity.

He leans into the shower, turning on the water before his attention turns back to me.

I don't say anything as I allow him to pull my shirt off, followed by my bra, pants and panties.

Once I am bare to him, he takes a step back before quickly stripping his own clothes off his body. It's impossible to not ogle his impressive body. His age hasn't denied him the ripped body he has been hiding beneath his clothes.

Again, no words are spoken as he grabs my hand again and leads me towards the now steaming shower.

The hot water hits my skin and I can't help but groan at the feeling of it.

It's been a long fucking day.

God, it's been a long fucking life. Which is ironic considering I am a few years over a quarter of my life. I shouldn't already be feeling these kinds of things, yet here we are.

Turning me so the water can hit my back, Vic pumps some shower gel into his hands before he lathers the suds into my skin.

I feel no shame being bare in front of him. Rather, the way he looks at me makes me feel comfortable. Like I don't have to cover myself up or put on some kind of front to not feel vulnerable.

His gaze doesn't stray any further than my face. I'm impressed at his restraint. I know it's not something that I was able to control when he undressed. But as his eyes remain focused on mine as he lathers my body, I develop a different kind of respect for him.

He could very well take liberties that I know a smaller man wouldn't hesitate in jumping at. But, I don't think that is Vic's style.

I think Victor is the kind of person that wants enthusiastic consent. That when the time comes for us to take the next step, he won't want me to hold any kind of hesitation.

I know as I stand here, holding back desire for the man that respectfully has his hands all over my body, I want to be able to give that to him.

I want to be able to sit in the frame of mind and not be terrified to hand my body over to an Alpha. That when I do, all I will feel is pleasure. A pleasure I know will be so fucking worth the wait. Especially if it is to feel even remotely close to what I have already felt with the Duran twins.

Hands on my arms have me blinking back into the present. I must have blacked out, lost in my thoughts.

Vic is looking down at me, a fond look on his face.

"Are you ready to get out?"

His voice is quiet; a gentle edge that helps to sooth me. I nod, continuing to remain silent.

He leans around me, turning the water off before stepping out of the shower and grabbing a towel. Forgoing his own comforts, he wraps the first towel around me before wrapping the next one around my head.

Once done, he takes a step away, quickly grabbing his own towel and drying off.

He reaches out a hand to me—one I take willingly—and follow him into my room. He guides me over to the bed, indicating for me to sit. He holds up a single finger before leaving the room.

I frown in confusion as I wait for him to come back. It's only moments before he is walking through the door with a handful of clothes.

Sitting them on the bed, he picks up the top item—a shirt—before pulling it over my head.

Victor's oakmoss and amber scent overwhelms me as I am cocooned in nothing but him. It's euphoric in a way that is surprising. I feel my heart thunder in my chest. My core clenches, desperate for relief. Goosebumps cover my flesh; the need to shiver becoming overwhelming.

Never before have I reacted to an Alpha in this way. I never reacted positively to the Andrews pack. Rather the opposite. It was always something they enjoyed punishing me over.

Because how dare I turn up my nose to the pack that abused me.

Yet, here I am, huddled up in an Alpha's T-shirt and I am ready to say fuck it.

Popping my head out through the hole, I suck in gulps of air, desperate to remove the cloud Vic's scent has put over me.

He doesn't seem to notice my turmoil as he steps away, dropping his towel and pulling on a pair of gray sweats.

Either this man is completely oblivious to the phenomenon gray sweatpants currently have on the world, or he knows exactly what he is doing. Because at almost eye level, Vic's very impressive cock is perfectly outlined and teasing the living fuck out of me.

I don't know who exactly I was kidding when I swore to myself that I was to never entertain an Alpha. I can feel my body screaming for the man she has decided is hers.

I gulp as I watch Vic walk around the bed, salivating as I watch his body contour as he pulls back the sheets.

I huff out a breath, needing to wipe the sweat forming on my forehead.

What the fuck is wrong with me?

I shake my head and stand up, walking around to the other side of the bed and hastily climbing in.

The bed dipping beside me has me looking over to Vic. His face is void of any kind of emotion as he looks at me. When I look into his eyes though, they give me everything.

They tell me of his desire. The desperate need that he has for me and what he believes I can give him. But I can also see the need for him to give to me. The want he has to provide for me. To be the Alpha I didn't know I needed.

That even though he believes that I am still a Beta, his want for me overrules any kind of body autonomy.

It feels as though all of my previous insecurities just diminish.

Why am I so scared of letting people close to me when they prove that they want me for me?

Not once has my designation come up in question with these men. Well apart from Conall but that is a whole other story.

It makes me think that maybe these three want me for more than my biology. That maybe I am worth more than a wet hole that can provide them an heir.

It has been years since I have felt that feeling. It's as foreign to me as a mother's hug or a father looking upon you proudly.

A need inside of my chest arises with aggression. It claws at me. Refusing to be buried like I have done with any of my previous feelings.

Because at the time, I couldn't feel them. Because if I did, it would have killed me. Either that or I would have walked out on the other side as nothing but a shell. Something I could never and would never do to myself.

I make a vow to myself as I remain locked in some kind of trance with Victor, that I will actually give him a chance. That I will give all three of them a chance.

Because maybe, just maybe, this is my one last chance for happiness.

The door behind me opens, startling me and forcing a small scream. Conall sticks his head through, a guilty expression on his face.

"Shit, I'm sorry. I just…" he trails off as his face falls. For a man that I know has seen the horrors this world has to offer, it's clear that what happened tonight has rattled these three men more than I know they were expecting.

Wiggling over to the middle of the bed, I tap the now free side of the bed.

Cal sighs in relief, making his way into the room in only his boxers. He makes quick work of settling in beside me before snuggling his way into my arms. He wraps his entire body around me, but somehow still manages to push me up against Vic in the process.

Nuzzling his face into my tits, he sighs, his whole body deflating in what I am sure is relief.

"I don't know how, but you make everything better."

CHAPTER TWENTY-FOUR

OLIS

Sleep refuses to claim me. I swear I have tried every single trick in the book. I have lost count of the sheep I was hoping would pull me under.

After endless hours of staring up at the ceiling, I decide to give up.

It's been a long time since I have had a night like this. Years in fact.

There is at least some kind of silver lining to it. I know what is keeping me from rest.

Seeing that Omega who had been raped, abused and finally murdered feels as though it is seared into my brain. It's rare that we have had to deal with any injustices against Omegas. I guess that means that the OPA are actually doing their job.

It's just the big cases that seem to slip through the cracks and reach us. Much like this one is turning out to be.

I wish I could be one of those ignorant people that continue to go about their lives while terror is wreaked all around them.

But I'm not.

The thought of the killer being out there, unchecked and laughing at our faces has me on edge.

The last time someone dared to go up against us, too much blood was shed. We lost our Omega. Our sons were motherless and we became widows far too early.

That's not something that I want to happen again.

Not when I feel like my second chance at love is within reach.

My obsession with Valentina has grown in the short time I have spent in her presence today. I feel like an addict, constantly needing another fix of the drug that is her.

I grunt as I roll out of bed but pause with a groan as something in my back twinges. Fuck this getting old bullshit.

Righting myself, I stand and make a beeline for Valley's door.

I feel something in my stomach pulling me towards her. That maybe all I need right now is her.

Reaching her door, I silently open it, taking my time to ensure it doesn't creak. I don't look up as I take a step inside before turning and shutting it behind me.

When I finally turn, I pause as I take in the situation on the bed.

Valentina is sandwiched in between both Conall and Victor. The twins' bodies are wrapped around her impressively so, to the point it is impossible to tell where one ends and the other begins.

The beauty between them remains fast asleep even though I know she wouldn't be comfortable. Those two are like furnaces.

I take a seat in the chair in the corner of the room, relaxing as my eyes remain locked on my girl.

I startle as I realize the direction of my thoughts. I don't know when I decided to mentally begin referring to her as mine but I find that I don't hate it. Rather the opposite actually.

I want her to be mine. To be ours.

She may not be an Omega, may not be able to take our knots, but I don't care.

Valentina is mine. Something about her speaks to me. There is something that I can see in her that is reflected in me.

Loneliness.

My girl is fucking lonely and that kills me.

She may have Amity and I have seen her laugh with the other dancers at the club but that doesn't mean that at night when she goes to bed, she doesn't long for something else.

Something more.

Something I know that I could give her.

Maybe it isn't just her that's lonely either.

Fuck, it's been a long time since I have felt the comfort of sleeping next to a warm body. It's something that until you lose it, you don't realize just how used to it you are.

I don't realize I have spaced out until a soft voice is pulling me out of my thoughts.

"Are you okay, Olis?"

I try to find the words but each time I open my mouth to say something, anything, they become lost to the wind.

I hear Valley grunt and watch as she carefully untangles herself from between Cal and Vic.

By the time she makes her way over to me, I am already desperate for her. The need to breathe easier just by her touch alone, is almost impossible to keep contained.

Valley steps up into the space between my legs, her touch setting me alight, taking any of the negative and lingering feelings that had been plaguing me.

She doesn't just stop at standing in front of me though. Maneuvering both of our bodies, she settles herself down into my lap, so she is face to face with me. Her hands settle on my stomach and I suddenly notice the lack of clothing both of us are wearing. The same thought seems to occur to Valley as she stiffens slightly before relaxing again.

I follow her movements, not willing to give up this rare alone time with her.

Even though both Cal and Vic are already awake—knowing just how light sleepers they are—I am thankful that they are giving us this time together.

"Talk to me," she whispers, her tone sending shivers over my body.

I sigh, dropping my head between my shoulders.

"Today was a lot."

She nods, giving me an encouraging look to continue.

"I thought I had hardened myself against this life a long time ago. That there was nothing that could rattle me anymore. I became known amongst the ranks of being a force that couldn't be broken. Today proved that I'm not that person."

Valley looks at me sadly, her hands move up my chest to cradle my face.

"Thats because you are human, Olis. Humans break. We were never built to be impenetrable even though it would solve majority of our problems."

I snort, knowing just how right she is.

"The thing I have come to learn about breaking is that it isn't the end. Because you can heal from that which you feel has broken you. And in the end, maybe you aren't so damaged. Maybe you are stronger than you ever thought possible. Even on the days when it doesn't feel like it."

I stare up at my girl in wonder. How the fuck did I become so lucky to have found her? Is this the god's way of repaying me for everything I have lost? Because at this moment, that is exactly what it feels like. Instead of an angel and devil sitting on my shoulder, it's just Valentina.

Not for the first time tonight, do words evade me. Instead of telling her just how far I have already fallen, I close the distance between us, allowing my lips to press against hers.

Butterflies soar in my stomach, a feeling of elation overcoming me as she moves against me.

The kiss is sweet and gentle. A feeling that is foreign to me but everything I didn't know I really needed. It becomes impossible to not lose myself in the feeling of her. To not completely forget myself and just drown in her.

Eventually though, Valley pulls away from me but doesn't go far. Her forehead rests against mine, our breaths becoming one as we soak in the moment.

I feel the moment my body relaxes even further under her hold. Valley leans back and smiles down at me before standing up again. She holds out a hand, one I instantly take.

On silent feet, I follow her, not surprised at all when we reach my door.

The moment she steps inside, I curse myself for not tidying up properly. Even though it is just my shoes from the day on the floor, I still feel a hint of embarrassment.

I know I shouldn't. Cal's room puts mine to shame tenfold but the lingering commands of my parents from all those years ago still linger. Longer than they deserve to. God knows those two would find delight in middle aged me still abiding by their rules even still.

It's a good thing they are dead now.

I continue to follow Valley as she slides in under my rumpled covers, her small frame becoming lost in the sheets. I could almost picture her snuggling up in a nest of her own.

Carefully, I slide in next to her. Opening my arms, she quickly adjusts herself against me—her head coming to rest on my right pec.

In an instant, the sleep that evaded me before comes rushing in like a freight train. My eyes become heavy and I begin to doze.

"Goodnight, Olis." Is the last thing I hear before sleep claims me.

I wake with a groan blinking my eyes against the sun shining through the windows. My body feels surprisingly well-rested considering just how hard sleep seemed to evade me. Looking up at the ceiling, I smile at myself as I think about who I shared a bed with.

I know that the difference in my ability to actually fall asleep last night was her. She gave me the ability to relax.

Not only that but she gave me an opportunity to talk about what I was feeling. To get it off my chest rather than bundle it up like I would have if she wasn't here.

I rub at a spot in my chest. Conveniently, it's the same one that has been giving me issues since I first saw my girl.

Speaking of, I roll over to face her but pause when I find the bed beside me empty.

Kicking off the blankets, I throw my bedroom door open but come to an abrupt halt as I find my missing girl right in front of me. Holding two cups of coffee.

Ignoring the steaming cups, I pull Valley into me, wrapping her up in my arms.

"Fuck, I thought you were gone," I mumble, buring my head into her hair. Inhaling, I curse the fact that I can't scent her. I know that it would have calmed me down instantly. I just have to work a little bit harder now, which is fine.

"It's okay. I'm right here."

Her whispers of reassurance and the way her body melts against my own help to ease the panic I felt finding her gone from beside me.

After what is surely way too long, I let her go, dropping my arms from her body. The minimal space between us is enough for her to hold up the coffee she had gone to make for me.

I don't thank her with words as I take the cup. Instead, I place a gentle kiss on her forehead. A shiver runs over her body and I smile in delight as I take a sip.

"Sorry that I wasn't here when you woke. My body alarm is set for stupid o'clock and I had to go make sure that Amity was alright."

I nod, understanding all too well.

"It's okay," I reply, feeling a hint of embarrassment. "I think after last night, I instantly thought the worst."

Valley nods before setting down her mug. Grabbing my hand, she directs me over to the bed. I sit, looking up at her as she glances down at me.

"Now that you have processed it, what is your plan?" she questions. I don't miss the glint in her eye. It's one that I know all too well.

It's the need for vengeance. A thirst in your blood that calls for justice to be done. To rid the world of filth.

Not everyone can stomach it. Because the path there is littered with gore and deception. One that will have our souls knocking on Hell's door.

Something that I now know I won't be walking alone because she will be right there beside me.

I knew she was perfect for us but I didn't understand the depth of it.

Looking back up at Valley, I smile. It's a cruel, cunning one. One I don't bother hiding from her. If she is to be mine. She needs to know the depths I will go to to ensure those that I love are kept safe.

"We go on a hunt."

CHAPTER TWENTY-FIVE

VALENTINA

I go over the same documents for what feels like the millionth time in a matter of days with Cal, Vic and Olis.

The week with the three Alphas goes surprisingly fast even amongst the pressure of sifting through what we know about the Omegas.

The majority of the time we spend together is just simply that; spending time. The rest of our days are filled with information sent through from OPA.

Mornings start with a cup of coffee and a plate of breakfast from Olis. After that first morning when he woke up without me beside him, he seemed to make it his mission to be up before me. I'm becoming dangerously used to the princess treatment.

I know that I shouldn't, but fuck if I don't just want to enjoy whatever time I have with them.

It has been strange watching my little girl develop a relationship with these men as well. Due to my hate for the opposite designation, Amity has never interacted with an Alpha before. It was a surprise to me that she didn't even think twice about allowing them into her life. Her little mind doesn't hold the same reservations that mine does.

If anything, she adores them. Something she reminds me in whispered tones when the four of us tuck her into bed each night.

While I have been hesitant in adjusting to the more mundane parts of living with these men, the more nefarious side has been like sliding on your favorite pair of jeans.

There have been three more deaths since finding that first body behind Flame. It brings the death toll to fourteen.

Each bit of news in regards to the now extensive case about the Omega murderer heightens tensions tenfold.

I have found Vic multiple times pacing his office with a very unsettled look on his face.

The murders have also changed how the Alphas have been in regards to me.

Especially Cal. He has hardly left my side since that first night. I can see the terror he tries to hide behind his jokes and laughter.

It's because he knows.

He knows what my true designation is. That without the blockers and sprays, I am a perfect candidate for the killer.

Maybe even more so than any of us first realized. Because the similarities between these Omegas and I are staggering.

Cal's breath hitches beside me, making me pause reading the document I have been reading.

Looking over to him, I find his eyes already on me. Terror and disbelief dampen his once bright features. The expression on his face has my stomach twisting because I know that whatever he has found, I'm not going to like it.

I remain frozen as his gaze travels across my skin. Normally, that kind of attention from him sets me on fire.

But not tonight.

Conall looks back down at the A4 size images of the victims he is holding before looking back up at me. He repeats the same process a few times before Vic becomes sick of the silence.

"What is it, Cal?" he questions, drawing my attention towards him. Vic's glasses are perched on the end of his nose. His hair is a mess from where he has spent the last few hours torturing himself with information.

Looking back at Conall—finding him looking frighteningly similar to his brother—he finally clues us into his findings.

"Something about these images of the Omegas has been bugging me for days. While the pattern of their deaths has been consistent, there was something else that I couldn't understand."

He takes a moment before he looks back at me.

"Each of these Omega's holds a striking resemblance to Valentina."

You could cut the silence with a knife, the room is that quiet. I remain frozen in my seat as I all but glare at Conall.

I hadn't wanted to admit it to myself. It was much easier to just deny it. To say that it was a brutal coincidence.

But apparently, I was wrong. Because it's not just me that has drawn that conclusion. Because Cal sees it too.

Vic snorts, drawing our attention back to him as he stands. "No, Conall. No. There is no fucking way that our girl is related to the situation."

Vic paces, shaking his head repetitively before pulling out a cigarette and lighting it. I look over to Olis who is looking down at the images Conall was analyzing before looking up at me.

"I see it." Is all he says, making Vic pause his pacing.

The Alpha scoffs, shaking his head looking at his brothers with a hint of disappointment on their faces.

"How the fuck could you think something so vile? It is clear that Valley has gone through enough. Now you are wanting to tie her in with the likes of murder victims?"

Shaking his head again, this time in disappointment, he goes to leave the room but pauses when I speak up.

"I see it too, Vic."

He turns towards me before eating up the distance between us.

"What the fuck do you mean, you see it?"

Grabbing the images in front of Conall, I fan them out so they are side by side.

"It's impossible to not see the similarities between myself and these Omegas, Victor." I point at each of them as I list it all.

The hair, the face shape, the color of their skin. Fuck, even down to the fact that these women were all single at the time of their death.

"It's not only these physical attributes that are similar to me, Vic." I swallow roughly before looking down at Conall. He rises from his chair, coming to stand beside me for what has to happen next.

It's time.

Time that Vic and Olis know the truth of who I am.

Olis comes to stand beside Vic, no doubt able to see just how precarious what I have to tell both of them is.

Swallowing roughly, I look up at them. Slowly, I begin telling them my story. I don't let a single detail slip my mind as I explain to them my life with my parents, the events around the time I designated and then finishing with my life as the Andrews Omega.

"Once I left that god's forsaken house, I knew that my old life was over. That everything about the old Valentina was gone. That I had to start anew. Not only for me, but for my daughter."

Taking a deep breath, I look up at Vic and Olis who remain frozen in front of me. Their faces are completely void of emotion as they process my words.

"For the last four years, I have been an Omega hiding and living as a Beta."

If I thought the silence earlier was thick, it is nothing compared to what it is now.

I feel raw, split open. My deepest and darkest secrets laid bare for the two men before me to hold judgement over me.

I know that nothing will ever be the same as it was between me and these two. While I know that Conall will remain steadfast—like he has both times I have laid myself bare—I can't seem to say the same for these two.

They are the wild cards. The ones that I can't say for sure will be okay with what I just said. Especially not Vic.

I watch as he takes a step forward before he takes another. Each inch closer to me seems to darken his features.

"You fucking lied to me," he growls, the sound making me gasp sharply. In an instant, I sink into myself under the weight of his stare. I try to stop the shake of my body but it is futile.

After years of running away from this exact situation, it's nothing short of terrifying facing it again. My stomach threatens to empty itself. My bladder not fairing much better.

But I fight it. I won't be what my designation demands of me because fuck that. And fuck Victor if this is how he is going to react.

Doesn't he realize that I did it to protect myself? To protect Amity? To not allow us to become another fucking statisic! To run from the same damn thing that we have strawn out in front of us.

"You have been an Omega this whole fucking time and have hidden the truth from us. You fucking deceived me and my brothers."

Victor chuckles but there is nothing remotely funny about what he is saying, "You had us all fooled, didn't you? You just thought you could play hard to get, shake your ass on stage and we would come crawling. Like the fucking idiots we are, we did exactly that. We fell right into your little Omega trap"

"That is enough, Victor!" Olis growls, but it falls on deaf ears.

"Who sent you, huh? Are you a spy? Is Amity even yours? Fuck, is any of what you have shown us even real?" His voice is like ice, each word hitting me like barbs.

Stepping around me, Conall comes to stand right in front of his twin. It seems to anger Victor more as he faces off with him.

"That's fucking enough! Tell me brother, when the fuck did Valley ever lie directly to your face about not being a Beta? Huh? Fucking never. Why do you think she has tried to deny all three of our advances no matter how fucking insistant we have been?"

Conall shakes his head in disappointment before continuing, "It's for this exact fucking reason. Your reaction to her letting you both in on her secrets is why she has had to hide herself from our designation!"

Vic takes a step back from his brother, processing the weight of his words. It doesn't seem to process in his brain in the way that Conall had planned.

Victor is beyond angry. In fact, I think it would be fair to say he is almost feral. His eyes are almost completely black. His hands keep clenching and unclenching like he is trying his best to hold back the beast. A vein in his neck throbs as he glares at me. If we were still wolf shifters, like we had been hundreds of years ago, he would have shifted and torn me apart by now. A fact I have know isn't an over statement.

Never in all my years facing off with angry Alphas have I ever seen one in this state. Not even when the Andrew's pack killed my parents.

"Because what happens when an Alpha thinks he is slighted in some way? They turn into fucking monsters. Which is exactly what you are proving to be right now."

I bring up a hand to my mouth as Conall's words wash over me too.

He is right. Damn him.

Vic takes another step back, looking between both Conall and me. His expression is a mixture of emotions; each fighting the other to win.

He shakes his head before retreating completely, his hand coming to land on the door. Fear fills me as I watch the knob twist, knowing that whatever happens now is it.

That whatever he does now will change whatever we were building between us.

"Fuck this and fuck you. I can't fucking do this right now," he says through gritted teeth before turning his back on us. Turning his back on me.

The moment he is out of sight, I collapse into myself. The tears that I had been fighting flow down my face in streams. My sobs turn guttural.

I knew that this was all too good to be true. That once I had found an inch of happiness, it would just all blow up in my face.

Maybe I was never meant to be happy. That being damaged beyond repair doesn't mean that you are somehow entitled to find your happily ever after.

Hiding my face in my hands, I allow myself to break. To grieve what could have been. Because once I leave this room, I am on my own again.

Maybe Conall will decide to stick around. Not that I expect him too. I'm not in the business of breaking up a pack.

A hand touching my shoulder has me jerking up right allowing me to come face to face with Olis. His face is blank—void of all emotion—and I prepare myself for a dressing down. Again.

"Did you mean to hurt us by hiding your true designation?"

I rear back at his words, a mixture of hurt and disbelief at the accusation.

"Never. I would never hurt any of you," I reply, shaking my head.

Olis nods, remaining silent as he moves his hand from my shoulder. I wait for him to back away from me completely, but he doesn't. Instead, he wraps his hands around my calves. The hard expression slips from his face. A bright smile, one I didn't know he was capable of sliding into place instead.

"I knew from the moment I saw you in the park that you were ours. Whether you are a Beta or an Omega doesn't change anything for me. It just reaffirms to me what you truly are."

I tilt my head, giving him a questioning look. "And what is that?"

His smile brightens impossibly so as he leans in closer.

"Mine. It means that you are mine."

I never gave much thought about what it would be like to be with a man like Olis. That is until he carries me the entire way to his bedroom in the main house. He doesn't hesitate for a second as we pass by soldiers whose mouths drop as we pass by them.

He doesn't even stop to say anything to Kennedy and Ledger who are looking after Amity in the living area. He only stops when we finally make it to the bedroom. Placing me down in front of him, he immediately shrugs off his shirt, gracing me with the hard lines of his chest I have become obsessed with.

Deciding to take matters into my own hands, I push Olis' chest hard enough to get him to sit on the edge of the bed. His eyes widen with surprise and lust as he looks up at me.

I chuckle as I step back and remove my own T-shirt. Olis' answering growl to what I have been hiding all day makes the discomfort worth it.

I had been planning on teasing Conall after we were done going through the documents Jaiden had sent over but this is just as good of an opportunity as any.

I shrug off my jeans, revealing the full outfit.

A corset top cinches in my waist giving my body an hourglass look. A barely-there thong covers my aching core while suspenders and stockings help to elongate my legs.

A fire lights itself in my core, burning me from the inside out.

I give Olis the time to take me in. The heat from his gaze only seeming to heighten the need in me.

Eventually I take a step, coming to stand in between his legs.

His hands reach out to hold my hips. They grip me tight before loosening slightly to move further up my body. They come to a stop at my back where they pause.

"You are so fucking beautiful, Valentina. God, I want you."

I smile, bringing my hands up to rest on either side of his face.

"Then show me," I demand. "Show me how much you want me."

My voice is laced in a heavy arousal, something that Olis seems to notice as he keeps moving his hands.

"It would be my honor," he chuckles and pulls at the ribbons holding my corset together. Once they have been loosened, he pulls the top off completely, allowing my breasts to fall free.

My nipples tighten as the cool air hits them. Olis doesn't waste time in appreciating them as he leans in, sucking one of the pebbled peaks into his mouth.

I groan at the sensation, my fingers grip his neck tighter.

He chuckles, continuing to suck and lick, teasing me until I am nothing but a puddle at his feet.

Pulling away, he grips my thong before tearing it off my body. I gasp as I watch the tattered piece of material fall to the floor.

"Don't worry, Sweetheart. I'm positive Vic will have a new set brought for you by morning."

I roll my eyes. "I highly doubt that asshole gives a single shit about what I wear. Especially after dropping that bomb on him."

"You shouldn't have to after the way he acted but just give him time. He doesn't always think clearly when he is under stress. This situation with the Omegas is a lot for him to handle. Mix that in with the fact that you are now somehow involved," he shakes his head and sighs, "Just ... don't give up on him just yet."

I blow out a breath as I look down at the Alpha.

"I will." I eventually nod but know that it won't be that easy. Men like Victor are complex and after the way he spoke to me tonight, I plan to make him earn it.

"Now, enough talk about my pack brother. All I want you to focus on is you."

I gasp as Olis stands, his hands holding my waist before he is turning me and throwing me onto the bed.

I giggle as he crawls his way up my body. The heat of his skin on mine making my core clench around nothing.

I know that if I wasn't taking my suppressants, I would be a bundle of slick. As it is, this man already has me wet beyond what is considered normal.

My body heats and my toes curl as Olis' lips meet mine in a breath taking kiss. I allow my hands to explore his body, his dark skin impossible to not appreciate.

"Fuck, Olis. Please..." I beg, desperately needing more.

He chuckles darkly, "Need more do you, Omega?"

I nod insistantly, my arousal heightening at being called Omega for the first time in years. It's like its own special kind of aphrodisiac.

"Please, Olis. I need you to touch my pussy. Please!"

"Fuck," he groans, his grip on me tightening. "You beg so fucking prettily. Even more so when you use that filthy mouth of yours to tell me what to do."

I don't have to ask him again, the Alpha listens to my demands just like I knew he would.

Sliding down my body, he stops, reaching the apex of my thighs. The first swipe of his tongue through my slit has me moaning, my stomach clenching as the feeling of ecstasy overcomes me.

Olis eats my pussy like a man starved. His tongue rolls, licks and vibrates against my sensitive clit. It feels like only seconds before my body tightens and an orgasm barrels down over me.

I come with a scream. My thighs clench around Olis's head holding him close to my centre. My back bows off the bed and I feel the evidence of my release drenching his face. I know that I am making a mess but I can't seem to find the will to care. He should drown in the evidence of what he has done to my body.

Once the waves of pleasure lessen, I drop my legs from around his face.

He chuckles and crawls back up my body. The evidence of my release visible on his chin.

"Fuck you taste so fucking good. Just like cherries."

My entire body tenses and I shoot upright in bed. That is until a wave of pain has me doubling over.

"Shit, baby. Are you okay?" Olis asks, rubbing my naked back. All his touch does is heighten the pain. I curl in on myself further as another wave of pain steals the breath from my lungs.

Just as the third wave of pain hits, my scent explodes from me. Olis staggers back, sucking in a breath of my sweet cherry scent.

His eyes widen as he looks down at me curled up on the bed. A look of astonishment adorns his features before he falls to his knees in front of me.

"I fucking knew it. You are my mate," he growls, his tone laced with a hint of possession.

"And I'm going into fucking heat," I grunt as yet another wave of pain cripples me.

Fuck. My. Life.

CHAPTER TWENTY-SIX

CONALL

I curse both Olis and Vic the entire time I spend cleaning up the documents that have been left sprawled out on the table in our war room. While I am pissed off at Vic, I can hardly blame Olis for taking our girl the way he did.

He is just as gone for her as I am.

It settles something inside of me knowing that he isn't mad at her.

Victor on the other hand needs a fucking reality check.

Never before have I been so disappointed in my brother. I would have thought that he would have had some sympathy for Valley considering all she has been through. Yet, all he could seem to focus on was himself and his feelings in the matter.

I have no doubt that he is already hating on himself. It was clear as day he was already regretting his words the minute he said them.

But that still doesn't change the fact that he fucked up.

He hurt our girl. He pushed her back to that dark place that she has worked so hard to escape from. He proved to her that we are all the same down to our core.

I just hope that she knows we aren't all like that.

I breathe a sigh of relief as I look around the now clean office. While our men know not to enter our offices without the say so, I don't trust anyone completely. Snakes are far too sneaky these days and I refuse to allow what I have built to come crumbling down around us.

Making my way back to the house, I give myself a moment to just take in what my life has become. From finding who I thought I was meant to spend the rest of my life with, to having the boys, losing Gwen and continuing to fulfill my role in the Syndicate, it feels as though I have never just stopped and taken in the world around me. I have spent my entire life trying to live up to the standards that were hammered into Vic and I at such a young age that now, I don't even know if I actually like my job.

Well, that's a lie to some degree.

I do love parts of what we do—especially since partnering with OPA—but I'm exhausted.

Maybe it's finally time that we hand over the family business to Theo and Jax. Ledger too.

Those three boys are more than capable of taking over from us. In reality, they have been for years. Even more so now that they have found the missing piece to their pack.

Since Valley stumbled into our lives, I have been feeling more selfish with my time. Fuck, I have only really paid attention to my job this past week when its been an emergency. Otherwise, I have been caught up in my girl and Firefly.

It has been near impossible not to.

I never thought I was a love at first sight kind of guy but these two have changed that for me.

I wouldn't admit it to my little devil but I am beyond gone for her. I have reached the point of no return and continued on through all of the warning signs that have told me to slow down.

Unfortunately for Valentina, slow isn't a part of my vocabulary.

The moment I step inside the house, I am hit with the most overwhelming scent of cherries. A haze comes over me and all I can think about is rut, claim, own.

Fuck, Valentina is in heat.

I don't bother removing my filthy shoes as I trip into the living room. I come to a stop as I find Kennedy and Ledger already looking at me.

"I think Valley is going into heat. I know it's short notice but..." I take a breath but before I can continue, Kennedy is standing and making her way over to me.

"We have got Amity. We caught her scent not too long before you came storming in here like a bat out of hell." She shakes her head and laughs before placing her hands on my shoulders.

"Go. Go and look after your Omega."

I do nothing but nod as I look over to Ledger waiting for his approval too. He gives me a curt nod, letting me know without words that he will lay down his life for my little girl.

Because fuck it, after tonight, they are both mine.

I don't hold an ounce of hesitation as I push through Olis' bedroom door.

The sight before me is one for sore eyes.

Olis is flat on his back, his cock deep in Valley's pussy as she works him over, doing her best to prepare herself to take his knot—something I can see she isn't too far from accomplishing.

The call of the rut is worse now that Valley's scent is straight from the source.

A grumble sounds at my arrival, the noise bringing my girl's attention to me.

My cock stiffens painfully behind my zipper and I have to squeeze my knot so I don't make a mess of myself prematurely.

Valley's eyes resemble that of molten lava. Her gaze burns mine, taking in her fill of my body. Her scent explodes on my taste buds.

I force myself to wait for her invitation into what I am assuming will be her temporary nest. For now at least. I want her to have something better than this.

While Valley and I have a history, I want her to tell me that she wants me here for this. There's a little part of me that needs confirmation that she needs me just as much as I need her right now.

"Alpha," Valley groans, continuing to work herself on Olis' cock.

"Omega," I growl in return, my voice deep and laced with lust.

"Please, I need you."

I groan, throwing my head back, inhaling more of Valley's cherry scent. It's ironic that our girl used her scent descriptor as her stage name. Its fucking cheeky and I love it.

A quiet growl has my attention shooting back to my little devil. Her eyebrows are drawn, her face pulled up in a scowl, eyeing me.

"I said now, Alpha. I fucking need you now."

I chuckle as I take a step towards her. "So impatient, Little Devil. I think you need something to fill that bratty mouth."

She moans again, the sound a mere whimper, throwing her head back and continues her assault on Olis' cock.

I reach her in only a few steps, very quickly becoming drowned in her scent.

The most interesting part is, I can tell this isn't even her full scent.

Even more than that is the fact her scent tells me everything I need to know.

She is fucking mine.

Somehow, we have been given a second chance at a mate.

I force back the tears that threaten to fall at the revelation.

The Omega before me is mine.

My beautiful Little Devil. My Valentina. Mine.

Fuck.

I shake myself out of my thoughts but only barely as I realize I have been just standing here staring at my pack brother and mate fucking.

Quickly, I remove my jeans, shucking them off my body in desperation as I close the rest of the gap between us.

My cock stands proud from my body, the sparkle of hidden jewellery on the underside of my cock catching the edge of Valley's attention. She gasps before her hands reach out to grip my dick.

My knot throbs as I watch my girl stop and turn her focus to run her hands along the Jacob's Ladder piercings. With each light tough to the silver barbells, I shiver, my cock leaking with the need to feel her mouth on me.

She pauses for a moment, turning her head to the side, assessing me. I didn't realize that she hadn't seen them last time I was bare before her. I don't know exactly what she was looking for but after a few seconds, the devilish smile that adorns her face lets me know that I am in for the ride of my life.

It feels like eternity as I watch my girl stick her tongue out. Each millisecond is torturous as I wait for the first touch of her tongue on me.

My resounding groan as she takes her first lick is guttural. Whether it's the taste of me or my reaction to her touch, Valley seems to take that encouragement in her stride, slowly taking me into her mouth completely.

Pleasure overcomes me as I look down at my girl who still rides Olis, with my cock completely swallowed down her throat.

Reaching a hand out, I rub her cheek with her thumb, falling under her spell as time and time again, I watch my cock brush against her plump lips.

Her tongue rolling and playing with my piercings has my breath quickening. My stomach clenches and my knot throbs as I slowly begin to fuck my girl's mouth.

Saliva escapes the confines of her mouth. Spit dribbles down her chest, rolling onto her tits. It's a delicious sight, one that has me falling over the edge.

My orgasm hits me the moment Valentina's hand grips my knot. I come down her throat with a roar, Olis following along with me. Judging by the choked cry around my length, I know that Olis' knot has slipped into place.

I don't move, not trusting that I would be able to even if I tried as I remain standing in front of Valley, my cock still deep in her throat.

I pant, attempting to catch my breath as I look back down at her.

I feel nothing but awe and love for my little devil as I take in her sweat and tear streaked face. She smiles with a weak but blissful smile, one still noticeable given the predicament she clearly doesn't want to end.

Everything is telling me that I should be laying her down. Making sure that she is hydrated. To pull back her hair and tie it into a braid so she doesn't come out of her heat with matted hair, but I don't.

Instead, I revel in my luck for just a little bit longer.

I thought that I was lucky when I first met my little devil. It felt as though I had won the lottery when I finally convinced her to give us a try. But right now? There isn't even a place that I can begin to describe the feeling as I look down at my forever.

Because that is what she is.

The moment Valentina Rossi caught the eye of the Duran Alphas, she was never going to escape without us.

Now, all I need to do is convince her to take my claiming bite.

One step at a time, Conall.

CHAPTER TWENTY-SEVEN

VICTOR

I lose track of time as I sit in front of the headstone that I haven't visited in years.

I could say that I have been busy. That the Syndicate has taken up all of my time. That I have been busy trying to educate my sons, preparing for them to take over so that I can finally retire.

But they would all be lies. Ridiculous excuses that I use instead of admitting that I couldn't come here.

The idea of seeing the place that my dead mate would rest for the rest of my life has haunted me.

At the start, I told myself that I would come and see her everyday. To remind her that I never would forget the love that we shared.

But after the first visit, I knew that I would break my promise. Because I haven't been here since that day.

Her headstone still looks the same as it did all those years ago. Her flowers are fresh, no doubt having recently been changed out. The grass around her gravesite is kept short and tidy, something I demanded when we chose this particular cemetery.

It looks peaceful. A complete polar opposite to how I am currently feeling.

Because Valentina is an Omega.

The revelation has rocked me to my core to say the least.

I was none the wiser that she would lie to me like this.

Not that I have deserved any kind of heads up from her.

But fuck. I had let her into my life. Let her into my home. I had begun to show her the deepest and darkest past of not only my life, but myself.

Was it all just a lie?

Some kind of cruel ploy into getting us to protect her? To get us to fall in love with her just so her and her daughter can be protected?

What's worse is I wouldn't have ever turned her away if she had come to me with the truth at the start.

I would have protected her and *piccolo* with my dying breath.

But now, it just feels like it was all a smoke screen.

It makes me think that maybe she just doesn't want me because I am the wrong twin. It wouldn't be the first time that Conall has been picked over me. I know he would see it the other way but that is only because I am feared. Not because I am actually liked.

I know that I am hard to love.

That was something that was always written in black and white to me when Gwen was still alive. She despised the side of me that demanded I be the Don. She could never accept that blood thirsty side of us. She would always shy away from that ruthlessness.

Is that what Valentina is doing right now?

I would have thought differently based on the way that she has handled the situation with the Omegas.

But I have been wrong before.

It also doesn't escape me that the signs that point towards Valley being part of these murders somehow is far from being a coincidence.

At the time, I just didn't want to admit it to myself. I was also under the belief that Valentina was a Beta.

But now the writing is on the wall.

The woman that I have been falling over my feet for is an Omega. An Alpha's perfect match. She is designed just for me. From the inside out, she is everything I could want and more.

But she lied to me. Or omitted the full truth at least.

I guess some blame could be placed on me. Because not once did I ever question her designation. I just ran with what I had been told.

Do I have a right to be as upset as I am? Do I even have a leg to stand on if I was to reconfront her with my feelings?

Now that I am thinking about it, maybe I don't. Because not once has she ever owed me anything. What have I done to deserve the full truth from her?

Fuck, she was abused from her previous pack.

They fucking *abused* her.

I grip the grass I have threaded my fingers through tighter.

No matter how I feel about any of this, the one feeling that comes through stronger than the rest is the immeasurable anger I feel towards the fucking Andrews pack.

Knowing that Valley disposed of them before she left is the only reason why I am not hunting them down as we speak.

Although, the thought of finding where they are buried, digging them out just to ensure that they are dead is powerful.

I continue to sit in front of the headstone, staring at the letters etched into the granite.

"I don't know what to do, Gwen," I whisper into the early morning air. "After you, I never thought there would be anyone that I could picture my life with. I had resigned myself to the fact that it would only ever be you. Yet with a single glance from this girl, I have turned to mush."

I shake my head, before sighing.

"Even from the other side, I can feel you laughing at me. But fuck, I am just so torn up. It feels like she has lied to me. Like she has betrayed me. That she has kept this massive secret from me."

I sigh yet again and look up at the slowly rising sun, "The worst part is, I don't think it is her that I am even mad at anymore. It's me that I am mad at. I allowed myself to become the person that she has been running from."

I sob escapes my throat before I can catch it.

"I fucking hurt her, Gwen. I have hurt the first person that has made me feel anything real since you were taken from us. I have fucked up. More than I ever thought I would be capable of. I was borderline feral, screaming at her!"

I brush a hand roughly over my face.

"I fucking questioned if her daughter was even hers."

Tears begin to stream down my cheeks and I rip the grass I had been gripping from the roots, throwing them to the side with a roar.

"I fucking love her, Gwen and I have already fucked it all up."

I grip my hair, pulling at the strands as I break down. I feel a part of me break as I all but collapse into myself. My pain feels inescapable as I allow it to pour from me.

"Sitting here wallowing in self pity isn't going to do you any favors in winning her back."

The voice of my son has me turning with surprise. I thought I was alone out here.

Theo's hands are tucked into his pockets, looking down at me with a mixture of pity and disappointment.

Quickly, I wipe away the tear streaks, knowing it's futile. Eventually, I clear my throat before looking back up at him.

"No amount of apologizing will ever be enough for what I did to her," I whisper, the emotion evident in my tone.

Theo sighs, the sound laced with disappointment.

"How will you ever know if you don't at least try?"

I shrug my shoulders, looking up at my son again.

"I don't know if I could handle being rejected by her for the last time. I have spent so much time and energy trying to get her to say yes to me that now it feels like if I push anymore, it will be too far this time."

I drop my head, bringing my hands up to grip my hair. At least if it is just me inflicting pain on myself, maybe I won't feel so fucking awful.

"I've already taken it a step too far."

I hear rustling beside me, indicating that Theo has taken a seat beside me. I don't look up. I can't see that look again on his face. It is so much like his mother's, it is terrifying.

"We all make mistakes, Dad. You know that better than anyone. But that doesn't define you. It's what you do after that matters."

I shake my head. "Using my words against me."

He chuckles, "Just calling it as I see it." Theo remains silent for a moment before he speaks again. "What are you truly scared of, Dad?"

That question has me pausing as I lift my head to look at my son. Just over twenty years my junior and he is more intelligent than I ever was.

Theo has a way of seeing the world in a different light. It was impossible to not be proud of him, Jax and Ledger and the way they handled the start of their relationship with Kennedy.

I know at their age, I wasn't thinking as far ahead as they had to. It took me years to be able to keep calm in particular situations—something that has clearly been forgotten in this circumstance. Yet they did it with a grace that was admirable. Even with the clean up bill at the end of it.

Right now, I feel as though I am the one that needs to be coached through this part of my life. While I don't hate it—having to rely on my boys more now—it makes me see that my time in my current position is coming to an end.

Knowing that isn't even remotely related to my problems tonight, I turn back to the unanswered.

What am I scared of?

I am terrified of not being loved in return. I am terrified of walking back into that house and being pushed out of my own pack. I am terrified of having to be the one to sit out on the sidelines, all because I am an irrational dickhead with no filter.

I tell Theo that and more, feeling as though I pour my entire heart out to him.

He is silent for a while before he breaks it.

"Well, I say, fuck that."

I snap my head up in surprise, my eyes going round as I stare at him in shock.

"What?" I question, feeling dumbfounded.

He just shrugs his shoulders as he leans back on his hands. "I said, fuck that noise. You are Victor motherfucking Duran. You are the Don of the Mafia. You are an Alpha. I have never seen you as the kind of man that shies away when things get intense."

He shakes his head before continuing, "When Kennedy was taken from us, you forced us to pull our heads out of our asses and think rationally."

He smirks and I know I am already dreading what he has to say.

"So Dad, you need to harden the fuck up. Because your Omega is waiting for you. She needs you."

He almost had me there but the idea that she needs me is what lost me.

"She doesn't need me, son."

It's Theo's turn to scoff as he looks over at me.

"Tell me then, Dad. Who the fuck is meant to help Valley through her heat?"

I choke on nothing as I process his words. Straightening, I move into a low crouch as I get closer to Theo.

"Speak plainly. What do you mean?" I mutter with a growl. I feel my heart racing, the organ threatening to burst from my chest.

Theo's lips tilt with a smirk. "Your Omega is in heat."

Crashing through the front door, my eyes are laser-focused on the stairs I very quickly run up. There is only one thing running through my mind as I come to a stop at the closed door of Valentina's nest.

My Omega is in heat.

That the Omega is also *mine.*

Her sweet cherry scent is thick in the air. Her arousal is just as potent, scrambling all rational thought in my brain.

Nothing has ever smelt as good as my *dolce ciliegra* does right now.

With more grace than I have shown in the ten minutes it took me to get from the cemetery to here, I slowly open the door.

Getting hit with a fresh round of my girl's scent, I look down at the nest.

I can't hide the genuine smile on my face as I look at Olis and Conall who have themselves wrapped around a very naked and asleep Valley.

From here, I can see a hint of Olis' cock still knotted deep in her pussy. They must have only just drifted off before I got here.

As quietly as I can manage in this state, I slowly begin to remove my clothes until I am left in only my underwear. I keep the clothing close to the side of Valley's nest, knowing she may find a need for them at some point during these next few days.

I don't step foot into the nest. Instead, I sit right on the edge.

My eyes remain locked on the beauty in the centre of the bed.

Even in sleep, she has this radiant glow about her.

It baffles me that I could ever have thought that she was anything but a Beta. There is this certain air that Omegas have about them. This ethereal beauty that screams for an Alpha to treasure them.

Because they deserve nothing less than that.

Il mio cuore deserves more.

Especially from me.

After my colossal fuck-up, I know that I don't deserve to be here right now.

If Valley woke up right now and told me to fuck off, that is exactly what I would do. I'd let her be happy even if that meant removing myself from the picture, I would honor her request.

I would and will give her anything that she asks from me.

My pack, my job, my house. Fuck, even my life.

Because she deserves it all. Every pitiful part of me. It's hers. I don't deserve to love her. But I am a glutton for punishment.

I become so lost in my thoughts and self-loathing that I don't realize someone is awake until a throat clears.

Blinking a few times, Valley quickly comes into focus.

Olis' knot must have gone down enough to allow her to sit in between the two Alphas who are still asleep.

I can't help but admire her naked flesh, my stomach in knots at the thought of finding a claiming bite on her neck. But I come up empty.

Instead of analyzing the mixture of thoughts I have about that realisation, I turn my attention back to her face. Blank features greet me and it makes my stomach roll further.

"You fucked up, Victor."

I cringe at the tone of her voice. The acid in it hits me right in the chest. She doesn't need to lay down the law any more than that because I *know*. I know exactly what I did and just how badly I fucked it up between us.

"I know, *dolce ciliegra*. I know," I murmur, my shoulders deflating. I drop my head, unable to bear witness to the look on her face any longer.

I deserve the pain, knowing I am unworthy of anything else. Like a coward, I turn away from it still.

I don't look up, even as I hear the rustling of sheets as she makes her way towards me. Her feet eventually come into view as she comes to stand in front of me.

Fuck, even her toes are perfect.

I remain locked on them as I wait for my beat down.

I jolt as her hand picks up my chin. That blank face is still comfortably in place, hiding her true feelings from me. She opens her mouth to speak but I interrupt.

"I'm so sorry, Valentina." I shake my head, huffing quietly, "I know that apologizing will never be enough. I showed you every single reason why you shouldn't trust me. I showed you why I am exactly like those Alphas that hurt you.

"For the last few weeks, I have pestered you to the point of immense shame on my behalf. Everytime you told me no, I pushed back. My want for you went beyond my control."

Diverting my eyes, so they are no longer locked with hers, I scoff at myself, "I was a fool for thinking that I deserved the truth from you. I have been so lost in my pain that I didn't consider yours. I didn't consider that you have reasons that I will never even begin to understand for why you kept the truth from us. Reasons that even now, I still don't deserve an explanation for. I allowed my anger to get the best of me."

I take a breath before looking back up at Valley. Finding her eyes easily, I lock in on them as I open myself up to her completely.

It feels as though I have splayed myself out for her to analyze. To judge me and all of my flaws. I allow her to see every last bit of me as I get to my knees.

I bend down and ever so carefully place a light kiss on the top of her foot.

"I am so fucking sorry, Valentina Rossi."

The room is quiet as I wait for her to speak. For her to yell and scream at me. For her to kick my ass out of the room.

Yet nothing comes.

Unable to bear the silence anymore, I look up at her.

My heart stutters as I find her tear-streaked face.

Quickly, I stand, my Alpha instincts scream at me. I don't hesitate for a single second as I wrap her in my arms.

The moment I do, she sobs; her tears catch on my chest.

I do my best to comfort her, whispering comforting words as I look around desperately for anything to help make it better.

Lifting Valley up into my arms, I step into the nest and make my way over to one of the corners that she has seemed to have put a bit more thought into. It's almost as though she has created a mini nest inside of her nest. The sight of it has a quiet growl of approval escaping me.

I settle the both of us into the mini nest, tucking *Il mio cuore* into me. She honors me through wrapping herself around me tighter, burying her face into my neck.

I lose time completely as we lay together. Breaking the silence, I begin to tell her about my life. I don't leave anything missing. I tell her about my childhood, about meeting Gwen and the life we had together. I tell her about her death and the years that followed. I tell her my fear of never being loved again. I tell her just how much I love red velvet cake.

I don't stop talking until my words begin to slur and sleep takes me under.

CHAPTER TWENTY-EIGHT

VALENTINA

I'm hot.

So fucking hot.

I groan, nuzzling into whatever surface I am currently laying on. It's hard but it smells like mine.

Just as I am about to get comfortable again, a sharp, stabbing pain has me crying out.

A soothing voice whispers to me, telling me how much of a good girl that I am. A hand rubs over my back as I ride though the spike. I curl up on myself as my memories come back to me.

The Omega killer. My secret. Heat. Victor.

My eyes shoot open, my head lifting as I find exactly who I am looking for.

His eyes are wide, looking at me in a mild state of panic. There is a desperation in his eyes as I watch him mull over in his head what he needs to do to help me right now.

I don't give him the chance to do anything though.

Moving my body so I am straddling him, I look at the Alpha below me.

“If you are to be here for my heat, you need to understand one simple thing. You are here to serve me.”

Before I can finish my sentence, he is already nodding. With my next words, I lace them with as much dominance as I possibly can.

“You will be at my beck and call these next few days. If I want your cock, you will give it to me. If I want your knot, you will say, yes Omega. If I want you to eat my pussy until I squirt in your mouth, you will do as I say. Do you understand?”

Victor’s eyes heat, nodding his head quickly. “Yes, Omega.”

I chuckle, biting my lip. Ever so slowly, I roll my hips over the hardening length I can feel beneath me.

“I want you to worship me, Alpha.”

Quicker than I can blink, Vic has me flat on my back. Kneeling between my thighs, he bends down, inhaling my scent. His pupils widen until his eyes are practically black.

“It would be my honor, Omega.”

I groan as he does exactly that, right before the blur of the heat takes me under.

My eyes blink rapidly against the light threatening to blind me. My body aches as I stretch. I cringe against the sheen of sweat, slick and cum that covers my body.

I slowly sit and give myself a moment to look around the room.

Fuck, how many days has it been?

Blankets, pillows and clothes are strewn about in a matter that makes it look like a natural disaster hit the nest.

Conall and Vic are on either side of me, the latter looking right at me. His hair is mused, the strands looking like they haven't seen a brush in days. It makes me think of my own hair. Reaching a hand up, I find two braids someone must have given me before things got too far. There are a few fly aways I can feel but I thank my lucky stars that one of my Alphas thought ahead.

"Conall made sure that your hair was tied back before you got too deep into your heat. You refused to sit still for him unless you had his cock in your mouth.

I choke, gaping at Vic as I process what he said. A blush reddens my face.

"Oh my god. I'm a fucking whore."

Vic growls, drawing my attention back over to him. I watch as he crawls towards me. There is this menacing look on his face as he gets right into my space.

"The way you commanded your three Alphas through your entire heat was one of the most attractive and pleasurable experiences of my life. You were so fucking beautiful."

He shakes his head as that ominous look he was wearing is replaced with raw admiration.

"You are so fucking strong. You ooze power in a way that is hard to not remain on my knees for you. You are a vixen. One that takes control of her pleasure."

He moves until his mouth grazes my ear.

"It was an honor to serve you," he whispers, causing goosebumps to travel over my skin.

My stomach clenches, my core already feeling needy and desperate for more of the Alpha in front of me.

Even though I know he can smell just how much I need him, he doesn't pay it any mind lifting me from the nest. I wrap my arms and legs around him as I blindly let him carry me. I turn my head as he opens the door of the bathroom. He doesn't let me go whileturns the shower on and waits for it to heat up before stepping into the spray.

I groan, earning myself a chuckle from Vic as the hot water crashes down over my body.

"We tried for days to get you to come in here and wash. You refused so we had to settle for a very protested against bird bath. You didn't want us to wash off the smell of us on your skin."

"Oh god," I mutter and wedge myself into his chest. I let him wash me as I hide in shame. Even though I know I shouldn't, I can't help but feel embarrassed.

The Andrews pack loved to tease me endlessly about how desperate I was for their knots during my heat. It always came with name calling and tears.

But as Vic tells me about my heat and clearing up the blurry moments, there is none of that shame I had once felt. It's the complete opposite. Vic clearly finds my actions to be sexy—his words, not mine.

It's strange, being boasted about in this way after being used to something so much different.

It helps me to see that maybe Vic isn't like the other Alphas. That maybe his anger was a momentary thing.

Because Scott, Matt, Jason and Trey never tended to me through my heats.

I would come out of the blur starving, dehydrated and covered in various substances. Bruises and bite marks would cover my skin for weeks before they eventually healed.

My last heat was the only time they gave me any kind of care.

It was only because they almost succeeded in killing me.

I shake myself out of my thoughts about my previous pack and think about my current pack.

Shit, when did I start referring to them as mine?

Because after this heat, I know that I could never refer to them as anything but. Conall, Olis and even Vic proved to me that I am safe. That even when my mind isn't my own, they will still honor my wishes.

Not only that, but they are amazing with Amity. They make my little girl happy, spoiling her with love from a male figure that I have always wanted for her. True father figures.

I don't have to do a thorough inspection of my body to know that they didn't claim me. I know that couldn't have been easy. There is no doubt in my mind that I would have begged for them relentlessly.

Yet, they resisted even against their own bodies' desires.

Because they care for me. They respect me.

It's a gift from an Alpha I never thought I would be entitled to, or ever see.

Even though they didn't give me their bites during my heat, I know it's not something that is permanently off the table, even without talking to them directly.

They have left it to be my choice. One I am able to make when I am of sound mind.

Lifting my head, I place a gentle kiss on Vic's cheek. He pauses halfway through undoing my braids to look at me.

"Thank you," I say in a whisper. His responding smile makes my heart clench. His eyes are filled with emotion. The strongest one being love.

"You never have to thank me for the bare minimum, *dolce ciliegra.* It is my life's honor to be here in this capacity for you."

A single tear rolls down my cheek as a feeling of euphoria settles in my chest.

"I don't deserve to be here, Valley. I hurt you in a way that's unthinkable. But if you give me a chance, I will never allow your heart to break again. I will love you and Amity until my dying breath. Everything that is mine will be yours. *Fino alla fine dei tempi, dolcezza mia.*"

Unable to speak, I close the distance between us. The moment my lips meet his, we are lost to each other.

Without words, I tell him yes. I tell him just how much I want him. How I want to be his. That I want him to be mine. That I want to grow old with him, Olis and Cal. To be his Omega and him my Alpha. For him to be my baby girl's step-father. To be my everything.

Eventually we pull apart. I rest my forehead against his as I catch my breath.

"Mine. My Omega. My Valentina," he growls, holding me tightly to his naked body.

"Yours."

After both Vic and I are clean, we make our way back to the nest, only to find it empty. Vic doesn't seem surprised, grabbing my hand, leading me back out through the house and to the kitchen.

The scent of freshly baked pastries greets us along with my two shirtless Alphas. It is a struggle to not turn into a goopy mess as I take in their hard chests.

Ones that are covered in scratch marks.

I gasp, dropping Vic's hand as I rush towards Olis. I inspect the marks, cursing myself as I come across a deep one. Fresh blood is dotted across the wound and tears fill my eyes.

"I'm so sorry, Olis. I can't believe I did this to you."

A deep chuckle shocks me. I look up at Olis whose broad smile covers his face, looking at the marks.

"Oh, my sweet girl. These marks are an honor for me to wear."

My mouth hangs open as I look at him in shock; even more so when Cal comes over to stand beside his pack brother. His chest is puffed, showing me his marks.

"I was kind of hoping for a much more permanent mark but these will do for now," he teases, making my eyes narrow as I smack his hard stomach.

He grunts, his wounded look an act as he approaches me. I squeal, unable to hold back a laugh as he lifts me over his shoulder, his hand slapping my ass cheek as he spins.

"Such a cheeky little Omega playing with her Alpha's feelings. I am wounded, Little Devil."

I am still laughing as he eventually sets me down. In true Cal fashion, he doesn't let me escape just yet, grabbing me around the waist and pulls me onto his lap.

Olis sets down two plates in front of us before placing a kiss on my forehead.

I watch as Olis fusses over one plate, making sure to get as much variety of the English breakfast onto a fork. He holds it up to me, waiting patiently for me to take it.

I open my mouth, groaning as he feeds me.

It's an odd feeling, allowing him to see to my needs in this way. Really, every green flag action has me shook to my core. It doesn't feel natural even though I know this is the life many of my fellow designation are given.

But for me, this is all new.

Cal takes over and finishes feeding me in silence. There is a blissed look on his face each time he offers me more food.

Once I am full, he turns to his food and begins shoveling it into his mouth. I watch, thoroughly impressed as the food is gone within a matter of minutes. Especially considering his plate was at least double mine, if not more.

They don't lie when they say that Alphas eat a lot.

The chiming of a phone has us all perking up to attention. Olis pulls out his cell frowning as he reads the new message.

His expression doesn't change, the only indicator he isn't happy about whatever he is reading being a slight lift of his lip.

Looking up, he finds Vic. They hold eye contact for a moment before he looks at Cal, then finally, me.

"They found another body. This one at the Throbbing Knot."

CHAPTER TWENTY-NINE

OLIS

I feel more tense than usual as we pull up to our newest club. For days, my pack and I have been heat-deep.

Even though there is a part of a heat that is draining, it also was refreshing in a way.

Because in Valley's nest, all that mattered was her. I was able to get lost in my Omega. My mind was able to clear itself, focusing only on her and seeing her through her heat.

Reality always seems to find a time to come crashing down on you.

I open the car door with more force than I needed to as I quickly take in the scene before me. It's a complete replica to every single other scene we were painstakingly analysing not even a week ago.

"Where is boss man?" Jaiden asks, coming to stand beside Conall and I.

"Our Omega just came out of heat. We couldn't leave her alone so early on. Vic stayed behind to be with her," Conall replies.

Jaiden's eyes widen, looking at us in shock, just as surprised as we were when he told us to go.

Never in all the years we have been a pack has Vic ever stayed behind. Its unexpected but about fucking time.

It has been hard for Vic to let go of situations and just let Conall and I handle it. He has control issues, especially when it comes to the Syndicate.

But, Valley's influence is already changing him for the better.

That's the benefits of a true scent match.

While Gwen was our scent match, Valley is different.

Maybe it's because she is our second, or maybe because she is something more. It feels that way at least.

Turning my attention back to the situation at hand, I listen carefully as Jaiden explains everything to us in detail. It's nothing that we haven't heard before though.

Omega found behind a dumpster. The word 'mine' carved into her torso. Bruises and signs of rape evident amongst the blood covering her flesh.

I sigh as Jaiden says he will send through the case file for us to add to the rest.

The car ride back to the house is bleak.

It's hard to feel that post heat happiness when this has very quickly dampened it.

I guess there is no rest for the wicked.

"Quicker, men! My daughter-in-law can level her enemies quicker than you lot even while pregnant. Fucking move! Harder, quicker, smarter!" I yell at the new lot of recruits.

Normally, Ledger is given the newest arrivals until they have been weeded out and ready for the next stage.

But today, I needed more.

After getting back from the latest Omega scene, we have spent hours going through surveillance, 'interviewing' potential suspects and doing our best to get into the head of the killer.

It's tolling.

We are all exhausted. Especially, Valley.

After Kennedy and Jax dropped Amity off after having her for the length of the heat, our girl has been run into the ground.

She refused to take time off to rest after her heat. She claimed that she had already rest enough, no matter how much we protested.

Late nights have become our new norm. Coffee has been our only saving grace at being able to keep us somewhat alert and functioning.

It doesn't help sugarcoat the fact Valley already wants to return back to work. While it has been enough time since the end of her heat, the idea of her not being able to have us with her 24/7 is unthinkable.

Vic has already added more security measures to the club. More guards at doors, cameras covering every point of the club and a vetting process at the door.

It's over the top, but necessary.

Especially considering our heart will be there.

I had never given much thought into my scent match being a stripper. I never really thought much about another potential partner after Gwen. But given how much Valley's face lights up when she dances, it's impossible to not support her; even if she is dancing for other men.

Because at the root of it all, dancing is what gave Valley her freedom. It gave her the ability to support both her and Amity after she ran from the Andrews pack. It became more than just a way for her to live. It became a hobby. A place that she is able to interact with other women, a lot from situations like hers.

It's her sanctuary and it would be wrong to take that from her just because we don't want other men to see her body.

My attention quickly turns from my thoughts as the scent of cherries hits me. Turning my head, I find my girl walking towards me. Her hair is up in a messy bun with a few strands framing her face.

Her outfit is simple; a singlet top and jean shorts with strappy flats, but she is still as beautiful as ever.

Fuck, she could wear a hessian sack and would still be the most beautiful person in the room.

Her face lights up when she sees me and makes her way over. From the corner of my eye, I find a few of the soldiers turning their heads and ogling her.

Immediately, I am on edge.

The moment Valley is within reach, I pull her into me, pulling her face to mine and drowning myself in all that is her.

We break away from each other eventually. She smiles up at me with a dazed look on her face–one that says she wants more. I chuckle, brushing one of the strands of hair from her face.

"Hey, baby," I whisper.

She chuckles, shaking her head, "Hey, yourself. Putting on a show for your men are we? I didn't expect you to be into voyeurism."

"When it comes to you, I'm into everything," I tease but am forced to suck in a breath as Valley perfumes for me. Pulling her closer—something that is almost impossible—I bend down, my nose touching the side of her neck where her scent gland is.

It's the same spot I plan on putting my claiming bite so everyone can see that she is mine.

I breathe her in, feeling my eyes go dark as the oxygen in my lungs is overrun by the potency of her. It's addictive and certainly the beginning of my downfall but I can't seem to find the will to care. Let me drown in her. I would die a happy Alpha.

Adding fuel to the fire, Valley rolls her body against mine. A groan escapes my throat as I grip her ass, pulling her into me even more.

Feeling eyes on the both of us, I lift my head finding our newest recruits staring at the two of us.

"Dismissed," I growl, the sound instantly making the men and women jolt back to attention as they start to scramble.

"And," I begin, my growl dropping a further octave until I sound otherworldy, "Next time any of you fucks make eyes at my girl, you will fucking lose them."

The scent of fear sours the room and I can't help but smile in glee as my promise hits its mark.

"Fuck," Valley groans drawing my attention back too her. Her eyes have darkened with lust, her breath quickening as she sucks in oxygen.

"I didn't think violence would ever turn me on like this," she breathes. I chuckle darkly as I lift Valley up into my body. She yelps but wraps her legs and arms around me.

"I think it's time to introduce you to the darkside," I whisper in her ear, chuckling as goosebumps travel over her skin.

Slamming the door open to the torture room beneath the warehouse, I walk straight towards the chains hanging from the ceiling.

Dropping Valley back to her feet, I find her arms, lifting them one by one to secure them in the chains.

She remains silent which is a good thing. I don't think any words that I would have tried right now would be tangible. I am too worked up.

All because Valley is feeding my inner demons, even if she is doing it unknowingly.

I don't really know what first drew my attention to the BDSM lifestyle. All I know is, I love the control it gives me. Knowing that you have that person at your mercy. Holding their pleasure over them until the time is right. And finally, watching as ecstasy floods them.

Once the chains are in place, I turn my attention to her clothes. Gripping the fabric at the centre of Valley's chest, I rip the fabric apart and quickly snap the straps of both the singlet and the bra. With a quick snap of fingers, the latter falls to her feet, leaving her chest bare for me.

Even though I spent days with her naked, the thrill it gives me seeing her like this doesn't fade. She is the woman of my dreams. So fucking beautiful, it becomes painful to look at her sometimes.

I trail my fingers down her torso, watching as she squirms beneath my touch. Her chest rises and falls rapidly as I reach the waist band of her pants.

In a matter of seconds, Valley is strung up before me, completely naked.

While I want to push Valley's body to the extremes, I know this first time needs to be slow. Chains are enough for now.

Besides, I want her in my bed the next time we play.

I give myself a moment to breathe her in. I watch her intently, admiring the way her body reacts. The way her breathing continues in rapid pants. The slight twitch of her thighs that she longs to rub together against her aching core. The tremor in her body as she waits for my next move.

She is just as desperate as me.

Just as much of a slave to her needs as I am.

But this time, she has a master. A puppeteer that will command her body and pleasure.

"The three of us have been having mixed feelings about you going back to the club," I murmur as I start walking around her dangling body.

"You can't stop me from going back there, Olis. Just because we are doing..."

She trails off trying to find the right word. Not being able to find it, she shakes her head with a huff, "Well, whatever the fuck we are doing, doesn't mean you have some kind of control over my body."

Holding up a finger, I come around to stand directly in front of her.

"That is where you are misplaced in your thinking, baby. Because it's not you working or dancing that we have a problem with. It's the people you are dancing for."

She sighs, clearly seeing where we are coming from.

"You know that I don't dance for them, right?"

I nod, taking a step into her until our bodies are flush with each other.

"I know, Valley. But that doesn't ease the beast inside the three of us. We want those fuckers to know that you are ours. That while you are dancing up on that stage, it's our bed that you come home to. Our cocks that you ride at the end of the night. That it's our knots you lock down on. Ours."

Her eyes heat, looking up at me. With zero hesitation, she knocks the breath completely out of my lungs.

"What are you waiting for then? Take me. Make me yours."

Time seems to evade me as I stare at Valley with a mixture of wonder, want and love.

Fuck, she is destorying me. Every single last bit of me that I have been holding back to appear as some kind of sane human is being destroyed. All by her.

With only a few words, she officially unleashed the beast, turning me feral in a matter of seconds.

She gasps, watching the transformation right before my eyes.

I feel the change happen through my body painstakingly. The Alpha roars, delighting in his Omega and her demands of him. Ones that he is all too willing to fulfill.

I pop the button of my jeans, hearing the metal ting against the wall. I pull them down just enough that my cock can spring free.

Because there isn't enough time.

I need her. More than I need air.

Gripping either side of Valley's hips, I lift and step into her groan as she slides down easily on my cock.

Her responding gasp gets caught in her throat at the same moment I lift her off me again and drop her onto my shaft.

"Fuck, Olis. Fuck!" she yells, her nails digging into my shoulders. The breaking of my flesh beneath her grip has me roaring in pleasure as my knot batters against her swollen lips.

I've always loved a bit of pain with my pleasure.

Abruptly, I stop, settling Valley down on her feet. Valley's eyes widen and she gasps, her features turning into a frown as I take a step from her.

She's pissed. Rightfully so. Her pussy was like a vice grip, clamping down around me in the lead up to the orgasm I just denied her.

"What the fuck, Olis!" she yells, whacking a hand into my shoulder. My responding chuckle only has her face reddening further as I look down upon her.

Quicker than either of us can blink, my hand snaps up, gripping Valley's throat.

"Present for your Alpha," I growl, sending a shiver down Valley's body. I feel her throat bob beneath my grip as I hold her in place, waiting for her to bend to my will. Her eyes are heated as I watch the internal fight.

The Omega side of her wants to submit. It's in every single facet of her nature.

But Valentina? The woman I have so quickly fell in love with fights against the act. No, the woman I love doesn't bend to the will of an Alpha. After what it has taken her to get here, not even the promise of ecstasy is enough to get her to submit for me.

No, my precious Omega will fight me every step. And I wouldn't have it any other way.

CHAPTER THIRTY

VALENTINA

This fucking Alpha.

The nerve Olis has believing a demand just short of an Alpha-bark would get me to submit to him.

But fuck, if it isn't one of the hottest things I have ever heard.

Slick drips down my thighs as I hang in the centre of a fully cemented room. There is a strong smell of blench that clings to the room ... along with the scent of blood and piss.

Its a dizzying feeling to know that you are being fucked raw in the torture room of the Mafia. Even more so that the Capo is the one who has your knees trembling for him.

Even as I dangle here completely at his mercy, there isn't a chance in hell that I am not going to submit to him.

Not this fucking easily.

No, if he wants me to bend to his will. He is going to have to make me.

Telling him exactly that has us both pausing for a moment. I'm not ready for him to move.

Within seconds, he grabs me by the hips, flips me so my back is to his chest, grips my hips and slams his cock back into my pussy.

I scream, my back bowing as pleasure courses through me.

"That's it, my little Omega slut. Bend that fucking back and give yourself to me. Show me just how fucking thirsty you are for my cock."

I do exactly that, becoming his little whore as I take every single thrust.

But it's not enough. I need more. More of him.

Feeling the need to be a brat, I turn my head, meeting eye contact with my Alpha.

"Is that all you got? I thought you were going to take me. To show me that I am yours."

Shrugging my shoulders, I level him with a look. "Maybe I need to go find someone else."

Olis' hand wraps around my throat before I finish the sentence. Any kind of further retort is cut off as is my oxygen.

Keeping my back bowed, he brings us closer together so his face is beside mine.

"Such a bratty little slut. Don't you think I can feel the way your pussy flutters for me? That I can't feel just how much you are loving this?"

Gritting his teeth, he growls deeply, "Now, shut the fuck up and take my knot like a good Omega."

My mouth opens in a silent scream as he shoves his knot so deep inside me, it's impossible to know where I end and he begins.

An orgasm hits me at the same time as he bites down on my scent gland. A mixture of emotions flood me as my newly forming bond increases my pleasure tenfold, my voice becomes hoarse as I scream my Alpha's name.

I feel the chains bruising my skin, my bones riot against the pressure I am putting on them.

But I don't care. Because Olis claimed me.

A man that has done nothing but support me and care for me from the moment we first met.

I have an Alpha.

A pack.

A real home.

Tears begin to stream down my cheeks. I hiccup a sob as emotion barrels down on me.

I never thought that I could have this. That I would be able to genuinely be happy to be a packed-up Omega.

But fuck, I am.

Because I am so irrevocably in love with these three Alphas.

"Fuck, Valley. Baby. Are you okay? Fuck, it was too much. Fuck. Fuck. Fuck!"

Olis fusses with the chains still holding my arms above my head. My limbs ache as they finally drop, the blood rushing back into them after being denied for so long.

Olis wraps me in his arms the best he can as I all but hang on his knot. After a claiming bite and sex, there's no way that thing is going down any time soon.

My head rests on his shoulder as I continue to cry.

Olis carries me over to a chair in the corner of the room, the old wooden frame creaking under our combined weight.

Olis' hands begin to travel over my body, his attention focusing majorly on the redness on my wrists.

"I'm so sorry, baby. I fucked up. I got too caught up in the moment," he mutters, continuing to gently rub my skin.

I shake my head and clear my throat, "You didn't hurt me, Olis. It's the bond. It's the fact that you are mine. That finally, I have a pack. One that I love."

Olis' breath hitches in his chest, his hands freeze. Turning my head, I find him already looking at me. His eyes are blown wide; his mouth dropped in disbelief.

"I love you, Olis Duran. So fucking much. You saved a part of me that I thought was damaged beyond repair."

A single tear drops down the Alpha's face as he snaps out of his stupor.

"You say that I saved you but sweetheart, you saved me. I was numb before you. I spent years believing that I would die alone. That my chance of happiness was taken from me to pay for my sins."

He smiles, a look that is so breathtaking on him, it breaks my heart a little.

"But you changed everything. You healed my heart."

Lifting a hand up, he pushes hair out of my face.

"I love you, Valentina Duran."

My eyes blow wide at my new last name. I never was particularly attached to my last name after having it ruined for me by the Andrews pack, so it feels nice. In a new and slightly scary way.

But after all these years, I'm ready. Ready to finally be happy.

A grin stretches across my face as I embrace the club. It feels like a lifetime since I have been here, when in hindsight, it's barely been a fortnight.

Luna's face lights up the moment that she sees me—even more so when she catches the men at my back. After my heat, I knew I had to come clean to my best friend at some point.

It was time for me to be honest with her.

She took it surprisingly well. I think there was a part of her that maybe knew the entire time.

Running up to me, she envelopes me in a hug before pulling back with a slight disgruntled look.

"Damn, I thought being an Omega would mean that your scent would be out on display now."

I roll my eyes as Cal growls, the Alpha pulling me into him. "That scent is *ours*."

After Conall and Vic found the claiming bite on my neck, they have barely left my side. I think it has something to do with only just having had my heat and only been bitten by one of their pack brothers.

Or they are just over protective bastards.

I think it may be the latter.

I push him away, rolling my eyes at the caveman behaviour. I grab Luna's hand, dragging her along behind me as I head to the dressing room.

"Fucking brutes, the lot of them," I grumble, frowning at their protests.

*

The club is already packed by the time I get out on the floor. Against my regular first night tradition, I decide to wear something a little bit simpler.

A black sequined bodysuit with a cut out over the stomach gives the illusion of a bikini, crisscrosses over my chest into a halter neck. I am by far one of the most modest dancers tonight but that does nothing to distract from what I have allowed on display.

Other than my claiming bite, of course.

It hurts to cover up the one thing I wish to show off for the world but Olis and I both know if I want to continue dancing, I will have to sacrifice these things.

Doesn't make it suck any less.

My scent was the next thing that had to go. While I'm not taking my heat suppressants anymore—seeing as that train is now long gone—scent-neutralizers are still a must.

My schedule for tonight is quiet, which is unexpected.

Normally I would have had a few privates booked by now. But there's nothing apart from my stage sets. I have a sneaking suspicion it has something to do with the three Alphas in one of the dark corners of the room.

The moment I walked out of the dressing room, I could feel their eyes on me. It's a heady feeling having their attention on me. It makes thinking fucking hard.

Like the fact that I need to somehow come up with two different stage sets that I haven't done a second of practice for.

I need to ask one of my Alphas if they can set up a pole for me in the gym that I can use to practice on.

Before them, I used to come into the club early or go around to Lulu's and practice. Now with everything that's going on, I doubt those two options would even be considered. We can't become lax just because of the title that my men hold.

That would be naive of us.

Instead, every moment we are outside of the gates of their mansion, we are automatically on edge.

Vic has even mentioned moving his boys and Kennedy back in so both of us Omegas are safe. Knowing that Kennedy is pregnant had me agreeing with them without a second thought.

I shake myself out of my thoughts in time to hear my name being called up onto the stage. For a moment, nerves hit me but I push through them as I make my way up the stairs.

The stage is dark, the lights completely dimmed as I make my way to the pole.

Deciding to add a little flair to my dance, I grip the pole and flip myself to the dragonfly pose. The moment I nod my head, the music flares to life, as do the lights in the room.

They illuminate my figure, highlighting the curves and dips of my body.

I spin for a moment before I lift my body back up and begin to spin around the pole into a carousel. The crowd cheers and I can't help but smile as I contour my body into the next move.

I continue to work the pole as the music inclines. Money is thrown across the stage as I continue to tease the front row, who are all but panting.

But this dance isn't for them. It's for my Alphas.

Eventually, I slide to the floor with grace that I once struggled with when I started dancing. Now, it's as easy as my next breath.

I become lost in the sway of the music and the peace it offers me. After the stress of these past few weeks, it's nice being able to close my eyes and just be in the moment.

That is until the entire room goes dark.

The sounds of gunshots echo throughout the room. Shouts join the chaos as the patrons and dancers scream and run.

Pained groans sound from around me as bullets hit their targets.

"Valley! Valentina!"

Conall's terrified voice reaches me, filling me with fear as I try to get my bearings.

I go to call back out to him but the scent of rotten apples freezes in place. A dark chuckle from behind me has my stomach threatening to spill its contents. My body goes uncharacteristically still as hands grip me, pulling me off the stage.

I don't realize I am crying until a fist hits the side of my cheek.

"Fucking pathetic. You had the balls to try and kill me all those years ago and now faced with your failure, you turn into a sobbing mess."

The sound of Scott Andrews' voice is a living nightmare.

One I thought I had escaped.

I thought I was safe.

But I was wrong.

"You and your used-up cunt are going to fucking pay for what you did to us. For what you did to my brothers," he grunts, his grip on me tightening.

Bile rushes my throat. Attempting to bend, I empty my stomach contents off the side of the staircase I am being dragged down. Scott recoils, dropping my body and allowing me to fall the last few steps.

I don't allow myself even a second to get my bearings as I stumble to my feet. I curse my heels as I begin to run but am quickly stopped by a strong grip on my hair.

I scream as Andrews pulls me back into him.

He chuckles darkly as one hand wraps around my stomach, the other holding my head back to his shoulder.

"My scared little mouse finally found her fight. It's going to be fun breaking you all over again."

I scream and struggle against him even as a hessian bag is pulled down over my head. The scent of rotten vegetables is nauseating but I don't stop fighting.

Not as I am dragged out of the club and into the frigid night air. Not even as I am thrown into the back of a van and smashed into the metal walls.

I won't stop fighting.

Not this time.

This time, I will fucking win.

CHAPTER THIRTY-ONE

VALENTINA

I can already feel a bruise forming on my eyebrow from the amount of hits I have taken since being tied to the chair in the decrepit cabin Scott took me too.

I have seen a few other unfamiliar men who have come and gone from the moment my blindfold was removed.

It's been hard to keep my attention on them though.

No matter how hard I try to breathe through the hits rained down on my body, I struggle to keep consciousness.

But I won't stop.

I can't.

Because the moment I finally do is the moment I sign my death wish.

It would be so easy to do too.

The thought of going back to the same spot I was in all those years ago is enough to make the grim reaper weep.

But it's them.

Amity, Cal, Olis, and Vic.

It's them I fight for.

Now that I have had the taste of what my life could really be, I could never just give it up that quickly. It's something that Scott seems to understand, landing his last hit before standing back and panting.

The Alpha before me is a mess.

The wolfsbane I used to poison him did some kind of damage.

If every single feature of his wasn't etched into my psyche, I wouldn't have recognized him.

He looks as though he has aged thirty years. His hair is a fowl gray color, the strands matted which only seems to bring out the insanity in his gaze even more. There is a scar on his face, covering his entire right cheek that never used to be there. The bags under his eyes hold a permanent darkness. His skin is wrinkled and leathery, adding the finishing touches to a feral Alpha.

I glare at him, shooting him daggers that I wished weren't just a part of my imagination.

He snarls at me before turning and kicking a chair across the room. His hands shake, the evidence of insanity as he grips is hair, ripping some strands as he paces.

He is feral, beyond the point of saving. Even if he was worth that.

Which he isn't.

In a way, the scene before me is hilarious.

Little old me was able to fuck this Alpha's life up to the point that he is completely gone. It makes me cackle out loud which I know is a huge mistake the moment those bleary eyes turn back my way.

Rushing me, he backhands me again, the action only making me laugh even more.

"You psychotic fucking bitch! Do you think this is funny, do you? You fucking killed my brothers! We gave you everything!"

I cackle a laugh, the sound perfectly mirroring this moment.

"The only thing you gave me Scotty, was fucking trauma. You really think you did anything right by me the entirety of the time you and those cunts you call brothers held me captive? You murdered my parents in front of me all because I told you 'no'."

He snarls, getting right in my face.

"You were just playing hard to get, you little slut! I've seen the way you dance on that stage for me. The way you teased me with your body. It was the same way you used to walk through all of those dinner parties. You pretended like you were too good for us."

His snarl turns into a devious smile that has my gut churning. "That was until you sat on our knots."

I spit in his face, grinning maniacally as he snarls before roaring in my face. The move is meant to terrify me and maybe a small part of me is scared but I don't let it show. Instead, I continue to laugh, fueling that anger and praying he makes a mistake.

I need to time it well.

I have already been spending the entire interrogation rubbing the rope that has tied my wrists against the wooden backrest of the chair I am secured to.

I can feel it beginning to fray.

I just have to keep his attention on me. Get him close enough when the time is right so I can strike.

I may be an Omega but since the moment I escaped his clutches, I refused to allow myself to be weak in a moment like this ever again.

So I wait, painstakingly.

After further abuse, my body sore and aching, Scott finally gave up and left the room.

It gives me the perfect opportunity to work on both the rope and my bond to Olis.

Years ago, there used to be rumors about a small fact relating to an Alpha and Omega's bond. That if the two were true mates, there was a possibility of being able to communicate telepathically.

While I don't have any interest in being a damsel in distress, it would be much fucking easier to get out of this position with a little extra help.

I know they are already looking for me. I can feel Olis' emotions down the bond. He is beside himself. His pain is raw and crippling, a struggle to breathe through.

I do my best to send comforting emotions down the bond but either it's not reaching him yet or something else is the cause of his pain.

I just hope it's not the latter.

Not being able to feel my other two Alphas in the way that I can feel Olis is a problem that I need to rectify the moment I am out of here.

I need to feel them. To know that they are okay. To reassure them that I am alright.

Mostly.

I'm sure this will all come to bite me in the ass before I know it but I don't have any other choice.

The front door opens and a new figure walks into the room. I blink my eyes, trying to clear the blurriness from them against the sun.

The figure walking into the room is much smaller than Scott but judging by the overall stature, I know that he is male. A Beta possibly.

My breath hitches as I finally get a clear view of him.

"I know you," I whisper, my voice laced in shock.

The familiar face nods, a bright smile turning up his lips at my words.

"I knew you would remember me, Mom."

I frown, my eyebrows raising at the use of the name that this grown-ass man should certainly not be calling me. The Beta, one that I gave a dance to not all that long ago, takes a few more steps into the room.

I can't help but feel sympathy for the male that is now on his knees before me, his features full of hope that I know I can't give him.

It's obvious that the poor guy is confused. That he potentially has some kind of mental health issue that has led him to be convinced of the impossible.

He is young, maybe eighteen so there is no chance of him being mine.

Softening my features as best as I can, I look down at him. "Sweetie, I'm not your Mom."

His face saddens as the hope that one bloomed in his eyes dampens. "But you are my Mom. Dad rescued you from those Alphas. He promised me that he would get you back for me. That I would finally have someone to love me."

Tears shone in his eyes as the Beta sunk in on himself. My heart breaks as I take in his emotions. They are raw and desperate. A poor young man in need of love and care.

I can see just how much he wants to be loved.

To be accepted.

Deciding to not cause him anymore pain or confusion, I give in. I nod back at him, forcing a smile on my face.

"You are right, sweetie. I am your Mom."

His bright smile returns, shooting to his feet. Engulfing me in a hug, he squeezes me as sobs begin to wrack his body.

I do my best to comfort him, wishing that I could do more for him. He needs help. Help that requires a professional touch.

But for now, I coo in his ear, giving him as much as I can. He eventually backs away, wiping the tears from his face, leaning back on his knees.

"What's your name? Your father has never gotten around to telling me your full story."

I can see a hint of heartbreak at my words, something that rips me up inside, but I need to know the truth. Not only so I can get out of here but so I can also help the Beta.

I refuse to just throw him back to the wolves.

"My name is Makari. My biological mother is named Gwen. My father is named Jason."

I blanch, hearing the names of his parents.

"G-Gwen?" I murmur, feeling the color drain from my face.

He smiles but I can tell it's forced.

"She died when I was only a few months old. Papa said that she needed to go be with the angels."

I see the war of emotions on his face. He knows just as well as I do that there was much more to his mother—Gwen's—death.

In fact, I think it's more than either of us could possibly fathom.

I feel my heartrate pick up in my chest as I mull over the next question. I have no doubt that my fears are true. But I need to confirm it.

"Makari, can you remind me of which of your fathers you call Papa?"

"Scott, of course," he smiles but it fades, obviously remembering something, "I used to have three other Dads but they had to leave me too."

Quicker than I can blink, his features change again. "It's okay though! Papa said that now that we have you and my sister back, we can finally be a family."

A gut wrenching sickness drowns me as the door behind Makari opens. Scott walks into the room, Amity following close behind him.

"Our son is right, Valentina. Now that our *daughter...*" he emphasises the word by putting his hands on Amity's shoulders and squeezing, "is here, we can finally be a family."

CHAPTER THIRTY-TWO

CONALL

I have lost track of the days.

There is no point in knowing where I am at anymore.

Because with each day that passes, any hope that I had at my last chance of happiness is gone.

My girls are *gone.*

Grief has become my newest friend as I wallow in the feeling.

Living feels useless.

A world that seemed brighter the moment my little devil and firefly walked into it is now pitch back.

Any hope I had in those first initial days is now lost to the wind.

I feel as though I am a shell of who I once was.

My brothers don't fare much better.

I have hardly seen Vic. Losing another love, one being a child, has been too much to bear.

Olis is the only one of us who has seemed to be able to keep a level head in all of this. While he has shed his fair share of tears, something I have never seen him do before, he hasn't given up yet.

I watch from the corner of the office as he frowns down at the laptop in front of him. He hasn't stopped scouring the surveillance that we were able to obtain. I have already been over the documents more than once, paying attention to each second of film.

But it was no use.

There was no surveillance recorded from the moment we entered the club over three weeks ago.

Just when we thought we were good, it appears that someone was better.

Much fucking better.

Olis slams his hand down on the table, his growl echoing through the room. Lifting a hand to his chest, he rubs the spot, feeling the emotions of whatever Valley is feeling.

While we have practically nothing on where our Omega has gone, at least we know that she is alive.

Somewhere.

I curse, and not for the first time, that I didn't claim Valley during her heat. I had wanted to give her a heat that she didn't come to from with a bond that she didn't want.

I wanted her to say yes to me. Wanted so desperately to hear that she wanted me just as much as I want her.

But now that chance is gone.

Continuing to wallow in my heartbreak, I don't realize that Olis has found something.

With a shove of my shoulder, I find an emotionless Alpha standing over me.

"What? What is it?" I say as I quickly get to my feet.

Olis remains quiet for a few moments before his eyes glaze over.

My heart thumps in my chest as I wait for something. Anything.

My pack brother eventually puts me out of my misery after what feels like a lifetime.

"I don't know how she did it but Valley just mind-linked with me."

My jaw drops as I stare at him blankly. I force a swallow that feels like nails but I don't give it anytime.

"W-w-what did she say? Where is she? Is she okay? Is Firefly okay? Who the fuck has her?"

Olis' eyes go glassy again, continuing to speak with our girl.

Mind-links were always something that our elders told us about whenever the beauty of true mates was brought up. For so long I had thought it to be a myth, much like the ability we once had to shift into a wolf. Olis proves it wrong, continuing to communicate with her, peppering her with questions.

He comes back to me eventually. A deathly smile turns his lips, putting a hand on my shoulder.

"Ready to go hunting, brother?"

CHAPTER THIRTY-THREE

VALENTINA

It didn't take me long to get the hint that I needed to play the dutiful Omega to survive.

After Scott walked into the cabin with my child, I knew that I had to be careful about my next moves.

For the first few days, he rained down abuse on me. Makari and Amity bore witness to every single moment.

After I changed my thinking, bowing to his demands instead of fighting them, the abuse stopped.

No longer was my anger important.

Because my little girl was at risk just as much as I was.

Scott knows Amity is an Alpha.

I listened to him boasting about how strong his sperm was. That he was able to not only produce an Alpha female but also, a male Omega.

It seemed I wasn't the only one that was able to fool people with my designation.

Makari is an Omega too.

An Omega that since he emerged, has been sold to Alphas to be used however they pleased.

I had originally thought that maybe Makari was deceiving me. That maybe he was in on Scott's plans more than I had first realized. It quickly became clear that that wasn't the case at all.

Makari was as much a victim as I was.

But where I held a deep loathing for Scott and the Andrews pack, Makari was the opposite. He had been brainwashed so deeply and carefully that he seemed to idolize the man he called Papa.

It meant that I had to continue playing my part in the male Omega's life as his mother.

It wasn't a hard task by any means. My nature seemed to call to protect him. So I did. Each night, I curled up with Makari and Amity in the hopes that I would be able to save them from Scott.

It was surprising that he didn't demand me to warm his bed the moment he finally let me out of the ropes. Evidence of the burns I had given myself from trying to wear the rope down are still prevalent on my wrists. Makari was beside himself when he saw the raw skin.

I let him take over my care. It gave him a distraction. It also allowed me the chance to get to know him better.

I haven't allowed myself to admit it out loud just yet but I have grown to love Makari as a son. While I can't do anything yet about our predicament, I can give him a mother's love. It's the one thing that I am able to give him with ease.

It also seems to make Scott happy. Not that I care about the way he feels, but it helps to weasel my way into a position that has me mostly unharmed.

At least physically.

Mentally, I am fucked.

Each time my ex-Alpha walks into the same room, I have to fight against the bile that tries its best to expel every time his scent invades my nose.

Bleach has been the only product that has seemed to give me any kind of reprieve. That is until it gives me a headache.

I guess it's the better alternative.

Each day that goes past without my Alphas is like a dagger to the heart. I haven't allowed myself to cry for them.

That doesn't mean that I haven't stopped making plans for how the fuck we are meant to get out of here.

I have been working at the bond in my chest that connects me to Olis.

At night, I have exhausted myself by mentally reaching out to him. By day, I have been the sweet Omega, luring Scott into a false sense of security.

He believes that he has won, yet again.

I see it in the way he watches me. There is this hint of elation as he struts through the house.

If I knew it wouldn't lead to further abuse, I would laugh.

Since seeing what a true Alpha looks like, it baffles me that I was ever terrified of him and his dead pack.

They are weak.

While Scott has managed to somehow hide what he did from the Durans, he is still pitiful in comparison.

In a one-on-one fight, there is no doubt who would win.

The only way that Scott was able to even snatch Amity and I in the first place was because he sold his soul to the Demons.

The moment I saw the cut of the Alpha that walked into the cabin one night with Scott, I knew it was never just him.

He had help from the deadliest motorcycle gang in the country.

I shouldn't be surprised that he is working with them. What Scott is able to give them though is still unbeknown to me.

Before their deaths, the Andrews pack had owned a semi-successful telecommunications business. It was why they were so desperate to marry into my family.

They needed a way to secure their position in society. My family and I were just collateral on their way to the top.

Another gift, besides the abuse, was the front row access to the boasting of a dozen Omega murders.

"You thought you were so clever, didn't you?" Scott snarls, getting right into my face as some kind of intimidation technique. I try to pull against the rope holding me hostage but it doesn't budge, it just burns the fuck out of me. I grit my teeth against the pain, refusing to show weakness.

"But you can't run from me. You are mine."

I shiver at the emphasis he puts on the final word in his statement. He doesn't miss my reaction, chuckling and standing to his full height. I curse myself at showing my hand so early. Trauma that I thought I had buried deep rears its head, wreaking havoc over my system.

"I knew that I would get your attention with the other Omegas."

I feel all of the color drain from my face, yet again.

"You didn't," I whisper as the first tear falls down my cheek. There's no way that the Omega killer is him.

It can't be.

But as he nods his head, a sadistic look on his face, I know that I am naive in my belief.

"Of course it is me," he laughs, crossing his arms over his chest that he has puffed out in pride. "You didn't think that you could just get away with trying to kill me, did you?"

When I don't answer, Scott laughs, the sound chilling me to my very core.

"God, you are so fucking stupid. You and your entire designation."

I stare blankly, unable to allow myself to even dip a toe into the turmoil that I know would consume me if I let it.

Those Omegas died because of me.

"It was easy to get them to come home with me. At the promise of a knot, they were like putty in my hands. It made it even sweeter to watch their flesh cut beneath my knife. Do you know I thought of you each time I did it?"

I swallow bile at his words, needing to breathe deeply through my nose to not make a mess of myself.

"I was picky with my selections. Not too tall, not too short. Long brown hair, the perfect kind to wrap my fist in as I had my way with their bodies."

He snaps out of whatever dreamland he had drifted off too and closes the distance between us.

I do my best to cover a whimper as Scott grips my chin in his hand, squeezing tightly and wrenches my head up to look at him.

"I could never find anyone with the same eyes as yours though. The kind that lures a man to his death. So fucking pretty."

I haven't allowed myself to give his candor any more time than I did on that first day. I don't think I could even if I wanted to. Because I know, without a doubt, if I hadnt have fucked up the day I tried to kill him, those Omegas would still be alive.

The next time I take my role as the Grim Reaper, I refuse to allow any mistakes.

No, the next time that I take the steps of removing the scum from this earth, I will be through. Now that I have seen what Scott is capable of, I can't allow him to continue breathing.

He needs to be eradicated.

As another day comes to an end, I tuck Amity and Makari in the makeshift nest that I built for us. Originally, I had hesitated at doing something so Omega-coded, but I needed some kind of comfort, especially now that the bond between Olis and I refuses to quieten.

His emotions are like a thunderstorm in my chest. I can feel his frustration, anger and heartbreak. I want nothing more than to kill Scott and get back to my pack but I can't be too hasty.

Sighing, I sink into the small nest and close my eyes. Finding that spot that I have come so familiar with these past weeks, I tug on it. Opening my mind up, I call down the bond.

The feeling of shock and disbelief from Olis hits me square in the chest. I hold my breath as I wait for him to respond or give me some kind of acknowledgement that it wasn't just a coincidence.

Baby?

I choke on a sob as the sound of Olis' honeyed voice echoes in my head.

Oh my god! It worked! I can hear you!

Relief floods into me as the connection between Olis and I grows. I can't stop the tears from flowing now.

Shh, my love. I am here now. Are you okay? Is Amity okay?

I can feel the bated breath he holds, waiting for me to reply.

We are both okay. There's a lot that I have learnt since Scott took me.

I can feel the growl he releases.

You have a lot to fill me in on, Omega. His words are strained and straight to the point but I can't blame him. If he was being held by a psychotic murderous ex, I would have burned the world down by now.

I mentally nod. Remembering that I need to warn my Alphas of who exactly we are dealing with. I fill in Olis on as much as I can, not leaving out anything. I won't let my Alphas walk into a gun fight with knives.

Got it. Hang tight my sweet Omega. We are coming.

I breathe a sigh of relief. While I wasn't counting on Olis, Vic and Cal saving me, it eases me to know that I will have back-up when the time is right.

It's hard to remember that I'm not alone in this anymore. That I have people that I can trust and lean on. That if I needed them to fight for me, they would in a heartbeat.

Olis and I continue to talk for the rest of the night. We talk about everything and nothing all at once.

For the first time since I was taken, I feel hope.

Since breaking through the blockade in our mind and being able to finally mind-link each other, Olis and I—along with the help of Vic and Cal—work out a plan to extract us.

Neither of the other two Alphas were remotely pleased about the fact that the Demons were the ones that helped Scott take me. Because they were the same club that took Gwen.

What they don't know is that it was actually the Andrews pack that took her. The Demons were just the lackeys for them.

I mull over the information that I am holding back from my pack as I cook dinner. I'm terrified of the pain that it will cause them when they find out—because they will. It's inevitable at this point. But I still want to protect them from it. They are going to learn that their first Omega was raped which resulted in a pregnancy.

And now the child of that pregnancy now calls me Mom.

It's a clusterfuck.

I glance at the clock for a final time as I dish up the pasta dish I prepared for the four of us. Right on six o'clock, I place Scott's plate down in front of him. He grunts before digging into the dish, not bothering to wait for anyone else.

I glance at the clock again as Scott swallows the mouth full of food.

Four minutes.

I place Amity and Makari's plates in front of them before collecting my own.

Three minutes and twenty-one seconds.

I pick up my glass, taking a deep drink of water. Placing the cup back down, I keep an eye on Scott as he continues to eat. My gaze travels quickly to his phone that remains dark.

I grab a small fork full of the pasta, eating quickly, but not quick enough to raise suspicion.

Three minutes.

I look over at Amity, smiling as she sucks the pasta into her mouth. Sauce covers her face already, the look only making her look even more adorable.

I glance over at Makari. He looks up to me at the same time. I nod my head enough for him to notice but not enough that Scott does.

Once my Alphas and I had concocted our plan, I filled Makari in on everything that was going on. Seeing the hurt on his face as I carefully explained to him what the Andrews pack had done to him and why it was wrong, took a heavy toll. After Makari asked me his questions and shed a few tears, the young Omega transformed in front of me.

Gone was the naive boy that did as he was told.

In his place was a man that understood that his abuse wouldn't be tolerated.

Thankfully, Makari was more than happy to keep acting as though nothing had changed, leaving Scott none the wiser.

The feral Alpha's phone flashing has me jolting to attention. Picking up the phone, he answers the call. I don't bother listening in though. I already know what is being said.

I look up at the clock.

One minute and forty-six seconds.

"Stupid, useless cunts. Can you believe that the Demons have just pulled their protection from us?"

Scott continues to ramble, cursing out the gang that left him high and dry. I take another mouthful of my pasta before setting my fork down.

One minute.

I take a final sip of water as Scott finally stops talking. It's not that the poor excuse for an Alpha has finally run out of profanities though.

It's because the concoction of poisons that I mixed into his pasta has already taken effect with fifty-two seconds remaining.

The sound of multiple vehicles pulling up into the driveway has me standing up from my seat.

Scott frowns up at me from his partially crunched over form. Pain is written across his features but even as the poison eats him from the inside out, causing his organs to fail one at a time, that doesn't stop him from being a downright cunt.

"Sit the fuck down, Valenitna."

I sneer at him, "I think the fuck I wont, Scott."

He goes to mutter something else but he doesn't. Because his face starts to turn blue.

"See, the last time I poisoned you, I was too light on with my measurements. This time though, I decided to get a little..." I watch as it finally hits Scott that he is going to die while I mull over my next words, "Creative. See, Wolfsbane is incredibly toxic on its own when given the right dosage. When mixed with cyanide..." I chuckle not even needing to finish my sentence as Scott slumps back in his chair. His body convulses, foam dribbling from his open mouth.

It seems I really did learn my lesson from last time.

I couldn't leave anything to chance.

So as Makari removes Amity from the dining room, leading her to the cars outside where my pack is waiting for us, I pick up a knife from the kitchen bench and slowly begin to walk towards the man that abused me.

It's an odd feeling to feel so elated watching as the man who caused me so much pain writhes in a world of his own causing.

I twirl the knife in my hand; the sharp point digging into the tip of my finger. I hear the front door open again but keep my gaze firmly on the man in front of me.

"How does it feel to know that I finally won? That all of the shit you caused in your miserable life was for nothing. That after today, no one will remember you. No one will mourn you."

I touch the tip of the knife to his forehead, pushing back his head so his dilated eyes can see me for one last time.

Blood drips down his face, quickly mixing with vomit and foam. It's a sickening sight but a fitting ending for a man that took my innocence for me.

"You lost, Scott. See you in hell, motherfucker," I say before plunging the kitchen knife directly into his heart.

I remain frozen, watching for what feels like a lifetime as the life drains completely from Scott Andrews' face.

I wait long enough that my hand cramps where I still have the knife clutched ridiculously tight in my hand.

I step back with a gasp.

Two more steps and I collapse to my knees. A sob wracks me and I break as my pack surrounds me.

I'm free.

CHAPTER THIRTY-FOUR

VALENTINA

I continue to cry even as I am lifted from my slumped position on the floor of the cabin. Not even the soothing words of my pack are enough to make me stop.

Now Scott is gone—for good this time—it feels as though I am actually able to grieve.

I get to grieve for the girl whose life was stolen from her. The woman she grew into who had to survive day in and day out. I grieve for my daughter who was forced into this life. I grieve for Makari who shares a similar story.

I grieve for my men who, for the second time, have had to save their Omega from the Andrews pack.

Rearing my head, I control my sobs for a moment as I find Vic. My Alpha looks tired. Black rings circle his eyes that are filled with a mixture of concern and relief.

"It was the Andrews Pack. They are the ones that took Gwen. They..." I pause, fighting through another sob, "they raped her. She fell pregnant and had Makari."

Vic looks as though he is going to be sick, processing my words. Eventually he nods, even as a lone tear streams down his cheek.

"I had a feeling that they did that to her. When we finally got her body back, the coroner said that there was evidence of a pregnancy in the last few months before her death."

He shakes his head before looking towards the door, the same one Makari walked out of not that long ago. "We tried to look for him for years but never found anything."

I nod, snaking my hand up to Vic's cheek. I wipe away one of his tears and hold him close.

"He has had a really hard life. What the Andrews did to him was unspeakable. But he is a warrior."

Vic nods, a proud look appearing on his face. "We will protect them."

Immediately, I agree with him. Since meeting Makari, I have felt a kinship over him. My instincts scream to keep him in my nest right where Amity is. He may not be my son, but I already love him as though he is mine.

My Alphas help me to stand before gently leading me away from the scene. Each of them touches me somewhere on my body, none of them wanting to let me go too far from them. In return, I grip on to them tightly, needing the strength they provide.

Before we get to the car, Jaiden, the Alpha from OPA comes to stand in front of me. He doesn't say anything, assessing my state. He gives my Alphas a look before turning back to me.

"Well done, Valentina. Go home with your Alphas and rest. I will take care of everything here."

With a nod, my men lead me over to one of the many black SUVs pulled up out front of the cabin, Cal guides me into my seat, but not before he pulls me into his arms.

I breathe in his vanilla tobacco scent, the smell calming me instantly.

"I'm so glad you are okay, Little Devil. I don't know what I would have done if I lost you."

I agree but refuse to speak. Instead, I hug Cal tighter to me. Eventually we let go of each other. Once in the car, I turn my head, finding both Makari and Amity sitting in the back row. The Omega rubs Amity's arm as she nuzzles into his chest. The moment both of them get a hint of my scent, they look up at me in relief.

Makari is the first to break, launching himself at me.

"You saved me, Mom. You saved me," he repeats, his words slurred against the tears.

Amity crawls over to us, working her way into my other arm.

"Are we safe now, Mommy?" she questions, her innocent little eyes blurred with her own emotions. Even though I did my best to shield her, it wasn't enough.

"Yes, baby. We are safe now."

She bites her lip before looking behind my shoulder to where Olis sits.

"Can we go home now, Pa?"

Olis chokes, and I feel his hand shake as he grips my hip. His eyes water as he gathers our three-year-old in his arms. She grips him just as tightly, needing the support only he can give her.

"Yes, my sweet girl. We are going home."

I don't leave my nest for days once we get home. Neither does my little family. Exhaustion claimed each of us the moment the adrenaline wore off. The second we walked through the door of the mansion, I ordered everyone to my nest.

It was almost as though I went through some kind of primal heat, the kind that instead of demanding that I breed, it demanded for me to protect my pack. To keep them by my side until the threat is gone.

Amity watches Vic, Cal and Olis with a keen interest as they dote both over me and Makari. The three Alphas were quick in claiming the Omega as their son, something that had us all in tears again. The moment that they could, Vic had adoption papers signed and filed with the court, officially making Makari one of us. They were also quick in officially adopting Amity.

I make sure to check in with each of my guys in the days after I get home. Together, we process our new reality. We cry together, grit our teeth in frustration and embrace knowing that it is finally over.

A week after the whole fiasco, I finally allowed everyone to leave the nest. It takes me a little bit longer to work up the courage to leave, but I force myself to, knowing that future me will be thankful.

Before I can get too far, Cal collects me in his arms.

"And where do you think you are going, Little Devil?"

I chuckle, turning in his arms to look up at him, "I was planning on stretching my legs unless you have other ideas."

"We have something we need to rectify before you get too far from your nest."

My thighs clench, my eyes widening as Cal bends down and throws me over his shoulder. I giggle, as Cal makes his way back through the door to my nest. During my heat, I hadn't given it much notice but after, I realized that there was an extra room in my suite. One with a nest. I spent hours during my heat perfecting it after finally being given a chance to listen to my primal side.

He drops me down on the nest, not allowing me to bounce before crawling up my body and slamming his lips on me.

He devours me, his lips moving across mine in a sensual dance. I grip his shirt, ripping at the fabric in desperation as my need escalates for him.

"Started without me, I see."

I groan, turning my head to watch Vic shed his clothes and step into the nest. His body ripples as he bends down, collecting my lips in his, allowing Cal to trail down my torso. His touch sends goosebumps over my flesh. I writhe between the twin Alphas, my need escalating the more they tease and manipulate my pleasure.

I squeal against Vic's lips pulling back from him to look down at Cal who ripped my clothes from my body.

"So fucking perfect," Cal murmers, bending back down. He dips his tongue out, ever so slowly licking his way up the inside of my thigh and to my core. I groan, my body moving on its own accord as I beg for more.

"Please, Cal, please."

He moves quicker than I can blink. Flipping me over so I am my hands and knees, I arch my back, moaning as he gives into my begging.

He licks his way directly up my slit, groaning into me before going back for more.

His tongue penetrates me, the noises coming from him heightening my pleasure.

Vic comes to kneel before me, his hand trailing over my cheek. I lean into his touch, soaking up the feel of him as I give in to the first orgasm that tears through me.

"Good Omega," Vic growls, lifting my chin. He presents his cock to me, the length swollen and red, desperate for my touch.

I give into him, sucking him into my mouth at the same time Cal slams himself inside of me.

WIth each trust of Cal's hips, I relax my throat, taking in as much of my Alpha as I can handle. Spit drips down my chin as I choke and moan on his length. It's messy but so fucking good.

Vic's hand combs through my hair before he grips the strands. I moan around his length, the sound spurring him on to begin fucking my mouth.

I give myself over to my two Alphas. My body becomes theres to do with as they wish as ecstasy courses through my veins.

Another orgasm peaks and I come with a shout. I feel Cal follow quickly behind me. His knot breaches my entrance before swelling to completion. Reaching an arm around my stomach, Cal lifts me up right. I lean back on his hard chest as I fight to catch my breath.

Vic closes in on my front, completely sandwiching me in between them both.

"Ours," the Alphas growl at the same time. Another orgasm rips through me as both Cal and Vic bite down on opposite sides of my neck, claiming me as theirs.

My entire world goes black the moment my orgasm subsides but I don't care.

After years of abuse, my body and soul damaged to the precipice of being beyond repair, I finally feel whole.

EPILOGUE

VALENTINA

Five years later

My fingers trail over the wet petals of my favorite foxglove plant.

A month after my kidnapping, I became lost in the what comes next portion of my life. I had never been given the opportunity to wonder what comes next. My life had been a consistent state of fight or flight.

Being with my pack provides me with a stability where I could explore my options. I knew that one way or another, I wanted to be an asset to the family business. I had mulled over the idea of nursing but quickly decided against that when my stomach rolled over the sight of blood. Kennedy is much stronger than me in that department.

While I am a half decent shot with a gun, weapons weren't necessarily my calling. It did take me down the track of a different style of weapon: poison.

I began to do research on the different varieties of plants, quickly falling in love with the research and soon thereafter, the plants themselves.

When I first took the idea to Vic, I was nervous that he would just laugh at me. That he would think my idea was childish or naive but when it came to presenting my idea of using a much more subtle style of fighting, he was eager to hear me out.

A few days later, he led me outside and to a greenhouse he had set up for me to begin growing my own poisonous sanctuary.

It became my savior as I processed my pain and my new reality.

Makari struggled a little bit more than I did in finding his place in the family. It took him a long time to accept that he needed therapy for what he went through.

It was hard watching him having to relieve his trauma. It hurt even more watching his anger take hold.

After four years of hard work, he finally is in a place where he isn't overcome by the memories of his childhood.

Makari ended up taking an interest in becoming a soldier. There was a lot of hesitation at first, being that he is an Omega, but when Makari all but saved the family during an altercation with an up and coming rival family, he easily solidified his position under Ledger.

The two quickly hit it off, becoming a dangerous combo.

On the day of our one year anniversary, Vic finally handed the reins over to Theo who slid into place as the new Don with ease.

It gave Vic a chance to become a stay at home dad which may have been an oversight on my behalf. My Alpha became obsessed with the idea of seeing me pregnant with his child.

I rub my hand over my swollen belly, cursing his strong will. It may have taken a few years thanks to the damage the suppressants did on my body, but nine months ago after a bit of help from Dr. Maddox, I was able to fall pregnant.

Hands worm their way around my stomach and I groan in relief as Cal lifts my baby bump, taking the weight of nine months of growth off me.

"How is my baby momma feeling this morning?" he whispers, nuzzling my neck and taking in a lung-full of my cherry scent that has blossomed this pregnancy.

"Sore, tired, desperate for this baby to evict herself from my womb."

Comparing my two pregnancies side by side, my current one puts Amity's to shame. From the get-go, I have had consistent morning sickness. Pelvic girdle pain has nearly crippled me at the back end of this pregnancy.

I couldn't have asked for better baby daddies than my three Alphas though. Not once have I had to ask for anything. It's almost as though they knew what I needed before I did.

Amity has been beside herself with excitement about finally getting a baby sibling. My now almost nine-year-old took her role as aunt to Koa and Enid—Kennedy, Theo, Jax and Ledger's children—very seriously.

Her new and rapidly emerging Alpha traits have been a completely different ball game. I don't know if I would have been able to survive these years without my pack. Especially now that she is hitting her pre-teen years.

Cal rocks me back and forth, slowly walking along with me as I check on my plants. I point out new growths, and talk about the plans I have to grow from here.

Poison has become an incredibly effective tool in the years since I first started in the greenhouse. Theo's running nickname for me, the

Poison Omega, making my name just as deadly along with those of my pack.

We nod at Jasper, my assistant who has taken more control of the greenhouse since I found out the news. Even though being in here and working with the plants is completely safe, my Alphas wanted me to have someone that I could fall back on.

Taking another step, I pause abruptly, looking down at my pants that begin to soak through.

"Hey Cal," I whisper.

"Yes, Little Devil?"

"It's time."

I hold our daughter Peyton Jean to my chest. Her little face is peaceful in sleep, looking so much like her biological father.

I don't know how I can tell, but I just know that she is Cal's daughter.

Fresh out of the womb and she already has an attitude that easily matches him.

"She is so perfect. Thank you, baby," Olis murmurs as we both admire her. His big hand cradles her face, making her seem so much smaller.

The opening of the door has my attention drawing to Amity and Makari who are both the picture of excitement. Cal and Vic follow in behind them with large bouquets of flowers.

Olis moves out of the road, making room for Makari who clambers onto the bed beside me.

"Oh, Mom. Just look at her," he cooes at his baby sister. Amity's face lights up as she too hops up on the bed on my other side. Tears form in her eyes, taking in her baby sister. Peyton takes that chance to yawn, making both Makari and Amity fuss over her.

I turn to Makari, nudging him with my elbow to get his attention.

"Do you want to hold her?" I ask, giving him a small reassuring smile. He immediately nods, readjusting himself and holding his hands out. Carefully, I place Peyton in his arms.

"Hi, baby sister. You are so beautiful. No matter what, I will protect you and your big sister for the rest of my life."

Tears begin to stream down my cheeks as I watch my Alphas come over to our adoptive son. Vic places a hand on his shoulder, giving him a half-hug. Cal picks Amity up, putting her on his lap and scooting in behind me. Olis comes to sit in front of Makari.

Moments later, Kennedy, Jax, Theo and Ledger walk through the door holding a large bouquet of chrysanthemums. I beam, even more so as my best friend Lulu walks through the door with her new partner. Mrs. Perry isn't too far behind, the older woman fussing over her grandmotherly duties.

I look around at each member of my new family allowing myself to soak in the happiness having them in my life brings me.

After years of fighting, convinced that I would never find happiness, here surrounded by my pack, I finally am free.

Free to love. To live. To make mistakes and learn from them. To heal and process the trauma that broke me for so long.

Because this is my family.

My life.

And no one can take that from me.

Not ever again.

THE END

ACKNOWLEDGEMENTS

And just like that, my forth book is done!

I cannot even begin to describe how insane that feels to say.

This book was never meant to exist. I had always planned for Knot So Broken to be a complete standalone. It was my book in between Greased and Thunderbirds 3. Yet, it seemed to have a mind of its own. Paired with my PA and editors fascination with the Duran Daddies, this book came to life.

Valentina, Victor, Olis and Conall were a completely different ball game to anything I have wrote before. They are so much older than both Scarlett and her men and even Kennedy and her Alphas. Not only that, but there was a cheeky little Alpha that I had to factor in. This book contains some of my favourite tropes that I absolutely had to write. I hope that you were able to relate to Valley and her men in one way or another.

Firstly, I want to say thank you to my readers. None of this would be possible without you all and your love for my characters and their journey's. From the messages screaming at me for the chaos I pull in these books to the way you relate to my characters never fails to make my day.

To my editor Callie, I can't even begin to describe how thankful I am to have you. You are the biggest hype woman and I can't thank you enough for giving me the courage to go that extra step. You help take my writing to another level. No doubt, I would be lost without you!

To my beautiful besties, Jess, Dani, Shan and Linnsy. God, I fucking adore you guys. From our late nights on discord to the chaotic group chats with endless videos sent back and forth, I couldn't ask for a better group of friends. I have never been one to have a big circle so to have you four, I couldn't be anymore thankful.

To my husband and babies, I love you so much. For the late nights I spend in my office to the many trips I take to signings, you three have been so patient and supportive of me. This year has been hard as I navigate through my chronic pain and all of the obstacles life throws at us. I hope that I am making you proud.

Now, onto the next one!

About Alexcis Morris

Alexcis Morris is a dark romance and Omegaverse author who lives in sunny Central Queensland. If you can't find Alexcis in her writing cave coming up with her next heart breaking plot twist or a cliffhanger that will have you screaming profanities and throwing objects, you can find her nose deep in a book that is most certainly not on her TBR.

You can find Alexcis on both Tiktok and Instagram (@alexcismorrisauthor) or if you would like more of the behind the scenes sneak peaks, be sure to join her facebook group, Alexcis Morris' Thunderbirds.

Also by Alexcis

The Thunderbirds Series

Summer Nights

Greased

Stranded (Coming early 2026)

Knot So Series

Knot So Broken

Knot So Damaged

www.ingramcontent.com/pod-product-compliance
Ingram Content Group UK Ltd.
Pitfield, Milton Keynes, MK11 3LW, UK
UKHW021940091225
9476UKWH00005B/730

9 781763 520493